# WIND THE CLOCK

*Wind the Clock*

Published by Blue Dragon Publishing, LLC
Williamsburg, VA
www.BlueDragonPublishing.com
Copyright 2014, 2022 Dawn Brotherton
ISBN 978-1-939696-79-3
ISBN 978-1-939696-08-3 (epub)
Library of Congress Control Number: 2019951844

2nd Edition, 2022

*Jo Ron*

# WIND THE CLOCK

*Dawn Brotherton*

# DAWN BROTHERTON

*Col, USAF, ret*

First edition published in 2014. Second edition 2022.

 Blue Dragon Publishing

# Author's Note

Don't let military time throw you off. It's a twenty-four-hour clock. Counting up to noon is easy. After that, keep going up instead of resetting. If you are given a time above 1200, subtract twelve to figure out the hour.

> Ten-hundred hours (1000) is 10 a.m.
> Fourteen-hundred hours (1400) is 2 p.m.
> Twenty-hundred hours (2000) is 8 p.m.
> Seventeen-thirty (1730) is 5:30 p.m.

(We really do talk like this…)

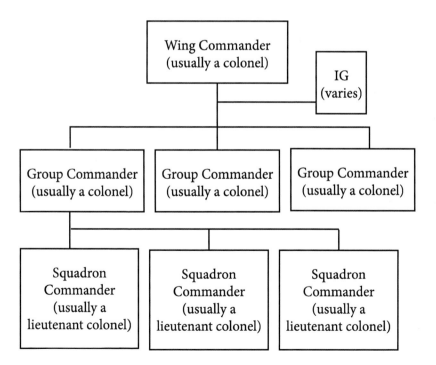

# Other books by Dawn Brotherton

**Jackie Austin Mysteries**

*The Obsession*

*Truth Has No Agenda*

*Eastover Treasures*

*The Dragons of Silent Mountain*

*Untimely Love*

# Chapter 1

He started to shiver violently from the cold. He couldn't get up. Someone would see him.

"Over here!" someone shouted.

Finally, he thought. A light flashed across his face, turning the inside of his eyelids red. He kept his eyes closed, but he couldn't control the shudders that racked his body.

"Hurry. Call the ambulance." Someone rushed off and the mutterings of a phone call reached his ear.

"Hang in there." Now the voice was directed at him. He felt relief as something warm and heavy was draped over his chest.

"He has cuts all over his body, and his leg is at a funny angle." This was a new voice. "He's shaking a lot."

There was a long pause and then, "Hey, Major, should he be shaking like this?"

Major Jackie Austin rushed to the prone man and quickly assessed his condition.

"Damn it, Bobby! Get off the ground!" Major Austin grabbed him by the arm and yanked the injured man to his feet. "Somebody get the ambulance here!"

"You idiot!" She picked up the jacket that had fallen to the ground and wrapped it around him.

Bobby was confused. Why was she mad at him? He played his part well.

The fake blood the exercise team applied a few hours ago covered most of his face, but his lips were blue, and that was real.

"You're supposed to be my medical expert. How can you evaluate the responders if you go into hypothermic shock?" She rubbed his shoulders violently, trying to get his blood flowing.

Bobby heard the sirens and willed them to move faster. He had made a stupid, stupid mistake. Within the next few minutes, the ambulance screeched to a stop only yards away.

"We got it, Major." The medic moved her gently aside. Jackie took a last look at Bobby, turned away, and stomped off, swearing at herself. She kicked a stone, and it rattled off in the darkness.

"Now what do you want us to do?" someone asked.

Bobby looked around at the medics checking his vitals. They had piled heavy blankets on him, and his shivering was quieting finally. He wanted to know how his mistake was going to affect the rest of the exercise.

Major Austin turned back to the waiting men, taking charge. "Read from the script. Give the responders the results they would have received from Staff Sergeant Ford and let them call it in." The young lieutenant rushed back to the waiting crowd and began to take control of the chaos that had quickly erupted.

Bobby watched as Major Austin dropped her head and shook it silently for a few minutes before walking to the ambulance. As they loaded him into the back, she leaned into the open doors. "You okay, Bobby?"

"Yes, ma'am," he replied from under the mounds of blankets. "I'm sorry."

"No, it was my fault. I should have known better. I didn't realize it would take them so long to find you. I should've planned better."

"You can't plan the weather," he said with a weak smile. Although early September in Germany was fairly mild, the nights got chilly. The day had started out beautiful, but with no cloud cover to trap the heat, the temperature dropped quickly when the sun went down.

She patted his booted foot. "I'll be over to the hospital in a few minutes. Do me a favor and evaluate how they treat you, okay?"

"Yes, ma'am. That'll ensure I get the royal treatment," he said between chattering teeth.

Jackie stepped back, and the medic closed the doors. Immediately the ambulance pulled away with its lights flashing. No sirens though. Bobby assumed that was a good sign.

# Chapter 2

Major Austin sat nervously outside her boss's door. She had sent him the incident report on Staff Sergeant Bobby Ford via email before she went home for the night, but now she had to explain how someone on her team ended up in the hospital for real while playing the part of a downed pilot during a training exercise.

She hadn't been able to sleep the night before. Her twelve-hour shift had quickly turned into sixteen hours and hadn't wrapped up until well after midnight. Although she had gone home with the pretense of sleeping, she had lain awake staring at the ceiling.

What could I have done differently? she continued to quiz herself. She was thankful Staff Sergeant Ford was fine. He'd been warmed up and released, but it could have been much worse.

Suddenly the door to her boss's office opened, and Jackie jumped to her feet. Her five-foot four-inch frame didn't even begin to measure up to the towering build of her boss, Colonel Mike Harris. She tugged at the shirt of her air battle uniform, or ABU, self-consciously. The colonel gestured for her to come in, and she followed without a word.

"Jackie, relax. I'm not going to bite you." Harris tried to put her at ease as he motioned for her to take a seat.

Jackie sat in the chair opposite Harris's desk but didn't sit back. How could she relax?

"Sergeant Ford is going to be fine, right?" Harris leaned back in his chair.

"Yes, sir. The hospital released him last night and he doesn't even have to go back for a follow-up. The doc said he was lucky." Jackie was hesitant to add this last part, but she knew that she had to come clean with all the details.

"Good. And what did you learn from this experience?"

A thousand responses popped into her head, and she sorted through them carefully to pick what she should say out loud.

"I should have had another medical representative on hand to watch over my role players in this scenario. It's too much to have the evaluator double as a role player and expect him to evaluate at the same time." She took a deep breath. "I should have waited until the last minute to have Staff Sergeant Ford lie down on the ground. I didn't even think about the cold ground zapping the heat from his body. Next time we'll put a layer of something underneath him to prevent it."

"Okay, sounds like a plan. Jackie, these things happen. We're all learning. That's what exercises are about. Think about what would've happened to the pilot if this had really been a downed aircraft. This incident highlights how important it is to get to the aircrew quickly, even in friendly territory." Harris swiveled in his chair and leaned his elbows on the desk. "Once you identified the problem, you reacted quickly and took action. Stop beating yourself up."

Jackie breathed a little easier, but she wouldn't let herself off the hook. "Yes, sir."

"The exercise still has a few more days to run its course. Don't get timid on me. We only have a few more practices before the Operational Readiness Inspection in March. Now get out of here," Harris said dismissively, but kindly. "I'll see you at the shift change briefing at oh-eight-hundred."

Jackie stood. "Yes, sir. Thank you."

As Jackie stepped into the bright morning, she realized how tired she was. Training exercises took a lot of work to put together and execute. The long hours cut into her workout routine to the point where she felt her body rebelling.

She wasn't complaining about her assignment though. As the chief of Wing Inspections, she had the latitude to delve into the various missions of the 52nd Fighter Wing; she was never bored. Spangdahlem Air Base was home to the 606th Air Control Squadron, the A-10 Warthogs, the F-16 Vipers, and all the support that goes along with getting and keeping the birds in the air.

Her husband, Major Stan Mason, was on cloud nine flying the F-16 Viper over some of the most amazing landscapes, complete with medieval castles and the ruins of historic cathedrals. Jackie envied his flight time as Stan animatedly talked about how gorgeous the countryside appeared from altitude. He loved boasting about his God's eye view, as if fighter pilots were more worthy of it than everyone else.

As she left Harris's office, she silently shook her head in disbelief that something like hypothermia had crept up on Bobby. She wasn't about to stop analyzing her misjudgment as Colonel Harris had suggested to her. That wasn't how she worked. When it came to her duty performance, she held herself to higher standards than anyone else. Her dad, a retired policeman, raised her to never settle for less than her best, and he didn't listen to excuses. For that reason, she would squeeze as much value out of her mistake as possible and never repeat the error or any related form of it.

Jackie walked toward the two-story, brick building that housed the 52nd Operations Group, where the group commander would be holding his internal hot wash on the events of the previous night. The hot wash was when everything was laid on the table—the good, the bad, and the hideously ugly. It was also where the lessons learned were collected to make things better for next time. Because she was in the field with the "downed pilot," she didn't hear how the coordination played out between the operations crew and the first responders. She was interested to see how the commander thought his squadrons reacted.

In this exercise scenario, the pilot reported trouble directly after takeoff, so the people in the tower were watching the prescribed flight path.

The simulated aircraft crash had to be expertly orchestrated to make the crash coherent and realistic. Jackie had an exercise evaluation team, or EET, member in the tower standing by to give injects to the supervisor of flying. The injects described what the reader would see if the scenario were really taking place.

The visual cues that would occur within a real-world situation, such as smoke, fire, and enemy planes in the sky, weren't going to be seen in a simulation, Jackie's team had to create injects to provide the necessary context.

For this scenario, a real plane lifted off with a pilot prepared to role-play his part. The pilot made a staged call over the radio. "Exercise, exercise, exercise, this is Dawgy One Four. I'm two miles north of the airfield with a CONFIRMED engine fire. Exercise, exercise, exercise."

At the same time, the EET member in the tower presented the supervisor of flying with an index card with a clearly typed inject:

EXERCISE EXERCISE EXERCISE

<u>Inject for the Supervisor of Flying</u>

- You observed Dawgy 14 and noted smoke trailing from his aircraft approximately one mile off the departure end of the runway

- He appeared significantly lower than normal for climb out

- You will assume the emergency locator beacon is from Dawgy 14's ejection

- You see a column of black smoke approximately four miles north of the airfield

The challenge was getting everyone to understand that, although the indications were showing a crash off base, for the purposes of the exercise, the fire department and rescue teams would respond to the simulated location on base where the emergency locator beacon was going off. Jackie had another EET member in place at the fire department to provide them with the proper response location once they received the call about the downed jet.

Jackie worried over the potential for confusion, but she couldn't think of a better way to simulate the scenario. She had to keep the location on base so the German nationals wouldn't be concerned and think there was really a crash. As for the Americans, they were so used to exercise-isms that the players didn't blink at the inconsistency. They would all respond to the simulated crash site and act as if they were carefully approaching a smoking hole in some German's cow pasture.

Of course, they didn't respond as quickly as she would have liked, hence Staff Sergeant Ford's close encounter with hypothermia.

# Chapter 3

The 52nd Operations Group commander nodded at Jackie as she slipped in the back but didn't stop talking to his executive officer.

"Lee, get copies of the last ORI's write-ups for the squadron commanders. Apparently, they didn't read them closely enough since we're seeing the same mistakes again." To the group he said, "Interesting that the engine caught on fire so soon after takeoff yesterday," he flashed a conspiratorial look at Jackie, "but let's not fight the scenario. The point was we had a downed pilot. What took us so long to reach him?"

The ORI, or operational readiness inspection, was a report card from higher headquarters on the wing's ability to do their mission. Everyone had a vested interest in making the most of the learning experiences Jackie brought to bear.

The conversation went on with a lot of discussion. Some good points were made, and the squadron commanders brought up things she hadn't considered. Jackie took notes on what processes they wanted to implement that she should test next time. The commander was right to tell his folks not to fight the exercise. The point of any good scenario was to create situations that weren't commonplace, forcing the participants to work through them using all their faculties and training. The twists Jackie and her team added to the action pushed them off balance, requiring them to exercise their brain in other ways to solve problems and move ahead. That way, when the unexpected happens for real, the players will have a starting point.

After the hot wash broke up, Jackie slipped out the back door before anyone could corner her with questions. She had a lot of notes to type up and a few more stops to make before the end of the day. Plus, she needed to meet with her team and get their thoughts. She made a mental note to call Bobby to see how he was feeling.

When she walked into the headquarters building heading to her office, she was lost in thought.

"Jackie," a deep voice called.

She turned at the sound of her name. "Yes, sir?"

"I wanted to let you know that was a hell of a scenario," Colonel Tim Polles said. The wing commander extended his hand to shake Jackie's.

She returned his firm grip and blushed slightly. "Thank you, sir."

"I know it isn't easy taking gruff from all the unit commanders on this base, but remember, I'm the only one who matters." He smiled easily.

She wasn't sure how to react. His intimidating demeanor made it hard to tell when he was just making conversation or when something more was expected. While she was still trying to come up with the right response, he went on.

"I know you can be awfully hard on yourself sometimes too," he went on. "It's okay to push yourself—but not over the edge. Do you hear what I'm saying?"

Jackie nodded. She wondered if he really saw that in her or if Colonel Harris had talked to him. "I'll work on that, sir."

He shook his head and laughed. "Go home and get some sleep. That's an order. I'll see you tomorrow."

She grabbed some files from her office to take with her, looking forward to working from home in her slippers and sweats. A sense of satisfaction swept over her. The wing commander was right. It had been a good scenario, and one that had never been tested before.

Now Jackie tried to relax and leave her worries of the mission behind. She loved the drive through the rolling countryside, still lush and green, even with the cold weather. As she topped the rise in Schwarzenborn, the small town of Grosslittgen was visible in the distance. She and Stan had lucked out when they came across the single-family dwelling nestled in the village. At first the thought of living next to a graveyard seemed a little creepy, but in Germany, even the cemeteries were beautiful examples of exquisite grooming and precision.

There weren't any other Americans in Grosslittgen, but a German frau had befriended them. Margaret was wonderful and helped them interpret their German bills and communicate with their landlord, whose English was sketchy. The other people in the town accepted Stan and her and invited them to neighborhood outings. It was fun to converse in the limited German they knew. As long as the sentences were short and spoken slowly in present tense, Jackie was usually able to follow along.

When Jackie pulled into the garage, she noticed Stan was already home. She was starving, so she hoped he'd started dinner. She opened the door and was greeted with the alluring smell of Italian spices.

"Stan, I love you!" she yelled into the house as she dropped her coat and purse on the stairs. She walked into the kitchen and put her arms around the man at the stove. She loved how her arms fit so perfectly around his trim but muscular waistline. With him standing at almost six feet, she had to stand on her toes to peer over his shoulder to see homemade spaghetti sauce he was stirring. His dark hair was military short and slightly unkempt after a day of wearing a flying helmet.

"You'd love any man who would feed you," Stan quipped, raising his eyebrows at her playfully as he continued his dinner preparations.

"Probably, but you feed me in my own house so that makes you extra special." She gave him one last squeeze and let him go. "I'm going to slip into something more comfortable," she said over her shoulder as she left the kitchen.

Stan smiled after her.

A few minutes later, Jackie returned in her old, gray sweats and her "Go Navy" sweatshirt. She was wearing the pink, fluffy slippers Stan had given her last Christmas. It could be eighty degrees outside, and Jackie's feet would still be cold.

"Comfy?" he asked with a smile. She liked wearing her Navy sweatshirt to taunt him about how the Navy had courted her before he did. She was glad she had chosen the Air Force instead.

"Very. Thank you. What do you need me to do?"

"Get the plates and then grate the fresh Parmesan that's in the fridge."

Jackie opened the cupboard to retrieve the plates. "What's the word on the street about the exercise? How did the squadrons do?"

"Well, as soon as I gave the call that I had a fire, I stopped talking to them and listened in. The guys were directed to another frequency to continue working through the response." Stan had been the pilot Jackie drafted into helping. Having an insider to the fighter community made Jackie's job easier. "We used the exercise frequency, and everyone did well throwing in 'exercise, exercise, exercise' once in a while, just in case."

Jackie smiled. That was one serious concern about this scenario—that someone would overhear the radio chatter and take it as real.

"How's Bobby?" Stan asked.

"He's fine. He was at work early this morning. I think he feels worse about the incident than I do."

Jackie took care to grate the cheese without slicing her fingers. She was glad Stan was in a good mood tonight. She went on. "All the scenarios went by the book today. More younger folks gave the deployment briefings rather than the people that usually do it. They did a good job."

Stan dished out the spaghetti and put the plates on the table. Jackie got down two wine glasses and uncorked a bottle of Chianti. She poured and offered a glass to Stan. He sipped the red. "Ah, 2002. A great year for red stuff."

Jackie smiled and took her seat at the table. She and Stan were by no means wine-snobs. They enjoyed the wine probes along the Mosel River and bought whatever wine caught their fancy, regardless if it had won awards or not. Mostly they had whites, but occasionally a red would find its way to their wine cellar.

"Now that the exercise is almost over, I told the Burketts we would meet them for dinner Friday night," Stan said.

Jackie looked shamefaced. "Not Friday. We still have reports to write and need to prepare for the debrief with the wing commander on Saturday."

He put his glass down hard, and a red stain formed around the base on the white tablecloth. He picked up his fork and pushed food around on his plate.

"Come on, Stan. You knew this was going to be a crazy few weeks."

"Jackie, this has been going on more than a few weeks. You're hardly ever here when I get home. When was the last time we went to bed at the same time? I'm out by the time you wander in or get done typing on the couch!"

Jackie immediately tried to think of the last time they turned off the bedroom lights together, and she couldn't help but extend that mental search to the last time they made love. Frustrated at not being able to get an answer in her mind, she lashed out at Stan.

"Well, it isn't like you keep a steady schedule either. I never know what your flight schedule is and when you might be home." Jackie was disappointed that their peaceful evening had turned into another argument. "And then you take off TDY for weeks at a time without so much as calling home." Jackie really didn't mind Stan's temporary duty assignments. They gave her time to work as late as she wanted, eat what and when she wanted, and sleep in on the weekends. But that was beside the point.

Stan pushed back from the table and stormed off up the stairs.

Jackie picked up her glass and slumped back in her chair. "Here's to us."

# Chapter 4

Getting into the cavernous hangar was as simple as she was told. No one was around, and everything was closed up. They had drilled her relentlessly through each step, but she was not prepared for the fear in her chest. Her heart pounded and seemed to echo in the silence.

It was dark inside the vast building. Even with the massive doors mostly open, the moon wasn't providing much illumination. She took a chance and flicked on her flashlight. Getting her bearings, she clicked the light off and headed toward the workbenches lining the walls. She felt around, groping for the area where she had seen the heavy black books. Her hand fell upon the rough cover. She tucked the flashlight under her chin to hold it in place and clicked it on again, keeping it close to the book. Her English was good, and her reading was even better, but these technical terms weren't in her normal vocabulary. Quickly she flipped through pages, searching for the key words her husband had told her to look for.

Finding the right section, she pulled out the pocket-size camera. She tried to hold the camera and the flashlight at the same time and get the picture, but it was awkward. As she tried to reposition, a sound outside caught her attention. Shutting off the light, she ducked under the bench and held her breath.

Music blared from the loudspeakers positioned all over the base. Americans were so senseless. They don't even acknowledge their god in public, but they worship a piece of material by putting it on a high pole by the headquarters building. Then they play music for it twice a day. She shook her head. It made no sense. Much of what the Americans did made no sense.

Several minutes passed before she nervously climbed out from her hiding spot. Once again, she tried to align her light, the book, and the camera. Frustration overtook her and she gave up, choosing to rip the pages from the three-ring binder and forgoing the pictures. She tucked the pages into her blouse and carefully made her way to the door.

Peeking out, she determined no one was in sight and there was no movement on the flight line. Moving swiftly, she slipped out, faded into the shadows, and made her way to where her husband was waiting.

# Chapter 5

The next morning, her team meeting went smoothly. Everyone was ready and knew their assignments for the day. She answered a few last-minute questions and then sent them on their way to get in place. The first event for the day would be at 0745, and she wanted to be in place at the mobile kitchen early to see how the set up for the deployable mess was going. Then she would throw in some exercise casualties to see how flexible the airmen were at responding outside their normal duties.

Jackie stopped by her office to pick up some paperwork before she headed out. As she rummaged through her desk, she heard a noise in the outer office.

"Sergeant Reynolds? Is that you?" Master Sergeant Derrick Reynolds was the senior enlisted evaluator on the IG team and often stored items in the locked filing cabinets in the common area they shared.

"No, ma'am. It is me, Mastana," came the reply.

"Good morning, Mastana," Jackie said coming out of her office. "You're getting an early start."

"So many people working around the clock. The cleanup takes longer." The thirty-something-year-old custodian was dressed in her typical garb—a flowing skirt that brushed the floor and long sleeves gathered at the wrists, billowing slightly all the way to her shoulder. With its baggy cut, her blouse gave no indication of her body build. As always, her dark hair was pulled back and covered with a head scarf.

Jackie thought of the messes she had to clean up from the errors made and smiled. "I know what you mean."

Mastana looked confused but smiled politely.

"Are you going to do something fun this weekend?" Jackie asked.

"My husband is working long hours. He will sleep all weekend." She retrieved the trash basket from Jackie's office and dumped it into the larger barrel she wheeled around with her.

Jackie shook her head in sympathy. This was usually the extent of their conversations. Mastana was nice and always polite, but she didn't really say much. Jackie had learned that asking her too many questions caused her to retreat more. She knew Mastana was an Afghan married to a younger German national who worked on base, but beyond that, nothing. She often saw Mastana's husband in the street where he picked Mastana up after work. He appeared to be of Middle Eastern descent, maybe Afghan, but it was hard to tell. She had spoken to him once briefly, and his accent was strongly German.

Jackie followed Mastana out the door and pulled it closed behind her. "Well, I have to run to my meeting. I'll see you next week." Jackie waved as she headed down the hallway.

She got to the outdoor mess at 0735. To seem inconspicuous, she picked up a tray and got in line with the others. She selected her food and took a seat at a folding table next to some security forces personnel. She didn't know how they sat comfortably with a gun slung over their shoulder, but she guessed, as the military police, they were used to it. They chatted about the scenario, and she withstood their complaints of how unrealistic some things were. They didn't understand it was really difficult to fit all the training objectives into a plausible scenario so everything involving crisis was tested in a five-day period. No one's luck was ever that bad.

About that time, a loud bang went off outside the tent. The cops rolled their eyes but quickly stood up and went to investigate. Jackie put on her inspector general badge, pulled out her notebook, and followed them.

Jackie spent the afternoon with the maintainers. Their job was truly thankless. It was all about keeping aircraft flying. The maintainers scurried around in the blistering heat of summer and the brutal cold of winter to service the aircraft, load its weapons, and then launch and recover sorties around the clock if necessary.

Since military flying began, crew chiefs have been closer to the pilots than anyone in the maintenance group. Their very personal sense of responsibility ensures the aircraft is ready to fly. Historically, the crew chief and the fighter pilot shared the same cheer or gloom depending on the outcome of a mission, whether in training or combat. Each jet has two names stenciled below the canopy—the pilot and the crew chief assigned to the aircraft.

Jackie listened to the load team inventory the cargo as they palletized it. The most crucial equipment had been packed, moved to the other side of the base to simulate departure, and unpacked during the beginning phases of the exercise to prove the squadrons could meet the required timelines for deployment. They had done a great job. Usually this was where exercise play ended for them. This time, Jackie was stressing their resupply and reach-back capability to home station. Their warts were showing through in some areas they hadn't practiced as often.

~

Major Stan "Mace" Mason stood at the ops desk copying down his schedule for the next week. He had an instrument check coming up, and he mentally noted he should review some emergency procedures before then.

Check rides had never bothered Stan, although some pilots really got nervous to have an evaluator grade their work. At this stage in his career, it was just another flight. The evaluators were the same guys he had been flying with for years and drinking with at the bar on Fridays. But that didn't mean they wouldn't rake you over the coals if you didn't know your shit. The evaluators were ultra-professional and good at separating themselves from friendships to do their job. After all, this was a matter of life and death. If a pilot couldn't pass a check ride, he was dangerous in the air—to himself, his wingman, and people on the ground.

"Ground control to Mace." Someone slapped Stan on the back.

"Kermit, you old dog! What are you doing here?" Stan asked.

Lieutenant Colonel Frank Carson was dressed in a flight suit and carried his flight bag. He, Stan, and Jackie had been in the same squadron in Korea, but Stan hadn't seen him in years.

"I'm stationed at headquarters on the USAFE staff, so I get to come fly with you bozos to maintain my currency." The United States Air Forces Europe staff was located at Ramstein Air Base a few hours away.

"Sorry about the staff, but at least they're letting you get out once in a while." Being on a headquarters staff was a necessary evil for promotion opportunities, but it usually took pilots out of the cockpit and tied them to a desk.

"You picked a bad week to be here," Stan went on. "Exercise scheduling isn't very reliable."

"I'll take what I can get," Kermit replied, setting his bag on the ops desk. "What's your better half up to these days?"

"She's the one messing with the schedule," Stan said. "She's in charge of wing exercises."

"What a perfect job for her!" Kermit laughed. "I can see her devious mind coming up with ways to torture people."

"Exactly." Stan smiled grimly. "Preparing for the ORI makes her schedule extra crazy, but she'd love to see you."

"Maybe next trip. I'm in and out today. I have a packed schedule tomorrow with meetings."

"Ugh, why not pour some lemon juice in that cut while you're at it?"

"It's not that bad. If you have to be on staff, Germany is the place to be."

"Well, I have to hit the books," Stan said. "Let's catch up next time."

"Will do. Tell Jackie I said hi."

Stan grimaced as he headed for the vault to study before his next flight. Jackie had been giving him the cold shoulder, so he wasn't sure when she would be talking to him again long enough for him to fill her in on his chance meeting with Kermit. When he saw their old friend, he had hoped meeting Kermit for dinner would soften her up.

He'd have to think of another plan.

# Chapter 6

The sun had set long before Jackie reached Grosslittgen, but there were no lights in the house as she pulled into the garage. She didn't see Stan's car either and suspected he got roped into working the operations desk for the late shift—or he volunteered. She felt guilty for the relief she experienced as she dragged herself out of the car and up to the door, fishing for her keys. She wasn't in the mood for another fight.

She sipped on a glass of wine as she changed from her uniform into her nightshirt. Settling into bed, she opened a book. Then on second thought, she replaced the book and shut off the light. She was so tired; she wouldn't need any help falling asleep.

Sometime in the middle of the night, a thump and "Shit!" sounded in the darkness. She was vaguely aware of Stan as he stumbled to his side of the bed and crawled in. Jackie rolled over and went back to sleep.

The next morning came too early. The long days were taking a toll on Jackie, but she knew they'd be ENDEXing, or ending the exercise, at 1200 and that boosted her resolve. She made her way to the bathroom practically sleepwalking. She turned the shower on extra warm and allowed the water to relax her. *Not a good technique for waking up but well deserved,* Jackie thought.

When the water started to cool, she shut it off and got out, tying the white robe tightly around her to hold in the heat. She spent ten minutes brushing out her hair and pulling it back in a neat French braid. She had been doing her hair this way for so many years now, she could do it with her eyes shut. Quickly she put on her uniform and went to the kitchen to forage for food.

While she sat at the table with a bowl of cereal, Stan came down the stairs. "Why are you up so early?" she asked.

He grunted something incoherent in return as he headed to the bathroom.

She got up and followed him. "Are you feeling okay?" Stan was usually a morning person and typically ran circles around her—even this early.

"I'm fine," he answered, but she wasn't convinced.

"Why are you up so early? You got home pretty late."

"I have an early flight. Can I have a little privacy here?" he said, pushing the door closed.

Jackie shrugged and went back to her cereal.

She had met Stan when they were both stationed at Osan Air Base in the Republic of Korea. He was flying A-10s as a flight commander and weapons officer, and she was the squadron section commander for his unit. She was responsible for the personnel actions for more than two hundred people, including their annual reports, medals they earned, and their follow-on assignments. She also had the Uniformed Code of Military Justice, or UCMJ authority, over the enlisted folks in the squadron. That meant she was very busy in Korea, where young, single, or at least unaccompanied-married individuals, tended to drink too much and get in a lot of trouble.

Within a few months of her arrival in Korea, Stan swept Jackie off her feet. They never looked back.

Shortly after they got married, Stan had literally saved her life when a man obsessed with Jackie had broken into their home. And then Stan stuck by her as she battled the nightmares that had followed the incident. Jackie had thought if they survived that, they could survive anything. But they had been drifting apart lately. Not for the first time, she wondered if a promotion for her would mean another wedge in her marriage they couldn't afford.

She didn't have any more time this morning to dwell on their state of affairs. Jackie rinsed her bowl in the sink and grabbed her car keys.

On base, things were still at full throttle. The lights on the flight line lit up the early morning sky as if it were noon. Although Jackie longed to look at the jets on the ramp, her first stop had to be the civil engineering squadron. She wanted to ask the commander a few questions.

The day went by quickly. No big explosions or plane crashes. At this point, it was a paperwork drill to ensure the administrative pieces of keeping the organization running were up to speed. It sounded trivial in a wartime situation, but the bullets and beans had to be reordered somehow.

When the message went out over Giant Voice, the loudspeaker system for the base, declaring ENDEX at noon, a cheer went up in the dining facility. For most people, that meant they could start packing up and still get home in time for the weekend.

Not Jackie. It was time to start preparing the debrief she had to present to Colonel Polles, along with his group and squadron commanders tomorrow morning. But the vice wing commander wanted something on his desk by 2000 tonight.

Back at her office, the evaluators were rolling in. Some were already working furiously on their reports, hoping to get out at a decent hour. Master Sergeant Reynolds was proofing work that had already been turned in. He had his red pen in hand as he furiously scribbled on Staff Sergeant Ford's slides.

Loud enough for everyone in the room to hear, he said, "Listen up, folks. You need to use the format template we gave you. I'm not going to spend all night reformatting because you're in a hurry. Do it right the first time and save us all the hassle."

When Jackie approached him, he stood, "Good afternoon, ma'am."

Jackie smiled at him. "Where are we?"

"We've been capturing things at each shift change so we're in pretty good shape. The team's writing up today's observations and then we need to sit down and prioritize what we want to brief the senior leadership. We'll keep everything for the detailed debrief next week, but for this presentation, we need to limit it to under an hour."

"Great," she replied. "Pull up the last exercise objectives and come up with a way to show whether the wing has improved or not in those areas."

"Yes, ma'am."

"It seemed to go really well. I didn't catch anyone gaming it. Everyone played it as if it were real."

"Having the ORI hanging over us tends to help people get their heads on straight."

Jackie agreed. "I'm going to my office to catch up on some paperwork. As soon as the first set of slides are ready, bring them in. Tell everyone we'll meet in the conference room at seventeen-hundred to go over the presentation."

By 1930, Jackie's vision had started to blur. She rubbed her eyes.

"Are you sick, Mrs. Austin?"

Jackie looked up to see a worried Mastana standing in the doorway. She smiled to reassure her. "I'm fine. Just tired. It's been a long week." She stretched and glanced at her watch. "You're here awfully late."

"There is much to do with extra hours this week. I will be quick," she said, backing out of the door.

Jackie shook her head. She had told Mastana numerous times to call her Jackie, but Mastana wouldn't do it. She also didn't seem to understand the rank structure enough to call her Major Austin. Mastana was going through her routine, emptying the trash, and running a feather duster across the items in the outer office. She never moved things around, but if the space was clear, it was dusted. That was more than Jackie had noticed other cleaning crews do. Most got in and out as quickly as possible. Mastana seemed to take more pride in her work, doing more than necessary and always with a positive attitude. Jackie wished she had a few more people like that working for her.

When she dropped the briefing slides off at the vice wing commander's office at 2000, he had a few questions for her. She went over the highlights with him and agreed to meet him at 0800 the next morning, after he had a chance to review the findings.

Finally, Jackie headed home.

She had already changed into her nightshirt and sweatpants when Stan fumbled with the door. She got up and opened it for him. He stumbled into her arms.

"Oops," he sniggered, wrapping his arms around her.

Jackie looked behind him to thank whoever brought him home. Seeing no one, she asked, "You didn't drive like this, did you?"

"Like what? Of course, I drove. I'm fine. I tripped." He squeezed her tighter, and his hand slid down to her backside.

Jackie pushed him away. "That's stupid and dangerous. What were you thinking? Oh, wait, you weren't!" She stomped back into the living room to pick up her book.

Stan sat on the steps and worked on untying his boots. "We had a few drinks to celebrate the end of the exercise. It was no big deal," he slurred.

"It'll be a big deal when you hurt someone or yourself. Stan, you're going to ruin your career if you're caught drinking and driving. There's no reason for it. You could've called me."

"Right. And you would have rushed on over, that is, unless anyone else needed to see you first."

Jackie wasn't going to fight with him when he'd been drinking. It wasn't worth it. She brushed passed him on her way to bed without another word.

# Chapter 7

The week was uneventful as Jackie and her team finished up reports and prepared detailed slide presentations for each of the units. Stan was on the schedule to fly three times, including a check ride, so he was spending long hours at the squadron. Jackie got back into her regular routine and even fit in a few volleyball games at the base gym.

All the same, Friday couldn't arrive soon enough. Following the exercise results, the wing commander had given the base a three-day weekend as a reward for meeting the impossible goals he had set for September, and it began with an early release to the officers' club. The operations group commander had a Commander's Call to discuss the next six months, and then the officers split off to the officers' bar while the enlisted went to their bar. Everyone with a significant other had summoned them to rejoin, and the music was live and loud.

Stan and Jackie met at the door and walked side by side into the bar. As they stood together drinking and greeting friends, Jackie saw Jenn walk into the club, and she waved her over enthusiastically.

Jennifer Collins's husband Jim was a major in the same squadron as Stan. Although Jackie typically didn't relate well to many of the squadron wives, she and Jenn had hit it off.

In the life of a modern military woman, not only did Jackie have to compete with men in the workplace, she had to contend with the traditional military wife. Most military wives couldn't be bothered to understand a woman like Jackie. Part of her assumed it was jealousy, but whether the jealousy was because Jackie spent so much time with their husbands or because Jackie had a career, she wasn't sure.

Through her friendship with Jenn, Jackie was beginning to see the flip side of this strange tango she played out with the other wives. She saw the important role military wives played in the careers of their husbands and learned not to take the snubs so personally.

Uncle Sam is not an easy employer. To stay in the service and have a family, someone must make a sacrifice. It takes a special partner who is willing to uproot at a moment's notice, giving up friends, family, and careers. Usually it's the woman who continually compromises—even if both spouses are in the military.

Jenn willingly and enthusiastically chose to focus on raising their four kids while her husband moved ahead in the mysterious path of promotion and success in a military career. Jim would succeed because of Jenn's amazing commitment.

Although military men and women got the bragging rights for their service, their families and spouses had to give up a lot to follow them. Because of Jenn, Jackie appreciated the dynamics at work around her so much more, especially the wives' network and its vigorous activity behind the scenes.

Similarly, Jenn told her she envied and adored Jackie. She saw her as the perfect model of what she would have liked to have been in some alternate universe. Their pairing was so unexpected, but it worked, and they treasured each other as dear friends.

"Hey, you two!" Jenn said as she hugged first Jackie and then Stan. "How's it going? Glad the exercise is over?"

"Of course," Jackie answered as she watched Stan's eyes searching the room like a caged lion.

"Have you seen my husband?" Jenn asked.

Stan pointed with his elbow to the back corner where Jim was standing with the group commander. In the fighter pilot tradition, finger pointing in a bar meant buying drinks.

"Figures." Jenn smiled. "If you don't mind, I'll hang here with you for a bit."

Jackie sensed Stan simply wanted to escape. "Honey, why don't you go tell your kind of war stories while Jenn and I exchange our own?"

"Good idea." He grabbed another beer from the bar and wandered off.

Jackie sighed.

"Not any better?" Jenn asked.

"Not really. He seems to be drinking more than ever." Jackie had spilled her guts to Jenn on more than one occasion. Jackie trusted her not to share details with Jim.

"For a while things will go fine, then something happens that makes everything turn sideways again. I can't even figure out what triggers it."

"Maybe you two need to get away. Go somewhere fun."

"Stan never wants to go anywhere," Jackie grumbled.

"*Make* him," she insisted. "Use your girly influence. It'll be good for you both."

Jackie took a sip of her wine and watched her husband make his way through the crowd.

Stan headed toward a gaggle of young fighter jocks who were incredibly animated about everything. They welcomed him into their circle where the chatter was loud and chaotic. Stan loved the energy and reduced his age by ten years to be one of them.

In the sweaty enthusiasm about him, Stan took notice of the maintenance captain, Renee Bennett. He had seen her orbiting around him in the past month and now she was there. She stood only ten feet in front of Stan, and he was perplexed at the coincidence. He shook his head as he reminded himself, although they had just completed an operations group meeting, the officers' bar was open for all officers, not only operators. He had to acknowledge she may have always been around. Strange that he had not taken notice of her until recently. She looked up and caught him watching her. Stan quickly returned his attention to his fellow pilots.

He took it in stride as one of his wingmen poked fun at him for a foolish move he had made earlier in the week.

*Let them laugh*, he thought good-humoredly. *That's nothing compared to what I did when I was a lieutenant.* He lifted his beer and took a long drink. As he brought the bottle away from his mouth, his eyes caught those of the maintenance officer again. They held for a moment, and then she turned her attention back to the fighter jock in front of her, who was in the middle of a grand war story.

It was like watching a toddler pretend to drive dad's car. Stan wondered how on Earth the young fighter pilot could make grand of his miniscule flying experience, but that was the way of baby fighter pilots. Stan was sure he was like that once. In fact, it was exactly what first drew Jackie to him—she loved it.

As the conversation went on around Stan, he continued to glance at Renee as she talked with the young jock, First Lieutenant Sam "Lopass" Mitchell. She wouldn't be as impressed if she knew how he got his call sign. Stan chuckled to himself.

Covertly, Stan studied Renee's face. She wasn't perfect, Stan noted as if checking a required block in an assessment, but she definitely had some worthy qualities.

Her eyes were beautiful and amazingly alive as she spoke. They were so clear, and their bluish gray contrasted nicely with her tanned skin. Her hair was back in a thick braid, but Stan imagined it was long and full when she let it down. It was an intriguing blonde, but with a vast depth of color and tone. Stan was entranced.

It's tough to make out the shape of a woman's body beneath the standard loose fitting uniforms; nonetheless, fighter pilots apply beer-laced barroom algorithms under these circumstances. Stan calculated she was well endowed on top and maybe a tad bit curvaceous on the bottom. That merited a score of good to excellent . . . but who could know?

Stan scanned back up to her face, turning his head to keep visual track of her as he took another swig from his beer bottle. She was smiling at Lopass, and Stan felt a strange pang of jealousy. He wished he were the recipient of her smile. Funny how he had never paid much attention to the blonde around the squadron. Sure, he had seen her and probably even talked to her before, but she never captured his attention like this. Maybe it was the beer heightening his awareness.

As fate would have it, she turned and looked directly at Stan. It took a couple seconds for him to realize they were actually locked onto each other. This was more than a passing glance. It was as if a line of fiber optic communications cable had been laid and an extreme amount of nonverbal messaging was passing between them.

Renee was the first to blink and, like a southern belle, bashfully dropped her eyes to the floor. From the red in her cheeks, Stan knew it was not about Lopass's story, but for the secret two-way she had exchanged with Stan.

Stan took a drink, nodded as if he was still listening to the guys talking around him, and looked around for Jackie. She was still engaged in conversation, not paying him any attention. He glanced back at Renee. She was checking him out now and not trying to hide it. His heart started pounding in his chest, and he felt a stirring below his belt. The feeling jolted him back into a clear moment of sobriety, and he turned back to his circle, rebuking himself. *What am I? Fifteen years old?*

Jackie picked that moment to take his arm to introduce him to some members of her team. It took all his willpower not to seek out Renee again.

$\sim$

O ver the next week, Stan recalled the look, tried to interpret the nuances, and fantasized about how that night might have ended if he hadn't been married. For one thing, he was pretty sure he would have gotten laid. Numerous times, he chastised himself for obsessing about what couldn't be. But the series of fantasies and lascivious thoughts were too good to be pushed away. They had to be revisited.

Tossing and turning Sunday night, he struggled to fall asleep. He glanced across at Jackie's still body, crowding the opposite side of the bed. Finally, he succumbed to the fantasy he tried so hard to suppress. He imagined he and Renee had run into each other hiking on one of the many paths in the countryside around Spangdahlem. He drifted off to sleep thinking about his hands exploring her body, feeling a passion he desperately missed. In his sleep, Stan smiled.

# Chapter 8

Stan and Jackie weren't talking much lately, and Jackie missed it. They weren't fighting, but they weren't clicking either. She wanted to get back on track. Thursday afternoon, she called Stan at the squadron to propose they go out to dinner.

"We can meet at Anna's," she suggested. "I could use the heart-clogging butter in her schnitzel."

"Sounds good," Stan agreed. "I'll be there by six."

"Do you want me to pick you up?"

"I won't be drinking," Stan said defensively. "I have flight planning to do."

He hung up without saying goodbye.

Jackie ordered a glass of Riesling while she waited for Stan at their favorite restaurant. She had already finished her first glass before he showed up.

Without an apology, he took a seat across from her and signaled for the waitress to order a beer.

"I was beginning to think you'd forgotten," Jackie said.

"I had things to do. I'm going to Aviano next week."

"Ah, okay," Jackie said. This was the first she'd heard about it. "What's going on?"

"I'm part of the advance team for our live fire training in a few months. We're going down to see what equipment is available and what we have to take with us."

"Sounds like fun. How long will you be gone?"

"Just a week. Depends on how things look."

"Maybe I can take some leave and join you," Jackie suggested. She loved Italy and hadn't been to Aviano since their first Christmas in Europe.

"I'll be working. I don't have time for sightseeing."

Anna herself came out to take their order. Both ordered the buttered schnitzel for which Anna was famous. They settled back for a long wait. Germans didn't hurry their dining experience, and Anna seemed to take an extra-long time.

They were quiet. The waitress brought another glass of wine for Jackie and another beer for Stan. Stan finally broke the silence. "Lucases got orders."

"Where to?"

"Laughlin, Texas. He's going to be an instructor pilot."

"Dang. What does Kim think of that?"

"She's not thrilled with Laughlin, but at least he'll be home every night."

"Maybe they'll finally have a chance to start a family," Jackie mused.

Stan took a drink and didn't reply.

The food was the highlight of the night. Jackie was relieved when the bill came, and they were able to make their escape.

～

Stan gave up trying to avoid Captain Bennett. It seemed wherever he went, she was there. Friday, she showed up in the squadron bar when the beer lamp was lit. She took the beer he offered her and downed half of it in one pull. Surprised, Stan took her glass and topped it off. "Hard day at work?"

"Hard week. I couldn't concentrate to save my life."

"Don't tell me that. You might have been working on my jet."

"I might have been." She took another drink, never taking her eyes off his face. "How was your week?"

"Frustrating," he answered honestly. He didn't elaborate that it was sexual frustration, but he had a feeling she understood his meaning.

"Shame. Maybe we should help each other out a little."

Stan almost choked on his drink. Did she openly proposition him? It was about as straight forward as he had ever heard, but he wanted to be sure. He'd never had it this easy, that is, if he was reading her correctly. "What did you have in mind?"

"If we put our *heads* together, I'm sure something will come up," she said artfully.

～

Italy was a beautiful country. The food was great, and the alcohol was cheap. Because there were no rooms at the American base nearby, Stan and his team were housed in a quaint hotel downtown. Like most places in Europe, it was small and run down by American standards—that's what made it quaint.

Stan cautiously responded to the knock at the door, and a blonde in tight jeans and a low-cut shirt pushed her way passed him into the room. He glanced down the hall in both directions and then shut the door.

Renee Bennett flung herself onto the bed and kicked off her shoes as if this were the most natural thing in the world.

"What do you have to drink?" she asked.

Stan went to the small dresser and opened the bag he brought from Germany in his travel pod. He pulled out a bottle of Absolut Vodka and a slightly chilled carton of grapefruit juice. "How about a greyhound?"

He wasn't sure what he was getting himself into, and he tried to pretend that it wasn't unusual for him to have a female officer in his room for drinks. He didn't want to make any assumptions in case he was reading Renee's advancements incorrectly. The last thing he needed was to make a fool of himself.

He mixed two drinks and handed one to Renee. "They aren't much for ice here, so you'll have to pretend."

Renee took the offered glass and looked at Stan seductively. "I have a feeling I wouldn't have to pretend with you." She sipped her drink and set it aside.

Stan smirked at her double meaning. The danger of the situation was exhilarating for him. Jackie's face flashed before his eyes, but he quickly pushed it aside. The multiple drinks he had before Renee had arrived had weakened his resolve, and he couldn't think beyond the moment.

The smell of Renee's perfume and the sight of her cleavage drew him in. His eyes roamed over her hips and tight jeans, which accentuated her thin legs. He thought of those legs wrapped around his waist and felt his passion growing.

He was tired of second guessing. He needed to know what her intentions were. He set his drink down and leaned in close to her without actually making contact. He breathed softly in her ear, making her shudder. "You mean you'd always be real with me?"

"Uh huh," she said, soaking in the attention.

"And you'd tell me what you'd really like?" He continued to torture her with his nearness but lack of connection.

She reached for him, but he captured her wrists in his hands and pushed her back onto the bed. He straddled her and pinned her arms over her shoulders.

"So you wouldn't have to fake it if I made love to you all night long?" He brushed his lips across her neck.

She raised her hips to show her willingness and felt him quite ready to please her. Breathlessly, she said, "I'm gonna hurt you if you don't get naked and get this party started."

Stan couldn't resist any longer. His mouth covered hers hungrily, and his hands began the satisfying chore of undressing her.

~

Time went by quickly while Stan was gone. Jackie caught up on her paperwork by staying a little later each night but still managed to get in a workout every day. When she got home, she wasn't stressed about the work awaiting her the next day, and she was able to enjoy her downtime.

Margaret, her German friend, came by a few times, and the two exchanged stories about their families.

"How's your lovely sister and that handsome groom of hers?" Margaret had met Jackie's sister Alison the previous summer when she and Lance had come to visit. Now Margaret always asked about them.

"They're doing great. Hopefully Alison will be coming to visit soon. I want her to experience Fasching." Karnival or Fasching officially began in most regions of Germany on the eleventh of November at 11:11 a.m., culminating in Fasching week, which began the week before Ash Wednesday.

"That would be perfect," Margaret agreed. "We need more women for the Fasching Day Parade."

"They're going to start trying for a baby soon so I know that will slow down her traveling for a little while. I want her to experience more of Europe with me before then."

Margaret smiled. "Tell Lance to bring extra ties."

Weiberfastnacht was the Thursday before Ash Wednesday. The day begins with women symbolically taking over city hall by storming the building. Then, women station themselves on the side of a street and flag down the men as they drive through the small town. They snip off men's ties in exchange for a kiss. Even the American military men join in the tradition and wear ties with their uniforms on that day.

Margaret's oldest daughter was getting married, so they spent a lot of time discussing the wedding preparations.

As Margaret recounted the tales of her wedding day, the phone rang. Jackie was still laughing when she answered it. "Hello?"

"Hey, Jackie, this is Jello. How's your Wednesday going so far?"

Jackie was instantly sobered. Lieutenant Colonel Brian "Jello" Mills, Stan's operations officer, had never called her before. But the use of his call sign rather than his rank told her it couldn't be too serious. "Fine, sir."

"Good. Glad to hear it. Well, it seems you aren't the only one having a good night."

She heard hooting and hollering in the background.

"I think Stan could use a ride home. I wouldn't mind dropping him off, but my wife is expecting me to meet her for dinner in a few minutes."

"Yes, sir. I'll be right there."

"It's no rush. We took his keys and stashed them behind the ops desk. You can pick up his car tomorrow."

"Thank you, sir."

"Jackie, don't worry about it. He isn't on the schedule tomorrow. It's no big deal."

It was to Jackie. Not so much that Stan was drinking at the office. After all, they had a bar in the squadron. But he had come back into town and hadn't even called her. She had a big reunion planned for him, but this wasn't the way it was supposed to start.

At least he didn't have a chance to drive this time. She was thankful for that.

~

Jackie needed to get out of the house. Two days had passed, and she was still mad at Stan for not calling her when he got back from his TDY. He acted as if nothing was wrong. Although he thanked her for the ride, he continued to argue that he was fine to drive. He had spent the whole ride home badmouthing Jello for calling her.

This morning he had slept in before going to play golf with some guys from the squadron.

As Jackie drove toward base, she tried to focus on something else—anything else. She always needed new material for the exercises. When the same scenarios were used over and over, it dulled the effect. People gamed the system and lost the chance to learn something new.

Jackie parked on the taxiway near the maintenance hangars and began to walk. As she strolled the length of the taxiway, she worked out objectives in her mind. What scenario would give the fire department a chance to respond to a fire that wouldn't be an airplane crash? Maybe this time she should get the security forces to respond. During exercises, first responders' objectives were usually pretty mild. It was hard to work them into a scenario when everything in the exercise was focused on deployment.

A sound from inside one of Hardened Aircraft Shelters caught her attention. The HAS was a large hangar built to protect the aircraft in case of an airfield attack. It was Saturday, and she was surprised anyone would be working. Although no lights were on inside, there was plenty of sunlight coming through the open bay door.

"Hello?" Jackie called. Her voice echoed. She noticed two jets in the hardened shelter, but she didn't see anyone inside. As she approached the jet, she had the same feeling of awe that always encircled her around these machines. She ran her hand along the metal skin in an almost romantic way. She wasn't qualified to be a pilot, but that didn't mean she didn't appreciate the job they did. The idea of shooting through the clouds at high speeds was exhilarating—especially being in Germany.

Eventually Jackie broke away from her reverie. She patted the machine one last time and turned to go. She sensed the slightest vibration in the air, and it made her shudder.

# Chapter 9

Hey, Jackie," Michael called across the room and waved her over. "Join us."

It was Monday afternoon, and two fellow officers were seated at the table already beginning their lunch. Jackie set down her tray and pulled up a chair. The officers' club was a great place to meet up with friends and catch a quick bite without having to go off base.

"What fun things do you have in store for us next?" asked Major Michael Spruce, a personnel officer in the 52nd Force Support Squadron.

"That's for me to know," Jackie answered. "I wouldn't want to ruin the surprise."

"You always give us at least one thing no one's thought about yet," offered Captain Brad Brody, a flight commander with the 52nd Security Force Squadron.

"Keeping you on your toes," Jackie said.

"I've got an idea for you."

Jackie rolled her eyes at the captain. "It scares me when you start off a statement like that."

"This is a good one," he said.

"Like your idea for aliens last time?" Michael asked.

"Not real aliens. People pretending to be aliens. I'm not that stupid."

"I'm thinking about ghosts," Jackie said.

Both men looked at her and burst into laughter. "What?" they said together.

"Okay, not really, but I was in HAS three the other day, and I heard some strange noises. It was freaky."

"Oh, we get reports of that all the time," Brad said. "It's usually a cat or the wind blowing through the cracks. They're pretty old buildings."

"Well, it was enough to send chills up my spine," Jackie said.

"I don't blame you," said Michael. He turned to Brad. "Now we have an idea what the scene for her next dastardly event will be."

"That's what I'm leading you to believe. Counterintelligence is important too."

∽

Jackie sat bundled on the sofa under a cozy blanket her mom sent her. One of her favorite authors was putting out books faster than she could keep up with him. She was determined to get through the stack of books she had been buying and setting aside for an opportunity like this.

Now, as she tried to concentrate on her reading, the thought of breaking the news to Stan that she was going to be filling in for her boss while he went on leave for the next two weeks filled her with dread. He hated when her workload increased for any reason.

A few nights ago, Stan had come home with a dozen roses. She knew it wasn't easy for him to admit he had done something wrong. Asking for forgiveness for not calling her as soon as he returned from his latest trip was a huge step for him.

Jackie smiled when she thought of the look on his face when, later in the evening, she brought him a beer on the terrace wearing nothing but lace and silk.

She was pulled back to the present when the back door open. "I'm in here," she called.

Stan stuck his head around the corner. "I'm going to change. Want to help?"

"How can I resist that come on?" Jackie answered, putting aside her book.

As they lay in bed, legs tangled together, salty sweat forming a layer between them, Jackie ran her fingers through his chest hairs. Stan's hand lazily stroked her back, while his breathing evened out.

"Colonel Harris is going on leave next week," Jackie started. She felt his hand stop moving in anticipation of her next comment. "I'm going to be filling in for him."

"But you hate the complaints-side of the IG."

Stan was right. Jackie loved working the exercises, but the other half of the inspector general's job was dealing with complaints. It was tough when, at any time, a complaint could be made against one of your friends and you had to be able to separate yourself from your personal feelings. She had seen it recently when a squadron commander was accused of having an affair with an enlisted person in his unit. Digging into dirt was not one of Jackie's favorite pastimes.

"I know, but it's a great opportunity," Jackie said.

"How do you figure? Sounds to me like more grief and longer hours."

"And more face time. The wing commander's going to be making his decision soon on who to give the DPs to. I want to be one of them." Definitely Promotes, or DPs, were given to the top ten percent of the people meeting the promotion board under that particular senior rater, in this case the wing commander. It wasn't really an automatic that a person with a DP would be promoted, but it greatly increased one's odds.

For Jackie, this was a Below-the-Primary-Zone opportunity, which made selection even harder. The senior rater may nominate a small number of officers for an early promotion to lieutenant colonel. Because Jackie was not expected to the meet the board for her primary zone for another year, to be named as one of the few BPZ-selects would be a huge boon for her career. As a non-pilot, if she wanted to keep advancing in the Air Force, this was one of the few ways to distinguish herself from the pack.

Stan extricated himself from Jackie's embrace and swung his feet to the floor. "Do what you need to do," he said with a sigh.

～

Jackie pored over the paperwork in her inbox. Some of the accusations infuriated her. People could be so petty. In some cases, she wished she was allowed to tell these people to grow some and move on, but she had to stay politically correct. She felt that the mountain of minor issues lessened the impact of those who had legitimate concerns or complaints. Because the inspector general's office was required to validate and, if necessary, investigate every accusation, their resources were stretched very thin. She finally realized why her boss stayed late so often and didn't smile much.

Jackie's thoughts pivoted back to Stan. She knew he wasn't happy with her working late, but it wasn't like he was sitting at home waiting for her. His flying schedule varied greatly, and when he wasn't flying, he spent time on the golf course or at the squadron bar.

Jackie jumped when Mastana appeared in her doorway.

"Sorry, Ms. Austin," Mastana said.

"No worries," Jackie said. "I didn't hear you come in."

"I will be quick."

Jackie was still thinking about Stan's attitude. "Does your husband mind you working?"

"I do what is necessary for the good of our family."

Jackie thought about that. Did she and Stan alone constitute a family? They didn't have kids. She didn't really need to work, but she wanted to.

"Mastana, do you have kids?"

Mastana froze her dusting mid-swipe as if she had been struck. Then she re-doubled her efforts as she attacked the imperceptible dirt on the shelf. "No."

Jackie was so caught up in her own musings, she didn't notice Mastana's discomfort. "Neither do I but I want them someday. I don't think Stan does." She twirled a pen around in her fingers absentmindedly.

Shaking herself from her depressing introspection, she tried to change the subject. "How long have you and your husband been in Germany?"

"Aashna was brought to Germany when he was a young boy as his father searched for work. He is Pashtun."

"He's Afghan?"

"His family is from Afghanstan, but he is a German citizen." Mastana never stopped moving. She emptied the trash and replaced the bag.

"Where's Aashna's family in Afghanstan?"

"They are near Kandahar," Mastana answered in a clipped tone.

"That's really dangerous."

Mastana had a look on her face Jackie couldn't translate. Mastana shook her head but didn't utter a word. Her eyes became dark, and her face looked moist with cold sweat.

Jackie was stunned by the change in Mastana's demeanor and searched for something, anything, to say. She wasn't sure what she had said wrong. Then a thought struck her. "Are you from Kandahar too?"

She nodded curtly. "After the war, I came here. Aashna's parents took me in. They arranged the marriage." She ran the feather duster over the shelves holding Jackie's reference books.

"Arranged?"

She paused in her work and looked directly at Jackie. "Mrs. Austin, our ways are not yours."

Of course Jackie had heard of arranged marriages. She just had never met anyone who had had one. She had many questions but didn't want to pry.

"Do you ever go back to visit?" she asked instead.

"There is nothing to visit."

# Chapter 10

Jackie cherished the rare opportunities to talk to her sister Alison. Between the time difference and the high price of overseas calls, most of their communication was via email, and that didn't have the same satisfying effect. When Jackie lived in the States, they spoke at least weekly. It used to be daily, but two years ago, Alison met Lance and got caught up in her own life. He was great to her, and Alison was very happy. They ran off and got married in Las Vegas last year. It wasn't truly an elopement because Jackie had shown up in time to stand beside her sister.

"What exciting things do you have planned for your anniversary?" Alison asked.

"Who says I'm planning anything?" Jackie replied.

"You don't know how *not* to plan something."

"Guilty." Jackie's sister knew her too well. Ever since they were little, Alison had been her best friend. Only two years her senior, Alison was close enough to guide Jackie through the most troubling spots of their teenage years, but far enough apart to not compete for boyfriends. It wasn't always easy growing up with their alcoholic father, and Alison was the only one who understood Jackie completely. Jackie knew her childhood had helped make her who she was today—a strong, self-reliant woman. She also knew adult children of alcoholics had demons to exorcise.

Thankfully, her father had overcome his addiction after many failed attempts, and Jackie had gotten much closer to him in the past few years. She was able to share her successes with him. But she would never be as close to anyone as she was to her sister—not even Stan.

"For years, we've talked about going to Switzerland. We both have plenty of leave saved up, and I think the timing should work out. I'll talk to his ops officer to make sure the schedule is clear."

"Are you sure surprising him is a good idea?" Alison asked.

"Stan doesn't plan things, but he's usually pretty good at going along with what I plan."

"Still," Alison cautioned, "think twice about it. I'd hate to see you disappointed. And waste a lot of money in the progress."

"Fair enough. I'll make the outline and share it with him before I buy the tickets."

"How are you two getting along these days?" Alison asked.

Jackie thought about the answer. "Okay. We avoid certain topics."

"Like . . . ?"

"Like careers."

"Great. Your work is your life—for both of you—and you have to avoid talking about it."

"Not work in general. Only the next step. My promotion board is meeting in a few months, and there's a good chance the wing commander may recommend me for early promotion."

"Of course there is. You're shit hot," said Alison.

Jackie smiled in appreciation at the confidence her sister had in her. "Considering you don't really know what I do, that's a big leap of faith."

"But I know you. You put everything into anything you take on. It's obvious."

"Thanks. But the real problem is Stan doesn't see that. Ever since he was passed over for lieutenant colonel last year, he's fed up with the military. He still loves to fly, but nothing else is important to him."

"Is there a chance he'll get promoted this time?"

"His records will meet the board again, but he hasn't corrected the reasons he got passed over the first time. He still doesn't have his master's degree, and he didn't finish his required professional military education. Besides that, he's got a very strong record. He's a great pilot, has been a flight commander, weapons officer, and safety. He's done everything else that was asked of him."

"It's a shame doing his job isn't enough to get him promoted," Alison commented.

"I agree." They were silent for a moment.

"So what are you getting Mom for her birthday?"

Jackie searched the internet for the best places to visit in Switzerland. She really wanted to see Zurich and knew Stan would love to ski the Alps. She printed out the most interesting places and put them together in a scrapbook when Stan wasn't around. She worked for weeks on the presentation in order to surprise him.

She talked to Stan's operations officer, and he didn't see any reason Stan couldn't take the time off. Jello agreed to keep her plans a secret.

All was prepared. Jackie set the table with their nicest dishes. She made his favorite dinner and opened a bottle of wine. As an afterthought, she added candles. She stood back and surveyed her work. She hoped he would be excited, and she was a little nervous. He had still been distant, and she wasn't sure what would pull him back to her. She hoped some time away, only the two of them, would reignite the old sparks.

Jackie went upstairs to change into something a little nicer than her usual sweats. As she pulled the sweater dress over her head and straightened it, she heard him come in. Still barefoot, she walked down the stairs and approached him as he sat on the couch taking off his boots.

He looked up. "Smells good." Catching sight of her dress, he asked, "Did I forget something?"

Jackie smiled and kneeled down beside him. "No, I wanted to have a special dinner. Is that all right?" She leaned over and kissed his cheek.

Stan looked at her suspiciously. "You're up to something," he said.

"But it's a good something," she replied.

She took his hand and led him into the small dining room. She gestured toward his chair. "Will you pour the wine while I get dinner?"

Stan watched her walk away and reached for the bottle.

Jackie came back in with a steaming dish of chicken marsala and set it carefully on the trivet they had purchased in Holland. She picked up his plate and dished out his food, handing it to him with a Cheshire grin.

As she dished out her own food, he asked, "You aren't pregnant, are you?"

Jackie froze. The tone of his voice was less than happy.

"No, I'm not. But would that be such a bad thing?"

Dodging the question, Stan cut into his chicken and took a big bite. "Hmmmm, you make the best chicken."

She sat down and put the cloth napkin on her lap. "You didn't answer my question."

"We've talked about it before. I'm not ready."

This wasn't the conversation Jackie wanted to have right now. She hadn't even been thinking about kids lately, but Stan's tone stung. She tried to shake it off.

"Have you talked to your parents lately?" Jackie asked, changing the subject.

"No. I sent Dad an email last week but haven't heard back from him."

"What about Kermit? When's he coming back?" Stan had told her about running into him at the squadron.

"It'll be a couple of weeks. He has some TDYs to visit the other bases as part of his orientation. He'll let us know. I told him to plan on dinner at least."

They made small talk through the rest of their dinner, catching up on the latest stories from the office. Jackie filled Stan in on Alison and her parents.

When they finished, Jackie stood up and cleared their plates. She came back into the dining room as Stan was refilling their wine glasses. She handed him the scrapbook she had been working so hard on.

"What's this?" he asked.

"Hopefully it's the plan for our anniversary celebration in Switzerland," she answered.

She went back into the kitchen to get their dessert as he flipped through the pages.

When she placed a slice of pecan pie in front of him, he picked up his fork absentmindedly and took a bite.

"I'm sorry, Jackie, but I'm not sure I can get away." He looked up to see her reaction.

"I already talked to Jello. He checked the schedule and said that was a clear week for leave."

"You what? You talked to my boss?"

Jackie was taken aback. "I only asked him to check the schedule for the second week of December. I didn't want to plan something that was going to be impossible."

Stan finished his pie without speaking and then pushed his chair away from the table. "This is very nice, Jackie. I know you put a lot of time into it. I'll think about it. There's a lot going on right now so I'll have to see if I can get away."

He got up from the table and went up the stairs, leaving Jackie to clean off the table.

She sat alone, trying to analyze what she had done wrong this time. Tears coursed down her cheeks, but she didn't make a sound.

# Chapter 11

For Thanksgiving, Jackie and Stan joined Jenn and Jim Collins at their place. With the four kids running around, ages two to nine, it was a lively household. Jackie took it all in stride and immediately began helping with dinner preparations.

"What did Stan think about the Switzerland idea?" Jenn asked as soon as they were alone.

"Don't ask." Jackie stirred the mashed potatoes.

"What? He didn't love it?" Jenn looked at her friend sympathetically.

"Nope. Not interested. He has to 'see if he can get away.' It's bullshit."

"Maybe you and I should go," Jenn offered.

Jackie chuckled. "Sounds like a plan."

"Now what are you going to do?" Jenn tossed the salad.

"What else can I do? Besides, why should I have to be the one doing all the trying?"

On the drive home that night, after a fulfilling turkey feast, Jackie reached over and took Stan's hand. "That was a lot of fun."

"Too noisy." He pulled his hand away to adjust the windshield wipers against the icy mist.

Jackie sat back and crossed her arms. *It's icy inside the car too,* she thought.

~

Stan sat in a briefing room, studying the maps for his afternoon sortie. He was having a hard time concentrating. He knew he owed Jackie an answer, but all their conversations were stilted.

Neither one of them brought up the Switzerland trip—Jackie because she was afraid of nagging him, and Stan because he didn't want to see the look in Jackie's eyes. Stan didn't feel like celebrating their anniversary. They had been married ten years, and for the most part, they had been great. Jackie was a wonderful friend and a good partner. They enjoyed many of the same things, and she wasn't the clingy type. But lately she was starting to get on his nerves.

She was always on the go. Her work hours were worse than his, and she seemed to thrive on it. Even his squadron commander loved her and complimented her presentations to Stan. Not that he really cared to hear.

He didn't understand why she wasn't satisfied to hang out with his friends and their wives at the officers' club. She spent more time wandering the flight line or chatting with the folks in the civil engineering unit. She used to be a lot more fun. In Korea, where they first met, she would do shots with him. Granted, she didn't hold her alcohol well, but at least she gave it a good try. He laughed to himself as he remembered the time he followed her home from the club, picking up the pieces of her uniform as she stripped them off walking across the parking lot.

The door creaked opened behind him. "Guess who?" Hands slipped over his eyes.

He grabbed her hands and slid them down to his mouth and playfully bit her thumb. "Tastes like jet fuel," he joked.

Renee swatted him and turned to push the door closed.

Then she moved to face him, circled her arms around his neck, and kissed him quickly. "When do we leave?"

"They haven't finished cutting the orders. I put in for the maintenance plane to depart Sunday. The jets arrive on Monday."

"Where are we staying?"

"There's no room on base so we're staying at Catalonia El Pilar."

"Adjoining rooms?" she asked playfully.

"Does it matter?" He kissed her again.

"No worries, Mace. I'm sure I know somebody who can make the change." She ran her hand along his arm. "So, did you tell her?"

"Not yet. I'm working on it."

"What's the big deal? It's a TDY. If nothing else, she understands work."

"You don't get it. Jackie plans everything. She'd plan her own funeral if given the chance."

"That's why this will be good for her. She can't control everything." Renee leaned in and whispered in Stan's ear, "She doesn't control you."

$\sim$

"What do you mean you're going TDY?" she shouted. "Jackie, get a hold of yourself."

"You volunteered, didn't you?" He couldn't hide the shame on his face that colored his cheeks. "How dare you!" she spat. "You know how much this means to me! Couldn't you do one thing for me for a change?"

Stan couldn't look her in the eye. He was starting to doubt the wisdom of his decision. He searched for a plausible explanation that she could relate to. "Volunteering is good when it comes to promotion, right? Haven't you told me that?"

"Not volunteering for flying! Everyone does that. Try doing something that's outside your comfort zone, not second nature. You are so selfish!" She was close to tears but was never one who cried to get her way. Before a tear escaped, she turned on her heels and walked away. Her steps were just short of a run, and her hand covered her mouth as though she were going to be sick. She took the stairs two at a time and closed the bedroom door surprisingly quietly behind her.

Stan watched her walk away, not sure how he was feeling. She sounded pretty pissed, but that was her way of covering up hurt. *"Well? What did you expect, moron?"* he asked himself. *"She'd planned this trip for our anniversary."*

He retrieved a beer from the refrigerator and opened it using the bottle opener he picked up on his last trip to Italy. He thought of Renee's smile and warm mouth on his. She didn't yell at him or try to tell him what he needed to do to get promoted. She accepted him as he was.

As he remembered his last TDY with Renee, he became aroused and all worries about Jackie's feeling were pushed aside. Instead he focused on his next TDY and the new positions Renee had so clearly described in her text messages. He went to find his phone.

≈

Stan had departed for a three-day out-and-back to Zaragoza, Spain, to visit the bombing ranges. Jackie was disappointed they hadn't made up after their fight, but at the same time, she was relieved to have him out of the house. It was less stressful. It had only been 48 hours and already she was more relaxed.

Instead of rushing home, she decided to go for a drive and let her mind wander. She loved to explore the flight line late at night. The weather was terrific. Clear and quiet. It was too cool for the bugs but unseasonably warm for December.

As she drove past HAS 2, Jackie caught a flicker of light out of the corner of her eye. She slowed to take a closer look. As she rolled to a stop, she stared intently. Nothing. Deciding it was her imagination, she drove on. Then she caught another flash, then another.

Her heart beat wildly in her chest. Something wasn't right, but she wasn't sure what to do. She wasn't about to go poking around inside the HAS at night. She pulled her car over to the side and put it in park.

"Wind the clock," she whispered to herself. She closed her eyes and took a few deep breaths.

Of all the pilot mantras Stan had shared with her, wind the clock was the most useful. The older planes had a mechanical clock in the cockpit that had to be wound as one of the steps on the checklist to prepare to fly. As new jets were designed, the mechanical clock kept making its way into the cockpit. No one would ever dare to replace it. The pilots were taught when they weren't sure what they should be doing, but feel like they *must* do something, "wind the clock." It slowed them down enough to clear their head and take the time to make the right decision.

Stan told her it was probably responsible for saving more pilots than the ejection seat.

She fished the cell phone from her pocket and searched the contacts for her friend from the security forces squadron.

"Hey, Brad, it's Jackie," she said when he answered his phone.

"Hey, yourself. What's up?"

"You wouldn't still happen to be on base, would you?" she asked.

"As a matter of fact, I am. I'm at the office but getting ready to leave. You need something?"

"Remember the ghost I was telling you about?"

Brad snickered. "I'm not falling for one of your scenarios."

"Okay, it *probably* isn't a ghost, but there's something weird at HAS two."

"What kind of weird?"

"Weird enough that I called you. I think I saw something."

"Okay, where are you now?" he asked.

"Sitting outside the hangar. Meet me at the entry point next to the A-10 squadron. I'll pick you up there."

"Be there in five," he replied, clicking off.

Jackie dropped her phone into her lap and put the car in gear. She drove the painfully slow five miles an hour to the entry point.

# Chapter 12

Her eyes were now adjusted to the darkness, and she was able to see more detail under the faint illumination cast from small exit lights by the two doors along the back of the hangar. The tool chests on roller wheels were lined up like soldiers within a precisely painted box on the concrete floor. It was in the exact location she was told. They were various sizes, but she was looking for only the ones that stood up to her chest and had five drawers.

Creeping toward the closest one, she listened for any sign of danger. *Five drawers. This is it.*

She gently pulled on the top drawer, but it only gave a little and would open no further. Crouching and straining her eyes across the face of the drawer, she tugged harder. A cord was drawn tightly through the metal loops attached to each drawer. The bicycle cable-like cord went up and across the chest where it was joined to a loop on top with a heavy padlock. The chests were all securely closed.

This was not in the practice drills she endured, and her anxiety rose as she thought about returning empty-handed. She knew this was her punishment for embarrassing her husband. Last time she had been told to take a picture of a certain page in the technical manual, and she had failed. Although she had secured the information, she didn't follow the directions exactly as they had been laid out. That made her husband very angry. He claimed she had shamed him in front of his friends because his wife wasn't obedient. She couldn't afford to fail this time.

Each chest she tried was similarly bound. Breathing heavily and darting from chest to chest, she tugged hard to see if any of the top drawers would open enough for her to snake her slender fingers through the opening. With each frustrated attempt, she moved more recklessly in the darkness, tugging on the drawers with all her strength and silently pleading for Allah to help her.

At the end of the row was one last chest. It wasn't aligned inside the painted lines on the floor like the others. She paused for a moment to steady herself, then pulled on the top drawer with both hands and all her strength. The drawer opened wide as the steel cord whipped over the top of the chest and struck the side of her head, sending her to her knees. The pain was paralyzing.

Gradually she pulled herself to her feet, and both hands fumbled hungrily across the tools nestled in perfectly cutout shapes in a layer of foam holding them snuggly.

*Could this be it?* She took the chance and flicked on the flashlight she carried with her. As quickly as possible, she ran the light across the other shapes to be sure there wasn't anything similar. No, only the one. She shut off the light, pried the tool from its hole, and held it close to her face to examine it. It was very similar in shape to the strange tool they had shown her but was about the length of her forearm. It didn't look like anything special. If they could get one from a hardware store, she wasn't sure why they needed this particular tool. She placed it inside her jacket, tightening the drawstring around her waist to hold it in place.

Something wet trickled down her face. A quick flick of the light illuminated red on her fingers where she had swiped at her cheek. At the sight of the blood, she panicked and bolted to the exit, tripping in the darkness on one of the chests she had pulled out of line. It slammed against the next chest with a deep-pitched thud that seemed to echo forever within the hangar. She tumbled onto the icy cold concrete. Sitting frozen and motionless, she listened for any response to the noise of the collision, barely breathing. After several minutes of hearing nothing unusual, she took a few deep breaths to calm herself.

Rising on shaking legs, she realized she had left the drawer open in her haste. She almost disregarded it but couldn't afford to be sloppy. Quickly this time, she reached the tool kit and closed the drawer, tightening the steel cord in place. She put all of her weight behind it and pushed to align the tool chest with the others. Another bang of metal on metal resounded as it rolled into place.

Sweating now and nervous that someone passing by might have heard the noise, she hastily she retraced her steps to the door and put her ear against the crack to listen. The gash on her head was swelling and pulsed with pain.

Brad jumped in the car as Jackie pulled to a stop beside the control gate. "What did you see?" he asked.

"Lights, I think. It may be nothing. It could be some poor airman working late, but it doesn't feel right."

"Are you sure you aren't playing a trick on me?" Brad asked dubiously.

"I'm not feeling that clever tonight." Jackie pulled closer to the HAS this time and parked the car. She left the headlights on but shut off the engine. She was feeling silly now that she had Brad there with her.

They got out of the car, Brad carrying his flashlight in his right hand, and headed toward the partial opening in shelter doors. The lights were off inside, but Jackie's headlights pierced through the darkness and illuminated some of the tool cabinets standing sentry nearest the entrance.

"Hello!" Brad called.

They listened but got no response.

"Hello!" he called again and clicked on his flashlight. He swung the beam around the shelter, casting long shadows across the floor.

Jackie walked around the tall, metal boxes and peered behind them. No one jumped out at her. She shook her head. "Sorry I pulled you out here."

"Maybe your headlights reflected off something when you drove by," Brad suggested.

"Maybe," Jackie murmured. She knew she didn't get close enough to cause a reflection of her headlights, and the light moved when she was still, but she didn't want to say anything more.

"Come on," Brad said. "You owe me a drink."

Jackie followed Brad's car to the Bierhaus located outside the main gate. This was a favorite dinnertime haunt for many base personnel, and Jackie couldn't resist their jaeger schnitzel.

As they parked and got out, Jackie asked, "Have you had dinner yet?"

"Nope. I have a TV dinner waiting for me at home."

"Think it'll keep for another night? Stan's TDY so I was going to eat a bowl of cereal."

"In that case, only to save you from yourself, I will have dinner with you, in addition to the drink you owe me."

They walked into the alluring aroma of grilled pork and pommes frits. A waitress met them at the table as they seated themselves, and they placed their orders without having to consult the menu.

"So where's Stan off to this time?" Brad asked.

"Zaragoza," Jackie answered as the waitress swiftly placed their drinks on the table and departed.

"Hardship. I never get to go anyplace that nice," he complained.

"Where have you gone?"

"Iraq once and Afghanstan once. Six months each time." He raised his beer mug in a mock salute.

Jackie tapped her glass to his. "That sucks. How was it?"

"Not as bad as you would think. But I'd much rather be in Spain."

Sensing he didn't want to talk about his deployments, Jackie changed the subject. "Are your parents coming to visit again this summer?"

When Brad's parents visited the summer before, Stan escorted them onto the flight line to get up close to the jet. He had the crew chief, Senior Airman Joe Suitor, pull out the rolling ladder used for distinguished visitors to climb the staircase with ease and look into the cockpit.

Jackie was in the squadron when the visit finished and took advantage of the ladder to take her own peek inside. Brad felt he owed the crew chief for doing him such a big favor, but Suitor later confessed to Jackie that he loved any chance to show off his jet.

"No, they're going to visit my sister in Texas. Her husband is stationed at Randolph, and she's due in March. I have a feeling they'll be spending a lot of time with their only grandbaby."

Jackie smiled. "Guess if you want to get their attention again, you'll have to start making babies."

"Perish the thought!" Brad held up both hands to ward off the suggestion. "I'd rather do things in the right order. First, I have to talk someone into marrying me."

"I suggest you start by dating. Weren't you seeing Beth from the hospital? She's nice. And smart."

"Too smart apparently. It didn't work out."

The waitress returned with their food, and they ate in companionable silence.

As they finished their meals, Jackie asked, "So do you have plans for your next assignment?"

Brad wiped his mouth and tucked his napkin under his plate. "I might be done."

"What?" Jackie was surprised. Brad had always come across as the gung-ho military cop who couldn't get enough.

"I still have another year or so here, and I'm not going to cut it short. I'm considering my options."

"Do you want to stay in law enforcement?"

"Yeah, I think so. But not a beat cop. Something more interesting, like an investigator. Maybe FBI. They hire ex-military."

"You'd be great in the FBI. Maybe they'll reopen the X-Files for you," she said.

"Ha, ha. Make fun all you want. Someday you'll call on me to solve your alien-invasion scenario."

# Chapter 13

Stan walked into the house, and the smell of scented candles assailed him. He was instantly attuned to Jackie's intention. The flickering light and soft music was her idea of a romantic atmosphere. A few months ago, he may have welcomed her advances. But not tonight. He still smelled a trace of Renee on his skin from their passionate morning goodbye before he departed Zaragoza.

Jackie entered from the kitchen holding two glasses of white wine. She was dressed in nothing but a rose-colored silk nightie Stan recognized from their Korean shopping adventures. Her hair fell over her shoulders in soft waves. She looked lovely.

She leaned against Stan, kissing him deeply before stepping back and handing him his wine. Stan kissed her back but read the disappointment in her eyes that it wasn't the tender response she was hoping for. The fact that she tried to smile anyway made Stan feel guilty.

"I'm sorry, honey," he said. "I'm exhausted. It was a long flight with multiple delays getting off the ground."

"That's okay," she replied. "Why don't you sit with me and relax a while?" She took his hand in hers.

"I really need to take a shower," he said, squeezing her hand and releasing it.

"Is that an invitation?" she asked playfully.

"Not this time. I'll be quick." He handed her his glass and left her standing in the hallway.

Frustrated, but trying not to read too much into his non-reaction, Jackie took their glasses into the living room, settling on the couch. She finished her wine, staring into the twinkling light from the candles on the coffee table. The shower water turn off, and she waited, curbing her impatience.

After finishing Stan's glass of wine as well, Jackie blew out the candle and went to find her husband. She followed the clicking sounds into the study where Stan sat behind the computer, dressed in his jeans and polo shirt, typing away.

Incredulously, she stood in the doorway until he looked up. "Sorry, Jackie. I wanted to get this email out while I was thinking about it."

"Forget it," she mumbled. She held her tears until she got back to her room. She had done her best to make up with Stan after their disagreement over the anniversary trip. It couldn't always be her who went the extra mile.

Stripping out of the silk, she pulled on an old t-shirt. She always felt self-conscious wearing that girly stuff anyway. Apparently, it wasn't interesting to Stan either. Admonishing herself for playing dress up, she swore to pack away all the ridiculous lingerie the Korean women had convinced her would keep a spark in her marriage.

~

Christmas came and went without anything remarkable happening. Her parents loved the European gifts she had picked up at the various Kris Kringle markets in the last few months. Alison and Lance appreciated the spices Jackie sent home to make their own mulled wine. They promised to spend next Christmas in Germany with her and experience firsthand the Weihnachtsmarkt in Frankfurt.

Stan called his parents, but as usual, Jackie didn't join in the conversation. She yelled hello from the background but found other things to do while they chatted.

She and Stan exchanged a few small Christmas gifts. It was hard to surprise each other because, with dual incomes and no kids, they pretty much had the money to buy what they wanted or needed as the urge arose. They didn't have to wait for a special occasion like Christmas or birthdays.

Jackie was delighted with the pair of diamond stud earrings Stan gave her. She presented him with a glorious, ugly tie for him to wear on Fasching, a new computer game that didn't involve killing things, and clothes. He hated to buy his own clothes. He would sooner let them fall to rags on his body than go shopping.

It had been more than a month since they had made love. Stan never mentioned his lack of interest in her silk display, and Jackie wasn't going to embarrass herself by bringing it up, but it haunted her. She wasn't sure what else she could do to turn their relationship around. She knew he was gearing up for another TDY. They needed to talk, but he wasn't a "talking" kind of guy. He felt if you ignored a problem long enough, it would go away.

Jackie sat at her desk finishing up the last of her day's work. It had been a long week, and she was ready to get out of there. She decided to go by the squadron and see what was going on. It was mid-January, and the new winter rotations would be in place.

Summer was the biggest time for reassignments, when most kids were out of school. The second highest rotation time was after Christmas and New Year's break. They would be bidding the old-timers farewell and welcoming the new guys with sophomoric fighter pilot games.

"Hello, Major Austin," said the noncommissioned officer standing behind the flight desk when she walked in the squadron.

"Hi, Jonesy. Ready for the weekend?"

"Very much so." He smiled. "Major Mason's in the back."

"Of course. Have a great weekend."

Hoots and hollers from the masses greeted her as she entered the squadron bar.

"Jackie, glad to see you could join us," Jello said with a big smile, handing her a beer.

She took it gratefully. The music was loud, and a few guys were well on their way to hangovers. She looked around and spotted Stan's back as he leaned over someone in the table booth built in the far corner of the squadron bar.

When he stood up laughing, she caught a glimpse of the maintenance officer. *Renee something*, she thought. *Begins with a B.*

"Hey, Jackie." She turned to the voice.

Jim Collins caught her in a bear hug. "It's great to see you. You've been scarce lately. We haven't seen you since Thanksgiving."

"Working hard," she replied. "But I'm here now."

"Just in time too. We're going to have a naming ceremony for the newbies."

"Ugh. You guys enjoy torturing the poor lieutenants."

"We also have a captain and a major this time."

"They don't have call signs already?" Call signs were a rite of passage for fighter pilots. Usually they came about from something stupid they did. The stories were shared during the naming ceremony, and suggestions for call signs were offered up. The squadron voted on the best and the majority ruled. The young pilot is stuck with the name unless he does something later in life that trumps his first exploit. Then of course, he must drink. Everything in a fighter squadron ends with drinking.

"Yeah, but that doesn't mean they get to skip the harassment that comes with joining the squadron. One of them already screwed up at the bombing range so some of the guys have a few options lined up."

"Well, I better get a good seat then."

Jim tipped his glass toward hers and headed off to greet someone else.

Jackie searched the packed room for an empty seat. The only availability was in the back at a table with older squadron members. In short order, Jello stood in the middle of the room, and someone behind the bar rang the bell. Rumor had it that this large, tarnished piece of art was stolen from a U.S. Navy ship that was docked in a European port where some young Air Force lieutenants were spending their leave. They decided to bring back a souvenir for the squadron. They were lauded as heroes, and even if the stories weren't true, it was a great conversation piece. Everyone quieted down and focused on the ops officer.

"It's that time again," he began, "to welcome new blood into the squadron."

"A new snacko!" someone yelled. The crowd burst into laughter. The snacko was the youngest pilot in the squadron whose additional duty was to keep the refrigerator and cupboard filled with snacks and, of course, beer for the bar. It was a thankless job.

"Let's start with Lieutenant Swanson then," Jello announced as a young lieutenant dutifully shuffled to the ops officer's side.

"Point of order," someone from the back called.

The pack turned to the voice.

"We have an outsider in the room," the voice continued.

The people looked around trying to identify the intruder.

"What am I missing, Captain Bennett?" asked Jello.

"There's a person present who's not a member of the squadron. She's a wife."

Jackie's face burned with embarrassment as all eyes turned to her.

"She's one of us," offered Jim. "She stays."

Jackie gave him an appreciative smile.

"The rules of the bar state only squadron members during a naming ceremony," a young lieutenant Jackie didn't recognize piped up.

"In that case, Captain Bennett isn't a member either," Jim said.

"She's the maintenance liaison, so she is actually," stated the same annoying lieutenant with a half-drunk smile on his face.

"Tell your wife she'll have to wait outside, Mace," prodded Renee Bennett from his elbow. A half dozen howls went up from the crowd, daring Mace to eject his wife because of the long-honored rules of the squadron bar.

Stan looked sheepish. Everyone knew he was trapped between loyalty to his wife and loyalty to the rules of the bar. "Jackie?" He begged for forgiveness with his eyes.

In unison, the entire room let out a dramatic, "Ooooo," indicating Mace had made a daring but dangerous choice. For them, it was all great theater for a Friday at the bar.

Lopass stood beside her. "Stay, Jackie. We want you here." More howls ensued as beer sloshed. The room was now divided, half daring Stan onward and half demanding Jackie remain.

Jackie stood. Trying to make a joke, she quoted, "I wouldn't want to be a member of a club that would have me anyway." The crowd chuckled along with her. She turned to leave but looked back in Renee's direction. "You realize this means you're about to lose the only lady in this room."

The crowd knew her target, and they let out another long, "Ooooo." Before anyone could stop her, she pushed her way to the door and was gone.

Jackie stormed through the door and was met by a crowd of wives waiting by the ops desk. "Hey, Jackie, are they done already?" asked Tina, Jello's wife.

"Not quite," she muttered as she kept going out the front doors of the squadron.

Her eyes stung with the effort to not cry. She paced back and forth in the parking lot ranting to herself. "Who the hell does she think she is?"

"Who, Jackie? What happened?" Jackie turned to discover Tina had followed her.

She scrambled to recall what she said, but she was too angry to regain her composure.

Tina touched her arm, and Jackie stopped moving. She took a deep breath. "That stupid maintenance whore," Jackie began.

"Oh," Tina said knowingly. "Bennett's a piece of work, isn't she?"

"What do you mean?"

"She's always got her claws out. You better watch out for her around Mace."

"She can have him. That bastard took her side over mine! They can both go to hell for all I care!" Jackie resumed her pacing.

"I know how you feel." Tina watched her walk for a solid five minutes until her steps finally slowed down a notch. "You doing better?"

"Yeah," Jackie replied. She stopped in front of Tina and hung her head. "Guys are pricks," she stated.

"Yep. You can't live with them; you can't kill 'em," she said.

"There's gotta be a way," Jackie said. "I'm going home. I don't want to have anything to do with him right now."

# Chapter 14

Stan stood outside the closed bedroom door, trying to muster the courage to open it. He wasn't sure what to say to her. It was an ugly scene in the bar, and Jim had really laid into him after a few beers. Stan knew the other pilots in the squadron respected Jackie. She always went out of her way to help them when it came to fixing their records or preparing for a promotion board. Despite all their playful encouragement that Stan should tell Jackie to leave, none of them ever thought Stan would treat his wife as he did. They were pretty disgusted at him for letting her get booted from the squadron bar.

Finally, he pushed the door open. It was dark in the room, although it was awfully early for Jackie to be asleep. Stan stood over her for a long while. He was pretty sure she was faking it, but not so sure he wanted to call her on it. He waited a moment longer before turning and walking out.

The next two days were frigid—at least inside the house. Stan and Jackie only spoke when necessary. She didn't say anything about the incident. Stan almost wished she would yell at him and get it over with. Of course, he couldn't bring himself to apologize. He wouldn't know where to start.

Technically he didn't do anything wrong. Jackie always stood up for herself. She didn't need him to rescue her. They had discussed that before. If he stood up for her, she would appear weak in front of the guys. She didn't want that. It was childish and indefensible logic, but that's how Stan tried to justify his actions to himself. By Monday morning, he was believing it.

As he loaded his TDY bags into his car, he waited for Jackie to lock the back door of the house. "See you in a week or so."

"Okay," she said without emotion. She got into her car and drove off while he watched her go.

**W**hat's wrong with you, Stan? You're all grumpy," Renee accused him.

Stan plopped down on the bed and swung his feet up. "I have a lot on my mind."

"Like me?" she teased.

He gave a weak smile as she sidled closer to him. She ran her fingers through his hair. He closed his eyes and tried to relax. She kneeled on the bed and straddled his legs. Meanwhile, her hands continued to tickle his ears and stroke his face. She leaned forward to kiss his neck.

He reached up to take her waist in his hands. He felt the tension seep from his body. As he let his hands wander up her back to pull her close, he felt Renee's body shake gently. He nuzzled her neck and asked softly, "Am I amusing to you?"

She sat up and tried to stifle her giggles with a hand over her mouth. "I'm thinking about Friday," she said with a wide grin.

Stan stiffened. "What about Friday?"

"The look on Jackie's face was priceless! When you asked her to leave, I couldn't tell if she was going to yell or cry." Renee leaned forward to kiss Stan.

He held her at arm's length. "I didn't ask her to leave. You called her out."

"Yes I did," she said. "It was classic."

Stan tried to get up, but Renee was still sitting on his legs. "Didn't you think it was funny?" she asked, attempting to lean into him and steal a kiss.

"Not particularly. You put me in an awkward position I'm now paying for dearly at home."

Renee rolled off and sat cross-legged on the bed, allowing him his escape. Stan stood.

"I thought things at home weren't good anyway," Renee said with a poorly disguised pout.

He waved off her attempt for reassurance.

She patted the bed next to her, trying to coax him back. "Sit down, Mace. I'll rub your shoulders." Stan had never noticed before that Renee always called him Mace. Jackie called him Stan. She said call signs were too phony for her.

Stan couldn't relax. He kept seeing Jackie's face as she tried to stay calm in front of their friends. He knew he screwed up. Things weren't good with them, but she didn't deserve to be humiliated.

"Forget about her," Renee said. "You deserve so much more. Come here and I'll give it to you."

"How can you be like that? What was the point of embarrassing her?"

"What do you mean? I didn't make the rules of the bar."

"But you were trying to make a point. If it had been anyone else, you wouldn't have pulled that shit."

"So? It's over. There's no sense worrying about it now." She tossed her hair out of her face and leaned back on her elbows, trying to lure him closer.

Staring at her in disbelief, he said, "You're a real ass, you know that? Do you ever think of anyone besides yourself?"

She stared back at him without expression, as if trying to decide her next move.

Stan walked to the door and opened it. "It's time for you to go," he said.

She stared at him.

"Now," he added with emphasis.

Slowly she got off the bed and grabbed her shoes. She stopped in front of him, close enough to smell his sweat. "You don't want to end it like this," she said.

He didn't answer, staring at the ground.

She kissed his neck. "Trust me; you don't want to end it at all."

Stan stepped back.

Renee smiled coyly. "We aren't done."

Jackie walked into the officers' club. Jenn Collins waved at her, and Jackie made her way through the crowd to a round table in the back. Jenn stood and gave her a hug. Nancy McCoy and Beth Davis greeted her warmly. Their husbands flew with Stan, and Jackie was sure they had heard about the scene in the bar.

She took a seat, and a waitress took her drink order.

"Hey, ladies," Tina Mills said from behind Jackie. She came around and pulled out the last chair to take a seat. "Did you already order?"

"Nope, waiting for you," Nancy said.

"I'm ready if you are," Tina said. "I've been craving the chicken salad all day."

"I always get the same thing anyway," Jackie said, setting the menu aside.

When the waitress returned with Jackie's drink, the ladies placed their orders.

Beth turned to Jackie. "Sorry about Friday."

Jackie shrugged. "No big deal."

"It most certainly was a big deal," Tina said. "You were fit to be tied in the parking lot."

"Stan can be an ass. I'm sure that isn't surprising to anyone."

The women laughed in agreement.

"If Paul had pulled that on me, I would have ripped his balls off then and there," Beth said.

"Paul doesn't have the balls to begin with. Have you already ripped them off?" Jenn asked.

"Now that you mention it." Beth tapped her chin and scrunched her eyes in concentration.

"You scared me, Jackie," Tina admitted. "I've never seen you angry before."

"I usually control it better."

"Yeah, she's more calculating than impulsive," Jenn teased.

"Can we talk about something else?" Jackie asked.

Jenn and Nancy exchanged a glance. Nancy spoke first. "One last thing."

Jackie waited.

Nancy fidgeted in her chair. She folded and unfolded her napkin in her lap.

"Come on," Jackie said. "It can't be that bad."

"You need to watch out for that Renee-bitch," she finally said. "There are rumors going around that she's getting it from somewhere."

"Somewhere? What does that mean?"

"People say she's having an affair with a married man. I don't know who for sure."

Jackie was stunned. "You think it's Stan?"

"We're not saying that, honey." Jenn touched her arm. "We're saying she can't be trusted. If she'd stoop to have an affair with a married man, it could be anyone."

"Just watch yourself," Tina warned. "She's slimy."

Jackie's mind raced as the women moved onto other topics. *Is Stan having an affair? Is that why he's so distant?*

# Chapter 15

The hills were gray and rocky. Heat rose from the landscape of granite boulders as the scorching sun weighed her down. But she was used to it. She adjusted her burka and shifted her pack. It was only a short distance over the next ridgeline, and she would be home.

As she approached the next rise, the roaring sound of thunder filled her ears. Without a cloud in the sky, she recognized the noise and started running. Dropping her pack, she scrambled up the last few yards in time to see the gray machines release their weapons to crash through the dirt and sunbaked mud huts below. The wails of the children reached her ears, even from this distance.

She stood in shock as flames burst from one, then another, of the homes. People, unsure whether it was safer inside the huts or out in the open, rushed from their homes and headed toward the woods. Mothers herded children as quickly as they could, gathering the smaller ones in their arms while older siblings dragged toddlers along behind.

As quickly as they had come, the planes were gone. Her feet were finally released from the stone, and she began to descend, stumbling over the rocky surface she had mastered long ago. As she began her descent toward her village, smoke filled her nostrils and burned her eyes.

Soldiers carrying weapons emerged from the trees. The leader walked calmly into camp, holding his gun comfortably in front of him but pointing at the ground. He was flanked by others who scanned everything with their guns nestled in their shoulders ready to fire. The soldier in front of the group lifted his voice into the now quiet air and addressed the men standing in the center of the village. He waited as the translator relayed his message.

"This is what happens when you act like Taliban by ignoring our warnings. We want to help you, but we can't have you shooting at us while we do."

The translator was an abnormally tall and slender Afghan wearing an indistinguishable uniform. He spoke in the local dialect, but also added a ferocious tone and wildly gestured with his arms. More soldiers appeared out of nowhere on the edges of the village and took up a vigilant watch looking outward. As soldiers rounded up the males in the village, the translator savagely barked instructions for them to sit in rows on the ground with their hands clasped behind their heads. At times, he slapped at the heads of those he considered moving too slowly.

Two of the soldiers entered a nearby smoldering hut and came out carrying a black, metal case between them. They dropped it in front of the man who appeared to be leading the soldiers and lifted the lid.

He spoke something loudly and paused while the other man repeated in Afghan, adding the harshest tone of accusation. "That's what I was talking about. How are we supposed to trust you when you lie to us?"

The Army medic worked hurriedly, going from one injured person to the next, applying bandages and giving painkillers where necessary. He tried to approach the women and children on the edge of the sparse trees, but they shrank away from him.

The woman from the hills moved closer, her feet feeling like lead. She skirted the village. As she approached, the man in front spoke again—that foul foreign tongue.

"Where are the rest of your weapons?" came the translation.

The scraggly men didn't respond. In response, the translator screamed at them and slapped the back of their heads mercilessly.

The leader said something impatiently, although his physical demeanor was calm. "I don't have time for this," came the Afghan interpretation. While the American waited for the interpreter to try to convince the men, he took in the scene around him and shook his head.

He turned back to the group of men who were glaring at him defiantly and asked another question. The words were repeated in Afghan. "I will ask you once more, where are the rest of the weapons?"

There was a pause as the translator spoke to the men and listened to their reply. Then the translator turned to him and said, "They say there are no more weapons in their town."

He shook his head slowly and turned to his men. He barked orders and gestured toward half the men, then pointed at the village. He waved his hand at the others and pointed toward the tree line. The men moved on, and the leader said something to the translator.

The translator nodded and relayed the message with a frenzy seasoned with ultimatums. "They are going to search your village. If you have any weapons left, you should tell them now." After hearing the message, one of the men looked at the officer and shook his head. The translator glared down at him.

Less than fifteen minutes later, his men were finished. Through a simple look and a hand gesture, they reported finding no other weapons.

The leader faced the men again and spoke, pointing first at his chest, then at the sky. He turned and walked away as the translator spoke. His men fell in step behind him silently, carrying the black, metal case between them. The Afghan said, "They are leaving now. He says if you shoot at them, the big guns will shoot at you."

As the soldiers moved away, the woman who had watched the carnage from the mountainside ran into the circle, searching furiously for her Samir. *Where was her precious Samir?*

She called his name. An elderly woman advanced and took her arms. The younger woman didn't like the look in her eyes. "Samir!" she yelled again, trying to break free. The older woman held fast. Now the other women of the village were joining them. They made a circle around her, reaching out to touch her. It was then that she knew.

She looked for her husband and didn't see him either. Why wasn't he the one to tell her? As she watched, two men carried a body from the bombed-out hut. They laid his mangled corpse in the grass at the edge of the village. She wanted to look away but couldn't. She recognized the robe and the worn-out sandals on those bloody feet. She had worked long nights making them.

Another man followed, placing a small bundle next to her husband's body. She couldn't take it anymore. She bolted for the retreating soldiers, and her screams paralyzed everyone in the village. The translator was yelling at her to halt, but she only ran faster toward the leader of the soldiers. The soldiers surrounded the leader, down on a knee with all barrels pointed at her. One of them fired a burst of automatic fire low at her feet.

The rounds blasted debris that dug into her skin, and she tumbled forward as the soldiers jogged to her, fingers on their triggers. In searing pain, she struggled to her knees as the translator screamed at her from behind the protection of one of the soldiers.

The leader calmly followed his men to her side. He poked at her with his barrel, and she looked up, blood running down from her scalp. He yelled something, and the man with bandages came running.

Suddenly, she grabbed his barrel and placed it against her forehead, stunning the entire detail. She wailed in Pashtun as if insane. "Kill me, kill me, you devil, kill me!"

He clicked on the safety and wrestled to get the barrel out of her hands. She hung on like an animal screaming for him to shoot. One of the soldiers struck her across the back with the butt of his gun, and she collapsed onto the ground, whimpering the same words over and over again. The soldiers motioned for the villagers to come retrieve her as they carefully backed away, unnerved by the incident. Two burka-draped women crept to where she lay as the rest of the village glared at the retreating soldiers. She continued to mutter the same words over and over again but fell silent from the pain. Her world went black.

Mastana awoke drenched in sweat from the awful recurring dream. Years had gone by, yet the scene was as real as the first time she lived it. She cried herself back to sleep.

# Chapter 16

A shadow crossed Jackie's desk, causing her to look up.
"Hey," Stan said.

"Hey, yourself," she replied cautiously. Stan hardly ever came to her office.

"I got back early."

"So I see."

"Want to catch some lunch?"

"Not really." She crossed her arms.

Stan stared at her.

"Stan, what do you want? I have work to do."

"I wanted lunch. Why do you have to make a big deal about it?" he snapped.

"Maybe Renee will take you," Jackie said sarcastically.

"Renee who?" Stan asked.

"Bennett. Isn't she your main distraction these days?" Ice formed around her words.

"Jackie, don't be ridiculous. You're acting stupid."

"Don't call me stupid!" She jumped from her seat. "You're the assohole chasing a skirt and not even hiding it very well."

"I have nothing to hide. I'm not chasing anyone." He opened his hands palm up, and his playful smile came easily to his lips. "I have a hard enough time keeping up with you."

Jackie tried to read his face. She was generally a trusting person and wanted to believe him, but he had really screwed up with the scene at the bar.

Stan came around the desk and took Jackie's hands in his. "I'm sorry for what happened at the squadron. I should have backed you."

At first she resisted his words. Then a rush of relief crossed her face. She wasn't one to hold a grudge. A simple apology is all she wanted to hear. She finally let him take her in his arms.

"I'm sorry I overreacted," Jackie said in a soft monotone.

"You have nothing to be sorry for."

They stood embracing for another minute. "I really am hungry," Stan finally said. "Can we eat?"

Jackie released him and, with a few quick keystrokes, locked her computer. She picked up her hat and led him to the door. "You're buying," she said, with a forced lightness that didn't sound quite natural.

Work settled into a routine. Jackie had a lot of paperwork to do, but for now, the wing was between exercises, and some of her key team members were enjoying leave back in the States. Jackie thought about visiting her family, but she didn't want to waste her leave stateside when she was in Europe. She'd have plenty of time to see her parents when their tour was over.

She and Stan were getting along better lately. It wasn't great, but it was an improvement. He was coming home directly after work, and they were eating dinner together. Their conversations were mostly about work, but that was normal as far as Jackie could tell. What else was there to discuss? Stan wasn't much of a dreamer, and Jackie's favorite thing to do was to plan their next adventure.

The Fasching parades had begun all around town. Jackie joined Margaret with her basket of flowers alongside the road. Together they gathered pieces of over thirty ties. Jackie gave the honor of clipping Stan's Christmas tie to Margaret while Jackie snapped a photo to send home.

As Jackie drove into work, she mentally reminded herself there was night flying next week. That meant she was on her own for dinner. Perhaps she'd invite some of the wives over.

Jackie had just walked into her office when Master Sergeant Reynolds stuck his head through the opening. "Morning, ma'am. Wing commander wants to see you right away."

She looked up in surprise. "Any idea what it's about?"

"Nope. The secretary told me to send you over as soon as you got in."

"Thanks."

Reynolds tapped the doorway twice in response and backed out of the room.

Not sure what the topic of the meeting was, Jackie gathered her notes on the last exercise and the next one she was planning. For good measure, she grabbed the binder holding the open findings from previous exercises and their status on improvement. She looked around the room one last time, trying to spark an idea of what the commander might want.

"Hi, Major Austin. Thanks for coming over," the wing commander's secretary said as she got up from her desk. "Give me a minute, and I'll let him know you're here."

Back at her desk, Jackie sat speechless, staring at the paper in front of her.

Colonel Harris cleared his throat from the doorway. "Well?"

She stood at the sound of her boss's voice. "Well what, sir?"

"Come on. I know the general was handing out PRFs this morning. Did you get yours?" The Promotion Recommendation

Form was how the senior rater gave his input to the board about individual officers.

Jackie's face broke into a wide grin. "He gave me a definitely promote below-the-zone!"

"Congratulations! I knew it! Well deserved." He stepped forward and shook her hand. "And . . . ?"

She glanced down at the paper again although it was already imprinted in her mind's eye. "He gave me his number one." She couldn't wipe the smile off her face, even if she tried. Although only a very small number of officers were promoted below the primary zone, being ranked as a number one was almost a sure bet she would be seriously considered on this board.

"Fantastic! You and Mace are going to have something to celebrate this weekend." With one last grin, he left her office.

A knife turned in her stomach. This was great news for her. She wanted to celebrate with her husband. But, as she had gotten her PRF today, Stan would also be getting his. He hadn't completed his master's or done his military continuing education. Jackie didn't have high hopes he would receive any higher than a "P" for promote. That meant another pass-over for promotion, and most likely, a quick exit from the Air Force and the life Stan loved.

It was the fourth evening of night flying, and the weather was clear for early February. While the wing was practicing maneuvers with night vision goggles, the pace during the day was quieter, and she had the evenings to herself.

The ground was covered in a white blanket, and everything smelled clean. Somewhere a dog barked, the sound carrying miles across the snow. In the distance, Jackie heard the roar of jet engines as they got closer. Somehow, she found it reassuring—the sound of freedom.

The week had gone by quickly without an angry word passing between her and Stan. He congratulated Jackie on her DP, but there was no talk of celebration. He didn't seem to begrudge her for her success, but he certainly played down the significance.

Pulling herself away from the window, she drew her bath. The narrow German-designed tub made her long for the spacious designs of modern bathrooms in the States. She poured bath salts into the stream of steaming water and watched it boil into foam.

Although she spent her days proving herself to be equal to her fellow male officers, it was a relief to come home and enjoy the simple girly-things like a long leisurely bath, a candle, and some bubbles. She had never met a man who would admit the same.

Her mind was in neutral gear as she enjoyed the changing tone of the water hitting the surface of the rising tub. She was so tired, and yet she still felt the jagged edge of stress that needed to be melted under the growing mounds of bubbles and foam.

The doorbell rang.

"No, really?" Jackie said aloud in disbelief as she dropped her head into her terry clothed robe.

The bell rang again. Jackie shut off the water. "You have to be kidding me!" she hissed, as if a sacred ritual had been violated. Jackie tightened her robe, tied the belt, and walked on her toes across the cold, hallway floor to the back door and peered through the port. It was Jenn Collins.

Jackie swung the door open and welcomed Jenn with a hug. "What in the world are you doing here on a Thursday night? Is something wrong?"

"I thought you could use some company."

"Well, I was getting ready for a bubble bath. You aren't the kind of company I was looking for."

Jenn smiled self-consciously at Jackie's glib remark. She knew Jackie and Stan had been having trouble lately, and she felt like she was preparing to rub salt into the wound.

"Jeez, what's wrong, Jenn?" Jackie took Jenn by the shoulders and looked her in the eyes. "Are you okay?" With sudden panic she asked, "Is Jim okay?"

"Yes, we're fine." Jenn paused and took a deep breath, "But it's time we had a talk." Jenn looked down to avoid Jackie's eyes.

"Is this a wine or a coffee talk?" Jackie asked.

"Get a bottle."

# Chapter 17

Jackie sat stunned and gazed into her glass.

"I'm so sorry, Jackie," Jenn repeated in a whispered voice, searching Jackie's face for a response. She had fallen silent as Jenn revealed the facts that had been circulated across the squadron. Jackie was the consummate fool and the last to know.

Stan had screwed that whore. He betrayed Jackie and humiliated her. She suspected it but had given him the benefit of the doubt when he denied it to her face.

"Thanks for telling me, Jenn," she said softly.

"I'm sorry I had to," Jenn admitted.

"I had a feeling, but I didn't want to be one of those wives who's suspicious of every movement her husband makes. I wouldn't want him to treat me that way. Look how many guys I hang around."

"What are you going to do?"

"I have to think," Jackie said as tears began to drip from her eyes. "I could kill him, but that's too easy. Not enough suffering," she tried to joke, but it came across dull.

"Do you want to come home with me?"

"No, thanks. I need to be alone."

Jackie walked Jenn to the door. Jenn gave her another hug. "If you need anything, call me. I'm here for you."

She didn't trust her voice to answer, so she gave a weak smile of gratitude and nodded.

Jackie closed the door and returned to the bathroom. The relaxation she had looked forward to was gone. The candle wax had dripped over the tub edge, and the flame had gone out. She drained some of the tepid water from the tub. She dropped her robe and gazed at her nude reflection in the mirror with a critical eye.

She was fit and still turned heads when she dressed up, but it had been a long time since Stan had paid her any attention. But which came first? His interest in another woman or his lack of interest in her? She slowly stepped into the remaining tepid bath and turned the water on as hot as it would go. She sank into the tub as the temperature rose, and she smoldered. Stan had cheated. He was unfaithful. Jackie was the last to know, and she was a laughingstock.

Jackie couldn't sleep. She tossed and turned for a while before finally going back downstairs to finish the bottle of wine. She was working out exactly what she was going to say to Stan but wasn't sure of the best approach. She had already directly asked him once about Renee, and he had denied it— and she had believed him. Everything Jenn had told her was circumstantial. There was no proof, and he would deny it again. Plus, she didn't want to drag Jim and Jenn into the hell this fight was going to be. As Jackie sat on the couch working through her dilemma, sleep finally came to her.

The next morning, Jackie awoke stiff from a night on the couch. Her head was still a little fuzzy as the grandfather clock chimed seven. She willed herself to move. Already behind schedule, Jackie dragged herself upstairs to get her clothes.

When she entered the bedroom, Stan was sleeping on his side facing away from her. She resisted the urge to throw something at him. Instead, she went about her morning routine, not taking any measures to keep quiet. He grumbled when she turned on the lights and covered his head with a pillow.

∽

Jackie pushed papers around on her desk without getting much done. She stared out the window, trying to see past the dirt and grime that stuck to the glass. As she let her thoughts drift, the feeling of being trapped grew—first by the building, then by her job, and finally by her marriage.

The phone rang, breaking her free from her despair. "IG, Major Austin," she answered routinely.

"So, did you challenge Stan?" Jenn asked without fanfare.

"No, I'm waiting for the right moment."

"Do you want Jim to say something to him?" Jackie heard the sympathy in her voice.

"No," Jackie said quickly. "I don't want to cause a split in the squadron. I'll take care of this my own way."

"Well, let me know. You can stay with us if you need to," Jenn offered.

"The squadron's not flying tonight. They're only scheduled a half day. I'll have a chance to confront him when he comes home. I left him a message that dinner would be ready at seventeen-thirty; I mean five-thirty," Jackie quickly translated the military time into civilian time.

Jenn laughed quietly. "I speak military. Hell, after all these years, I find myself writing military time more often than not." She paused and took a deep breath. "Good luck tonight. Call me."

"Thanks. I will." Jackie hung up and stared out the window.

She wasn't getting much accomplished, so she pushed away from her desk and went to check on her script writers for the next exercise. She needed something to take her mind off the inevitable.

She plopped down in the seat next to her noncommissioned officer-in-charge's desk.

"What did we do wrong?" Master Sergeant Reynolds asked suspiciously.

"Nothing. Why would you think that?"

"You look like your best friend died. Since work is your best friend, I assumed something has gone wrong." He smiled at her.

She gave a weak smile in return. "I'm avoiding my inbox. What's going on over here?" She gestured around the open room where a few folks were diligently typing away in their cubicles.

"They're trying to stay ahead of you. They've been brainstorming ideas to come up with something you haven't thought of yet. I think Sergeant Ford has one for you."

That made Jackie grin. She always offered a free lunch to whomever came up with the best scenario per exercise. It had become a matter of pride within the office to try to outdo each other. "But is it realistic?" Ford's last idea had storm troopers breaking through the front gates as robots cut through the back of the aircraft shelters. She gave him a cookie for his creativity but sent him back to the drawing board.

Master Sergeant Reynolds shrugged.

She and Master Sergeant Reynolds discussed the objectives of the next few exercises. They had a rotating list to choose from, fed to Jackie from various commanders across the base. But their main objectives were driven by the operational readiness inspection. These were the items higher headquarters would inspect them on to ensure they could get out the door quickly and to the fight.

Jackie's job was to ensure the wing commander knew his wing was ready to do their mission if and when called upon, at a moment's notice. They proved themselves mission capable on a daily basis as many of the squadrons rotated through ongoing military operations for years. It was the short notice reactions they needed to brush up on and test.

Satisfied her evaluators were well prepared for the coming weeks, Jackie made her way back to her office. She was biding time until her discussion with Stan, but she was also dreading it. She prayed to herself she would use the right words and not get overly emotional. What if he said he was sorry and wanted to try again? Would she give him another chance? Could she ever trust him again? Did she want to?

At 1700, Jackie stacked the papers neatly on her desk and grabbed her hat. Instead of heading straight for the gate, she drove by Stan's squadron. His Mustang was still in the lot. Jackie hit the steering wheel. "Dammit!" She knew he was off work hours ago.

She circled around and found a place far enough away from the door not to be seen, but where she had clear visibility to Stan's pride and joy, even in the fading light. She didn't have to wait long.

Renee Bennett pushed her way through the squadron doors and headed toward her car. A few minutes later, Stan emerged. He looked around the parking lot and spotted Bennett at her car. By the time he reached her, she was behind the wheel. He leaned down to talk to her through the open driver's window. Jackie couldn't see well from her angle. The next moment, Bennett was pulling quickly away from the parking spot. Stan shook his head, pulling his keys out as he walked to his car.

Jackie watched him get into his car, and she silently prayed he would choose his wife over the maintenance officer. Then, anger flooded her as she thought, *He better.*

Instead of making the left toward home, he turned right and circled back toward the maintenance hangars. Jackie paused a minute before following them. She waited until he parked and went in the hangar before pulling her car up next to his. Bennett's car was already there.

Quietly she got out and walked to the man-door. It was a cold evening, and her breath fogged the air. The hangar was closed for the weekend, but a faint light escaped under the door. Taking a deep breath to calm her shaking hands, she pushed the door slowly open.

An indistinct rustle and then a giggle broke the quiet. Near the jet parked in the middle of the hangar, she barely made out two shapes, or was it one? Staying in the shadows, Jackie approached the jet. She concealed herself behind the equipment racks neatly lined up and locked in place around the open space.

"Mace, let me give it to you like you like it." Renee said, her speech slightly slurred.

"Slow down," Stan said.

"I knew you didn't want it to end."

His reply was muffled. Jackie saw separation between the shadows.

More giggles, then a scuffing sound as the shapes rearranged themselves, becoming one again.

"Renee, I'm worried—" Stan started.

"You worry too much," she cut him off. "Your precious Jackie doesn't have to find out."

"It's not that."

The distinctive sound of a flight suit being unzipped reached Jackie.

She couldn't take it anymore. She had her proof. Disregarding any further need for secrecy, she stormed from the hangar, allowing the door to slam shut behind her.

Jumping into her car, she revved the engine. Without giving it a second thought, she threw the car in gear and flew forward fifty feet, tires crunching in the snow. Then, putting it in reverse, she gunned the engine and braced for impact as her car crashed into the side of Stan's Mustang. Then calmly, she put her car in park and emerged, leaned back on the hood and waited. The cold air had no effect on her.

As predicted, a harried Stan rushed from the hangar with Renee in tow. He looked first at his car, then at Jackie. "What the hell did you do?" he asked incredulously.

"It was an accident," Jackie said with a frigid calm.

"Are you crazy?" Stan yelled.

"No, I don't think so."

Renee stood by looking from one to the other. She wasn't sure what to do.

"I would suggest you leave quickly before the cops get here," Jackie offered to her. "You wouldn't want to get tangled up in our *affairs*."

Renee didn't answer. She backed unsteadily toward her car and took off.

"What is going on with you?" Stan snapped. "Look what you did to my car!"

"Your car? That's what you're worried about right now? Maybe you should rethink your priorities." Jackie opened her car door. "Your zipper's still down." She slipped behind the wheel and drove off, leaving Stan stranded by the hangar.

Jackie had to will herself to drive slowly. All she wanted to do at that moment was to go as fast as she could, as far as she could. But getting stopped by the police wouldn't help her right now. The rolling hills that usually calmed her after work only seemed to stretch on endlessly today.

When she pulled into the driveway, another flood of emotions hit her. They were so happy when they moved into this house. She remembered acting like a little kid, running from room to room to explore. The tunnel to the room under the garage was like the secret passageway she had imagined having as a small child.

And now her imagination was on autopilot. *How many places had he been with her? How many TDYs? Did his jet really break on the long weekend to Finland or did the maintenance officer arrange that?*

She didn't bother opening the garage. She had no intention of being here when Stan got home. Jackie opened the heavy front door they seldom used. Even company came to the back door. She took the stairs two at a time and went straight to their room.

Pulling out an overnight bag, she haphazardly threw things into it. As she searched beside the bed for her tennis shoes, she came across Stan's flight bag. In a fit of rage, she dumped the contents on the floor and flung the olive drab bag against the window. She kicked the paperwork across the room, the sound of ripping paper under her feet welcomed. His line-up card, which outlined his Monday morning cross-country flight, landed on her bag. She grabbed the pen from her pocket and angrily carved "GO TO HELL" across the page.

# Chapter 18

Jenn knocked on the guest room door. "Jackie, Stan's on the phone. Do you want to talk to him?"

When Jackie had arrived on their doorstep the night before, Jim and Jenn welcomed her without question. It wasn't until Jim had gone to bed, rather an early night for him Jackie suspected, that she had poured out her soul to her friend.

"No," Jackie said, "but I will."

Jackie trudged to the living room and picked up the phone. "What happened? Your girlfriend wouldn't give you a ride home?"

"Jackie, it's all a misunderstanding."

"Right. It's easy to misunderstand that whore going down on you in the hangar."

"It wasn't like that."

"The hell it wasn't! I was there, Stan. I heard you!"

Stan was silent.

"Was there a purpose to this call or did you call to gloat?"

"I don't want things to be like this," Stan said.

"You didn't want to be caught. Everything was okay up to that point."

"You know that's not true. Things haven't been right with us for a while."

"And whose fault is that?" she snapped.

"Why does it have to be one person's fault? I thought marriage was a two-way street?"

Inwardly she had to concede that point but wasn't going to let him make excuses. "Are you saying it's my fault that you chose to screw your way out of our marriage?" Jackie's voice rose, and Jenn peeked around the corner to make sure she was okay.

"No, that's not what I'm saying."

"So what are you saying?"

"This would be easier to discuss in person."

"Fine. Cancel your trip for next week, and we'll talk about it."

"Jackie, you know I can't do that."

"Is that whore going?"

Stan didn't answer right away.

"That's what I thought. You need to choose, Stan. I'm tired of being the dutiful wife while you go play with your bimbo. If you want to salvage anything, you need to stay home and fix it."

"I can't," Stan said. "What reason would I give?"

Jackie laughed dryly at that. "Who gives a shit?"

"Don't be like that," Stan said.

Jackie's voice rose again, and she didn't bother trying to quiet herself. "Be like what? A dedicated wife who has done everything possible to help you in your career while trying to balance my own? A want-to-be mother who is waiting for you to grow up and fulfill all the promises you made to me before we got married? Or a totally pissed off woman who walked in on her husband screwing another woman? I am all those things, and I'm tired of it."

Stan was defenseless against the onslaught; he couldn't dig his way out. He stayed silent.

"I'm done." Jackie hung up the phone.

She tried to hold back her tears, but when Jenn gently touched her shoulder and turned Jackie to face her, she gave in. Jenn held her as she cried.

~

By Monday morning, Jackie was cried out. She was exhausted and didn't want to do anything but sleep, but she was expected at work. Grudgingly, she forced herself to the shower and went through the routine of braiding her hair and putting on her uniform. She stared at herself in the mirror and wondered for the thousandth time what she should have done differently. How did their marriage spiral downward so quickly? Why Renee Bennett? What was she going to do?

She made her way to the kitchen, and Jenn handed her a cup of coffee. "You look like hell."

Jackie smiled. She could always count on Jenn to give it to her straight. Jenn had been watching Jackie closely since she had shown up Friday night. She even offered to change her Sunday plans in order to accompany Jackie back to the house to get her uniforms. Jackie wouldn't hear of it though. She had inconvenienced them enough.

"Why don't you take the day off? We can go get a manicure or something relaxing."

Jackie shook her head. "Me? A manicure?"

"Or something. Let's goof off."

"Not today. I've got work to do. We're kicking off a mini exercise. It's only going for two days. Maybe we can plan something for Thursday," Jackie suggested.

Jenn jumped on the opportunity. "Better yet, let's go to Tongeren for the weekend. We can be in place for the bazaar on Sunday morning when it opens at five-thirty."

"I'll think about it," Jackie conceded. "Thanks for the coffee." She got up and put her cup in the sink.

"You need to eat something. You aren't going to work on an empty stomach." Jenn grabbed a bowl and pulled out a few cereal boxes to choose from.

Jackie marveled again at how lucky Jim was to have someone so caring. She could sure use someone like Jenn supporting her and her career. Obediently, she sat down and poured herself some cereal as Jenn got the milk from the refrigerator.

# Chapter 19

Stan hadn't slept well the night before, or all weekend for that matter. He had really screwed up his life and didn't know what to do. He was not used to feeling out of control, but things were quickly unraveling. He continued to dodge Renee's calls but couldn't get Jackie to talk to him.

*How did I let things get so far off course?* he wondered as he walked into the squadron Monday morning. He was greeted by a few early risers, but his was the first scheduled takeoff for the day, so the squadron was mostly empty.

He stopped by the ops desk and saw red on the board next to his line. "What the hell?" he asked to no one in particular.

The young adjutant looked up in alarm. "Sir," he said standing, "it's a slight delay. The travel pod wouldn't mate with the pylon. We're hoping it's a bent pod and not something wrong with the suspension rack on the jet. They're fitting another one."

Stan was immediately irate. This should have been taken care of the night before. Reassigning him a different jet would take almost as long as fixing the travel pod because the maintainers would have to reconfigure it for his mission.

The phone ring in a nearby office and the ops officer picked up. "Lieutenant Colonel Mills." There was silence, then, "Well, get better. Don't worry about the flight. There are others who will jump at this chance. If this was a bad deal, I'd make you drag your ass in here." A few moments later, he hung up the phone and came out of his office.

"Mace, great timing. That was Foot. He's not going to make it today. Gotta case of the shits that won't stop. We need to find you another wingman."

"Dammit!"

"Relax. It won't take long. You have a hot date or something?"

Stan felt his neck burn red as he turned toward the briefing room. He sat pondering his position for thirty minutes before Lopass stuck his head around the doorframe.

"I just got the word. I'll grab my kneeboard and be right back."

*Great, now this little shit is going to be my wingman.*

~

Jackie had only enough time to stop by her office and answer a few emails before she had to be in place for the start of the exercise. There was an email from the security forces squadron commander. He had the report of a traffic accident involving the two cars registered in Jackie's name and wanted to get some details. The commander stated he needed to clarify the reason Stan had given as to why Jackie had left the scene before the patrol had shown up. Jackie sent him a reply saying she would stop by later that afternoon to answer any questions he might have.

For now, she had an exercise to kick off. She had wanted to place the exercise explosion at the Base Exchange, but the wing commander wouldn't hear of it. He didn't want to disrupt the revenue equivalent of a small department store, and he didn't want to spook the families. Jackie thought it would have been a great exercise to see how the civilians and dependents reacted. After all, living overseas, they were also a possible target.

Instead, Jackie had to settle for pretending to blow up the alert tower on the far side of the base. Normally, the area was deserted except for short periods of training because the U.S. fighters didn't maintain an air defense mission over Germany.

It was a no-notice exercise, and the wing commander had agreed to let the fire chief assist her with real smoke and a loud boom. The chief was interested to watch his team in action when they weren't prepared for an exercise.

When Jackie got to the flight line, she reached into her uniform pocket for her line badge to show the guard. She franticly searched all her pockets before giving up and pulling off to the side of the road. Two cars behind her, one of her exercise team members rolled down his window as Jackie got out of her car.

"What's up, ma'am?" he asked.

"I must have left my line badge at home. I'll have to watch the action from here."

"Should we delay?"

"No, you don't need me out there. You know what to look for."

He waved and drove through the gate. Jackie was frustrated. One more thing to go wrong.

As she waited for the explosion, Jackie scanned the flight line. Subconsciously, she looked for Stan's jet. As a cross-country flight, his flight was supposed to be the first takeoff of the day, leading a pack of Vipers to Aviano, Italy for another routine training deployment. At least that's what he had told her. She wasn't sure what to believe anymore. She half-hoped he had changed his mind and decided not to go.

Not wanting to stand on the side of the road drawing stares, Jackie decided to run home to get her line badge. She'd be back before the fire department had finished securing the area and check on the tower response.

~

When Lopass got back, they gathered at the ops desk to review the weather along their flight path and any notices that might affect their mission.

"There's a slight problem with your country clearance through France," Technical Sergeant Jones informed them. "We expect it to come through any minute now."

"Dammit!" Stan exclaimed. His morning thus far was living validation of Murphy's Law: *Anything that can go wrong, will go wrong.*

"That should have been done by now," Stan said.

"It was. I mean, at least it was submitted. There were questions in the French chain. We've answered their concerns. We're waiting to hear back."

"Perfect," Stan muttered under his breath. "We'll be in briefing room one." Lopass followed a few paces behind him, not wanting to further upset Stan's morning.

Stan led the brief. The last-minute change of pilots sliced the usual two-hour pre-flight period to under ninety minutes, and that was a huge impact to overcome.

After the briefing, the pilots rejoined at the ops desk. "Well?" Stan asked Technical Sergeant Jones, referring to the clearance.

"All is good, sir," he replied.

The duo then headed to life support to suit up. Stan was in a hurry to make up time. He tossed his bags on the floor and grabbed his G-suit from its assigned space on the rack. He wrapped the olive drab, green nylon around his waist and zipped it up. He placed his right foot on the bench, wrapping the straps around his upper and lower leg. He straightened and zipped the suit to a snug fit around his leg. He repeated the process on the other side, only this time, as he pulled the zipper into place, it caught. In his frustration, Stan yanked harder and the unforgiving fabric gave way.

"Damn it to hell!" he yelled loud enough to bring the airmen running from the next room.

When pilots subjected themselves to high levels of acceleration force—Gs—the G-suit's inflatable bladders pressed firmly on the abdomen and legs, thereby restricting the draining of blood away from the brain. The suits were fitted to each pilot individually and were like a second skin to them.

As the airmen realized the problem, most of them went back to their duties. The senior noncommissioned officer in charge stepped up to the challenge. "Sir, what seems to be the problem?"

"My zipper is broken. Can you grab me a spare suit please?" Stan said in the most controlled voice he could manage. He was irritated, but he tried hard not to take it out on the guy who was bailing him out of this situation.

"Right away, sir."

Another thirty minutes went by before they were able to locate a spare suit, fit it to Stan as closely as possible in a pinch, and get him out the door. Unlike his own, this suit felt like a stranger was wrapped around his legs and torso, and it was incredibly distracting.

Now, as they were finally stepping into their aircraft, a loud boom vibrated the air. Quickly their eyes searched the horizon and saw a cloud of smoke rising from the far end of the runway. No jets had taken off, so Stan quickly surmised this was another one of Jackie's surprises.

"Damn her!" he said loudly.

Lopass shot him a glance. "Who?"

"Jackie. This has got to be one of her stupid exercise injects."

At that moment, the announcement boomed over the Giant Voice. "EXERCISE EXERCISE EXERCISE." The microphone somewhere in the wing's windowless command post was open, picking up background noises mixed with popping and crackling. There was a shuffle of paper and a deep inhale as the controller prepared to read the script placed before him.

Stan didn't wait to hear the rest. He slammed the door and retreated back to the ops desk. They weren't going anywhere.

As the scenario unfolded, Stan listened half-heartedly. Twenty minutes later, they got the "all clear," and he looked around the squadron for Lopass. Voices drew him to the bar. In the back corner, still dressed in his G-suit, standing with his boot on the rung of a bar chair, Lopass tried to look comfortable and casual while he chatted up Renee Bennett.

Renee laughed at something he said. This time, rather than feeling jealous, a wave of disgust ran through Stan. Her demeanor toward Lopass was quite familiar, and he imagined she was hooking up with any number of testosterone-charged fighter pilots on base.

"Lopass, let's go. We're clear." Without another word, he walked out to the flight line.

Stan was met at his jet by his crew chief, Senior Airman Joe Suitor. With a quick salute, Suitor said, "Morning, sir. Great day for a flight."

"It can only get better from here," Stan answered wryly, handing him his helmet bag. "She ready to go?"

All aircraft, like ships, are referred to as females. Male pilots will say it's because they are as fussy as women. Female pilots say it's because you couldn't get anywhere without them.

"Yes, sir. She's recently back from the depot so take good care of her." On a rotating basis, every jet was sent to the depot for a complete overhaul. That preventative maintenance extended the life of the jet, which is very important with the constant budget cuts within the Department of Defense.

"I'll take care of her as long as she's taking care of me," Stan said with a smile.

Suitor carried the helmet bag up the ladder and prepositioned it in the cockpit as Stan did his walk around the jet. Suitor hurried back down and waited as Stan completed his inspection and climbed the ladder to get into his seat.

"Did you do anything exciting this weekend?" Stan asked Suitor, who had resumed his place at the top of the ladder.

"Slept mostly, sir." He reached across and pulled down the shoulder harnesses, making it easier for the pilot to buckle in.

"You need to get out more." Stan liked this young airman. He was a dedicated crew chief who truly cared about doing a good job. Not like some of the others who were only there to collect a paycheck and drink German beer.

After Stan clicked his harness into place, Suitor handed him his helmet and waited as he put it on. Then Suitor connected the oxygen.

Stan took a moment to marvel at the quiet efficiency of this young man. "Do you take care of your girlfriend this well?" he asked.

"No girlfriend, sir. No time." Suitor continued his tasks at hand.

"Make the time to find the right one to settle down with," Stan suggested. "Wives are a pain in the ass, but they're worth it."

"Yes, sir," Suitor answered distractedly.

Stan smiled at the formal response. Then Suitor was gone, zipping down the ladder in no time. Now it was time for Stan to put on his game face.

From the hurried briefing, to suiting up twice, to preflight inspections of his aircraft, Stan was unable to get into the groove. Fortunately, engine start and the taxi out to the end of the runway went smoothly. Yet the entire way, Stan was distracted, pestered by stray thoughts fleeting through his brain.

114

He transmitted on the UHF radio. "Ranger, check."

Stan's helmet briskly swung upward from his pre-takeoff checklist and stared at his wingman holding several parking spaces distant from him in the area at the approach end of the runway. Stan passively expected a curt, positive response of "toop!" from his wingman, but after a fraction of a second of extended silence, he knew his wingman had not automatically changed radio frequencies from ground control to tower control at the prescribed location on the parallel taxiway. It was one more glitch piling up on this very sensitive mission cloaked in a cover story about being a training mission.

Staring rigidly at his wingman, Stan slid his transmit switch forward and repeated with one level greater sternness, "Ranger, check."

As soon as Stan released the spring-loaded switch, Tower was already broadcasting a long set of changes to departure instructions for Snapper flight. Stan realized his transmission was stepped on and unheard outside his aircraft.

"Sheeeees Louise!" Stan yelled into the muffling grip of his oxygen mask. He was becoming increasingly irritated.

When it came to radio discipline, missing a simple radio check-in was flat out unacceptable. Yet, it was all too common in young pilots when they were inundated with cockpit tasks mixed with sensory overload from the surrounding environment. With the exercise inputs and the changes and delays they had experienced so far, Lopass was teetering on the verge of being task saturated, like a sponge that couldn't soak up another drop of water.

On top of that, the local exercise was being played out on the same radio frequencies as normal flying operations because no one was smart enough to shift to the exercise frequency. That caused communication jamming of all participants— simulated and real world. Crews were asking tower control to repeat their instructions concerning changes resulting from the simulated exercise scenario.

This made things even more confusing as flight leaders jumped on any gap in radio chatter to request clearances. Several flights were inadvertently competing for airtime, resulting in numerous cases where two or more flight leaders were trying to transmit simultaneously. One was stepping on the others' radio transmissions and no one was hearing anyone, necessitating even more repeat attempts.

It was frustrating for an experienced pro like Stan, but more importantly, it was distracting for an inexperienced pilot. The normal smooth flow of events before takeoff was anything but smooth now. This threw off a novice's pacing, and inevitably, checklist items were missed, causing pilots to move less confidently, cut corners, and consequently, make more mistakes. A young aviator wants nothing more than to please his flight lead, but in the high-tech cockpit, even a smidgeon of panic is counterproductive and works against that goal.

Stan had been coached a thousand times by his instructors and mentors to "wind the clock" to calm down in situations like these. He reflexively reached down to touch the mechanical clock that had escaped digital modernization and replacement in the F-16. He smiled as he realized what he was doing. It was part of the culture and karma of the cockpit; the touchstone everyone returns to in order to rebuild lost focus in times like these.

He probably should have applied that principle before getting involved with Renee.

Lopass's helmet was down deep in the cockpit, hurriedly pushing buttons, still setting up navigation, threat countermeasures, threat warning, and secure communications.

"You've got to be shitting me!" Stan shouted and then winced at having lost his cool over such a minor incident. After all, this was a takeoff from a friendly field. No one was shooting at him. The bad guys weren't breaching the fortress walls.

Nonetheless, the stress between him and Jackie, the internal conflict between temptation and conscience concerning his affair, his lack of sleep, and now this morning's rush had worn him thin. His edge was blunted.

Normally, Stan would try to contact his wingman on a separate radio dedicated to intra-flight communications. Standard procedure was to assign distinct intra-flight frequencies for each mission comprised of two or four aircraft. Upon entering the cockpit, a pilot would set that frequency and never touch it again. It was a perfect back stop for the very dilemma Stan was facing with his wingman.

Stan now understood why they had half the frequencies normally allotted to the squadron for this purpose. He presumed the other half had been commandeered by the wing inspector general to support the ongoing exercise. Somewhere out there, Jackie was probably barking orders on a handheld VHF using the very frequency Stan should have had. In the back of his mind, Stan registered another black mark on Jackie's ledger for her contribution to the ongoing chaos.

He had considered and vetoed any use of the VHF radio as he and two other four-ships were directed to use the same frequency. The other flights had lieutenant wingmen like Lopass, and there was an endless stream of chatter concerning aircraft starting malfunctions, missing maintenance documentation, and even a mini tutorial by a relatively young instructor pilot concerning boresighting of the Maverick missile. Stan angrily twisted the volume knob of the VHF radio to nearly zero to rid his cockpit of the incessant jabbering, while vowing to later rip into the knickers of the young instructor pilot for rendering the frequency unusable.

About that time, Lopass glanced up for a microsecond in the direction of Stan's aircraft, but immediately hunched back down into the cockpit. As Stan was generating pressure in his diaphragm to blast out another muffled expletive, his wingman looked again.

It took Lopass a few seconds to realize the dark sun visor of Stan's helmet was facing him, and that meant Stan was looking at him. Stan's body language signaled something was wrong, and it was the lieutenant's turn to act on instinct.

There were only a couple reasons why his flight lead would be looking at him. Option A was the flight lead was waiting for a thumbs-up indicating ready to go. Or B, something was wrong with the aircraft. Lopass looked around frantically for a moment. Then realization hit him—it was option C. The flight lead was about to kick his ass for being off frequency.

Lopass shot his hand down to the communication panel and twisted the UHF channel one click counterclockwise to Tower frequency without taking his eyes off his flight leader. He nodded his head like a circus elephant to let Stan know he was now up with him on Tower. He also transmitted in a low, soft voice, as if to sneak his mistake past the rest of his amigos monitoring the frequency. "Two's up."

# Chapter 20

Jackie kicked herself for such a rookie mistake. Her line badge was her pass to get her wherever she needed to go on the flight line. To leave it at home was a waste of valuable time. In her rush to get her uniform and get out before running into Stan over the weekend, she must have left it on her dresser. During the insufferable drive home, she ran through a checklist in her mind to see if there was anything else she had forgotten when she escaped to Jenn's.

Stan would be gone for a few weeks, and she'd have time to sort things out alone. She loved Jenn and Jim, but it's hard to be miserable around someone else. In her own house, she could cry, yell, and throw things without being scrutinized.

Jackie finally reached home and left her car running while she ran in the house. She bounded up the stairs and quickly searched her dresser. Finding nothing, she dropped to her hands and knees and looked under the furniture. Totally frustrated, she picked up Stan's dirty clothes from the floor and tossed them onto his dresser. Her eyes scanned the room one last time.

Downstairs, she rummaged through every conceivable place that could hide a line badge. Eventually she gave up. She must have left it at Jenn's. It was too late to go by there now. She needed to get back to base.

~

While Stan worked to calm his raw nerves and waited for his turn to takeoff, he considered what he needed to do to make up with Jackie. He knew he had been a louse. He wasn't sure she would ever forgive him, but he wanted to try.

*Shit. This isn't helping*, Stan thought. *I need to focus on one problem at a time. We need to get in the air.*

A loud message burst through the chatter on the radio. "Attention on the airfield. RAPCON has directed a real-world ramp freeze in support of the simulated aircraft mishap exercise. All aircraft hold your positions."

Stan slammed his head back against the ejection seat. His attempt to relax and focus vaporized. He was pissed. He had rolled into departure position on the two-mile long runway, having received clearance to depart. He knew what might come next.

And he was right. "Ranger flight, cancel takeoff clearance," came the call over the radio.

There was a high probability that Tower's next call would be for Ranger flight to exit the runway, requiring them to taxi a third of the way back. Because of the congestion of aircraft waiting in sequence, it would place Stan and his wingman at the end of the queue.

*It can't get much worse than this.*

Then a blaring emergency signal came across the Guard receiver. The Guard channel was designed for emergency communications. It was working splendidly at the moment as the beacon pierced into Stan's skull.

Almost always, the sound of the beacon on Guard was the result of a mistaken activation during routine maintenance activity. The fact that Stan was in the first takeoff of the day meant some buffoonery had occurred on the ground, and it would take some time for someone to discover and locate the gaff.

The wailing beacon was overpowering Stan's ability to hear calls on any other frequency. As he fumbled to turn the volume down, he thought he heard a garbled call from Tower about takeoff clearance. In frustration, Stan slammed the radio to a setting of UHF ONLY, thereby eliminating the Guard transmissions completely. Within the confines of his cockpit, the shrill beacon was silenced.

Stan queried Tower, "Tower, Ranger Eleven. Was that last call for me?"

"Affirm, Ranger. Can you make an expeditious departure?"

"That's affirm, Tower. Ranger Eleven is ready to depart now."

"Ranger Eleven, you are cleared afterburner climb to flight level two hundred. Fly runway heading to ten DME, then right turn direct Shamis, then flight planned course."

Stan read back the departure instructions.

"Ranger Eleven, winds are zero-two-zero for thirteen. You are cleared for takeoff. Contact Departure Control on local channel four."

Stan scrambled to reset a number of switches he had repositioned thinking he was about to taxi off the runway, and then realized he had not checked the status of his wingman. He looked over to see Lopass making a huge elephant nod that he was ready.

"Nice," Stan spoke aloud, thinking his wingman had finally caught up and was thinking ahead.

Stan raised his gloved fist and extended his index finger meaning the number one. He dropped his hand and then raised it again with all five fingers extended meaning the number five. He was reminding his wingman to take fifteen seconds of separation behind him on the takeoff. Another giant nod from Lopass.

As Stan released his brakes and began to accelerate, he called to Lopass on departure frequency in accordance with standard procedure. Silence.

"Obviously that was a bit too optimistic," Stan mumbled sarcastically, assuming his wingman had missed another frequency change. *I'll catch him after join-up.*

Stan placed his throttle into afterburner and all five stages lit smoothly. He scanned his engine instruments, and all were in normal operating ranges. He accelerated down the pavement, only needing a few thousand feet of its enormous length, and smoothly rotated the nose off the runway. He flicked the gear handle to the UP position, took one last look at his engine instruments, and let out a long sigh. At least the Germans gave the rare approval for him to make a screaming climb in afterburner all the way up to level-off altitude. Their jets were loaded with extra weight, but there was plenty of gas to burn. Stan pulled the throttle back just a bit to give Lopass some excess thrust to join up. He was finally airborne, all was quiet, and he left all the chaos of ground operations behind him.

∾

On the other hand, Lopass was assholes and elbows as he reset his own aircraft for takeoff. He was already sweating heavily despite the chilly cockpit temperature. As a drop of salty sweat rolled stingingly into his left eye, he muttered to himself, "Inconsiderate jerk. It's all about him. He rushes me, and then he'll rip me a new one later because I was twenty-five seconds behind rather than fifteen."

He should never have nodded he was ready. He lied, but he couldn't stand being the cause of another delay. He hoped for the best.

Lopass watched the butane-blue torch of Stan's afterburner lick the runway as Stan barreled ahead, rotated, and lifted gracefully from the runway. Much too delayed, he released his own brakes, engaged afterburner, and quickly checked to ensure he was properly tuned to Departure Control frequency. It was the fourth or fifth time he had checked. He did not want another breech of standard radio procedure.

"Lookin' good," Lopass spoke, reinforcing himself. As he picked up speed, he realized Stan had failed to check in on the departure frequency. Lopass noted to himself that his flight lead might be as harried as he was, and he reasoned it might make the mission debriefing a little less painful for him after they landed.

Jackie was in a hurry to get back to the base for the action. She hated missing the most exciting parts. As she sped along the winding roads, she tried to count her blessings. She had a lot in her life that was really good. She needed to keep her mind focused on those things.

Jackie slowed as she entered the town and made her way through the road curbs the Germans devised at the entrance of each village to keep people from speeding through. Not only were they functional, they were usually beautifully planted with flowers. As she rounded a sharp bend in the road, she swore loudly. A herd of cattle was being driven down the street, blocking both lanes. Jackie knew better than to be upset. Any other day, she would have found this situation funny. Now, as she sat being not-so-gently rocked by the dozens of cows as they bumped her car on their way past, she took a deep breath and released it slowly.

# Chapter 21

Finally, they were away. As the runway faded behind him, tension began to ease from Stan's body. He willed his shoulders to relax and settled down for the long cross-country flight.

"Mace, do you copy?" He thought he heard Lopass's timid voice.

*At least he figured out the right frequency,* Stan thought. Then he realized Lopass was talking to him on the VHF he had nearly extinguished in volume before takeoff. "Oh, shit," he mumbled as he looked at the radio settings.

Before he had a chance to respond, Lopass's voice came again. Still barely audible but with more intensity. "Mace, you're on fire. Ranger One, do you copy?"

Stan scanned inside his cockpit quickly then twisted around in his seat to scan the wings and airframe behind him. He looked first to his right to see if Lopass was rejoining on the expected wing inside his climbing turn back to the southwest. Lopass was lagging maybe 4,000 feet in trail.

Stan then twisted to the left and was stunned by the sight. A narrow pipe of flame was projecting out into the airstream perpendicular to his flight path. It was spectacular, like a gigantic blazing blow torch, so powerful it defied being bent backwards by the 300-knot airstream until it was about fifteen feet away from the fuselage. It then curled in the wind stream with a flickering yellow flame at the tip.

"Shit!" he exclaimed while simultaneously rolling out of his turn and pulling the throttle back out of afterburner and into mid-range. He twisted back again to locate Lopass and was stunned for a second time by a long trail of gray and black smoke. Stan was incredibly confused—how long had he been burning? He pulled the engine to idle and transmitted to Lopass, "Ranger Two, as soon as you can, take a look at my jet. Copy?"

From the lack of response, Stan was concerned that he had radio problems as well. He continued to scan his engine instruments and leveled his wings. He let the nose drop to pick up a slight gliding decent. Then it hit him like a mallet on the helmet. All those omens. He reached down and turned the radio knob from UHF Only to BOTH where it should have been. At the same time, he glanced at the channel window. "What the fff . . .?" he muttered.

Somehow in his rush to get airborne, he must have whipped the channel selector on the UHF radio past 4 to 7, which was an unmonitored frequency during good weather conditions. When he set the dial back on 4, everyone was screaming at him.

"Ranger One, this is Departure Control on Guard. Tower reports you are trailing flames and smoke. Come up two-eight-three-point-seven for a single frequency approach to runway zero-five. Do you need assistance?" Overlapping the call was the Tower calling on Guard for Ranger to come up departure frequency.

Lopass was screaming into his radio. "Departure Control, standby, standby. I'm rejoined on Ranger One. Ranger One is an emergency aircraft."

Stan had been burning for maybe two minutes, and he was fully aware he had cut himself off from ample warnings on the radios. He transmitted to Lopass on the interflight frequency. "Ranger Two, I'm up with you."

Lopass shot back instantly, "Ranger One, you were burning through the left side of your engine bay and the big fire is out, but you are still burning." Lopass was darting like a hummingbird around Stan's aircraft while keeping a hundred feet of distance clear. "Looks like part of your—"

Bam! Stan was knocked upward against the canopy as his jet fishtailed like a sports car at an icy intersection. It was followed by a loud crunch and pop. The nose of the aircraft pitched down violently.

"Ranger One, you lost your afterburner section and a big piece of the engine bay," Lopass announced.

"Copy all, Two." As Stan transmitted in a firm voice, the windup of the auxiliary power unit in the background indicated engine failure.

Lopass was having a hard time staying clear of Stan and not flying out ahead of him. Stan was flying well below a best glide speed without any assistance from the failed engine. Lopass took large weaving turns while fanning his speed brakes to maintain his separation from Stan.

Stan looked back at the fuselage and saw the entire left side had burned away, and the right side of his stabilator was gone. He considered himself lucky as the fire torched through the fuel cells without totally consuming the aircraft in a fireball.

He suddenly felt cold and wet as the cabin pressure deflated. The aircraft was drifting right and wanted to roll. Stan commanded maximum pressure on the control stick to stop the drift, but it felt unresponsive. He activated the trim motors, which seemed to have some effect. For now, the nose had stabilized about 45 degrees down. He had essentially stabilized the attitude as if he was flying a steep dive bomb pass, but his speed was accelerating in the plunge toward earth.

Stan reset the switches, shutting down the fuel control to extinguish the flames. It was useless. The realization hit him like a hammer. He was going to lose this plane. He looked down at the town stretched out below. He had been losing altitude quickly as he processed the emergency procedures. The houses were getting larger by the second.

In these final moments of light, infused with a powerful burst of adrenaline, Stan's senses became electrified, and the passing of time slowed sharply. An unnatural radiant heat flashed across his skin, as reality was ripped from his grasp. The intensity of his senses was stupefying, and it cast his dire situation as surreal. Stan felt separated from his body.

He was aware that his right hand was fiercely squeezing the control stick, the other bracing against the rail of the Plexiglas bubble canopy above the throttle. With every fiber of strength, his legs were uselessly mashing down against the rudder pedals. Yet, he was somehow lifted above the brightly flashing warning lights, the barking audio warnings, and the unresponsive craft to the status of spectator. He was uncannily detached, calmly aware that the outcome was forgone. Nothing further could be done.

"Damn," Stan muttered. "What now?"

He had to make a choice, eject and allow the jet to crash into the village below, or continue to fight the aircraft to miss the village. There was no time for both. "I've hurt enough people. No one else," he spoke through clenched teeth.

The Viper fought against his will, but he made it move ever so slightly. It was enough to miss the village, and it was enough to seal his fate.

$\sim$

Over the radio, Lopass's voice was shaky as he fought to keep himself calm. "Ranger—shit! Mace, eject, eject, eject!" Lopass already assessed there was no other outcome. "Mace, you have four thousand feet until min-controlled ejection. Do you copy?"

Stan responded in a strained, hard voice that communicated his struggle in the cockpit. "Lopass, stay high and away. My fault, my fault. Do not follow me below two thousand feet, acknowledge."

Lopass understood Stan's direction to stay clear. It was standard procedure, which would mean Stan was about to punch out.

"Copy, Ranger One, see you back at the bar."

Lopass lifted his nose to the horizon with a high-G pull. He was a bit startled when he realized how low, fast, and steep he had followed Stan and muttered, "Daaaaammmmm."

He inverted his Viper to regain a visual on Stan, immediately spotting the impact of the aircraft as smoke billowed. It was barely a hundred meters outside a fair-sized village. He scanned the atmosphere frantically for a chute but couldn't find it. He sliced his aircraft back toward the impact area, staying well above where he thought Stan ejected.

"May Day, May Day, May Day," Lopass transmitted to the world. "Ranger zero-one is down five miles due west of the airfield."

# Chapter 22

As Jackie waited for the last cow to bumble past, there was a loud explosion. *Wow, the EOD guys went all out on that one*, she thought. Exploded Ordinance Demolition was a specialty career field in the Air Force. They were the experts when it came to handling explosives.

Jackie had elicited their help in her scenario to create a controlled, realistic explosion without actually hurting anyone. For them, this was good practice, so they had jumped at the chance. Now Jackie started to wonder if they did *too* good of a job and if the wing commander was going to be ticked.

She put her car into gear and moved toward the base. She didn't see the corresponding smoke that should have been floating skyward to alert the fire department where to respond for the exercise.

When she finally reached the base, the guard checked her ID and waved her through the gate. She made a mental note to see if that was the proper procedure. If a bomb exploded on base, the procedure should be for a lock down.

She made her way toward the flight line, glad she hadn't missed all the action. When she arrived, she was surprised to see jets taxiing back to the shelters. No one was taking off. She had been told by her subject matter experts that jets ready to go would be launched to keep them out of harm's way in the case of a possible attack. They didn't want to be sitting ducks on the flight line.

A sense of dread filled her. Something had gone terribly wrong. Her stomach fell, and she felt disorientated. She wasn't sure where she should go first.

She was pulled toward Stan's squadron. From there, she would be able to listen to the radio chatter and figure out what was going on. She didn't have her line badge, so she'd have to find someone to escort her in. She grabbed her notebook and walked quickly to the guard shack facing the front of the squadron building.

Across the parking lot, a captain was talking to one of the new lieutenants Stan had taken under his wing. The captain had his hands on the lieutenant's shoulders and was talking intently into his face. Jackie gestured with a wave, and the captain immediately recognized her. He grabbed the lieutenant by the sleeve as he ducked his head and hurried inside.

She waited for someone else to walk by she could wave down to escort her. Shortly, Jello came out and approached her. "Jackie, you can't be here right now."

"What's going on?"

Jello's silence scared her. "We lost a jet, didn't we?" Jackie said quietly. "Which squadron?"

Jello shook his head. He wasn't allowed to answer any questions. When a jet went down, everyone instantly took a vow of silence until it was investigated. No one wanted speculation to get confused with fact. And then there was always the consideration of the next-of-kin notification; no one wanted them to find out through the rumor mill.

Jackie said a silent prayer of thanks that Stan had an early flight and was safely on his way to Aviano, even if it was with his whore Renee.

"Will you do a recall later and fill us in when you can?" she asked.

Jello looked sadly into Jackie's eyes, and she felt sorry for him. It must be tough to lose someone you work with and to come to the realization it might have been your plane. She wasn't sure how pilots handled that kind of pressure. It explained why some were devout Christians, putting their lives in God's hands, while others were atheists who believed *they* were gods with power over life or death. There weren't many who took the middle road.

"We'll be in touch," was all he promised. She understood the rules and their purpose, so she didn't press him.

As a personnel officer, she was trained on the notification procedures. The first time she had watched the training video on what a notification would be like, she had snuck out of the room to cry in private. And those were actors. She couldn't imagine having to go to the member's house herself.

She knew as soon as there was a confirmed death or serious injury, the wing would start the wheels in motion to pull together the people who would have the dreadful duty of notification.

The Casualty Notification Teams were chosen carefully for the right skills and maturity to handle the task, and they trained and exercised periodically to ensure they were ready. Notifications were handled professionally, compassionately, and with respect.

The chaplain on alert status for the team would be called. A senior officer, typically within the service member's chain of command, would have to don his service dress in preparation for the very somber event. If elderly parents were being notified, many times a health professional would be requested, in case the anguish of hearing tragic news brought on a medical crisis.

While this team was being pulled together, the personnel side of the house would be busy preparing messages that would report all the way up to the chief of staff of the Air Force. Not only were they concerned with taking care of the member, they needed to ensure the surviving spouse had everything they needed to keep going during this stressful time. That meant access to support personnel for the entire family, including the kids.

A tear slid down Jackie's cheek. She hoped the pilot didn't have kids. It was bad enough for an adult to have to experience this nightmare. To inflict it on a child would be devastating.

Jackie pulled into a parking space outside her office building. She wiped her face with her hands and tried to pull herself together before getting out of her car.

When she walked through the front doors, she was rushed by Staff Sergeant Ford and Master Sergeant Reynolds. "Ma'am, what's going on?" Staff Sergeant Ford asked.

Master Sergeant Reynolds added, "They told us all to come back here and wait."

Jackie shook her head. "I'm assuming we lost a jet. That's what all the secrecy is about. No one is allowed to talk about it until leadership fills us in. It'll be a while before we know what's going on."

"What squadron?" Reynolds asked.

"I don't know," she replied.

"It had to be an A-10," Ford offered. "I saw a two-ship taking off just before the crash."

"You don't know that for sure," Reynolds chided him. "There were a lot of planes taking off at that time. They were launching as many jets as possible because of the exercise."

In the silence that followed, the words sunk in. "Is this because of us?" Ford asked meekly.

"No," Jackie reassured him quickly, putting a hand on his shoulder. "Scrambling jets doesn't cause a crash. The pilots are trained for that. It had to be something else."

They lapsed into silence again.

"Okay, let's try to get something done and stop dwelling on this. We aren't doing anyone any good. Sergeant Reynolds, keep your eyes open and let me know how everyone else is taking this. If anyone needs to talk, we'll get them to the right people."

"Yes, ma'am." To Ford, he said, "Let's gather everyone together to collect what they observed during the scenario." They walked back toward their office space.

Jackie's feet felt like lead as she headed toward her own office. She knew the wives' network would be operating at full speed already. As if to prove her point, her phone was ringing when she walked in her door.

"IG, Major Austin," she answered.

"Jackie, have you heard?" It was Jenn.

"I don't know anything more than you do," she replied.

"I got a strange call from Jim. He called to remind me to take out the trash. It isn't even trash day."

"That was his way of letting you know it wasn't him in the crash. He knew if you heard his voice, you'd eventually put two and two together when you heard the bad news. No one is allowed to talk about who was in the air at the time. The family needs to be told first."

"Have you talked to Stan?"

"No, but he was first in line for takeoff this morning. He was probably preparing to land in Aviano before the crash even happened."

"Thank God," Jenn said. "Even with all that's going on . . ." she trailed off.

"I know," Jackie said. "A crash really puts things in perspective. Things could be a lot worse. Oh, I saw Jello at the squadron."

"I'll call Tina as soon as we hang up and let her know. Do we even know if the jet was from our squadron?"

"Not really. It's still early."

"Well, I need to make some more calls. I'll let you know what I find out. You'll call me if you hear anything, won't you?"

Jackie agreed, although she knew she probably wouldn't. Here was where her life as an Air Force officer intersected with her life as a wife, and her loyalty would always be to her uniform first.

Jackie hung up the phone and got up to close her door. She needed some privacy. As she fell back into her chair, she placed her head in her hands and began to cry. Gentle sobs, but the tears wouldn't stop flowing. Just when she thought she had things under control, visions of last year's squadron Christmas party entered her head. She saw the faces of the children light up when Santa entered the room. She thought about what their faces would look like when they were told their daddy was never coming home again, and her tears started all over again.

A knock at her door drew her back to reality. She glanced at the clock and realized she had been sitting in her office for over an hour. Embarrassed, she grabbed tissues and wiped her face as she got up to answer the door.

Standing in front of her in full-service dress were Colonel Eberhart and the base chaplain. Instantly Jackie's knees were weak, and she felt lightheaded.

Her first thought was somewhat detached. *So this is what it feels like*, but she quickly dismissed the pounding in her chest because she knew Stan was in Aviano. She fought through the panic that gripped her. She needed to be strong. Someone needed her.

"So it was one of ours," she confirmed. "Do you need me to go with you? Who is it?"

Looking past the first two, she saw her boss, also in service dress. She took a step back. The chaplain took her elbow, guiding her to a chair.

The next minutes felt like days as Jackie drifted in and out of a fog. She heard their words but couldn't process what they were telling her. It couldn't have been Stan. They must have made a mistake. Stan had left early this morning for Italy. He was scheduled as the first takeoff of the day. She hadn't wanted him to go, but he insisted.

They had been fighting. She didn't say goodbye.

Eventually the men stopped talking. She felt a hand on her shoulder, a gentle squeeze, then nothing. She felt nothing.

# Chapter 23

When asked about notifying Stan's parents, Jackie opted to have the Air Force contact them. She wouldn't know where to begin. Besides, she felt it should be done in person—someone needed to be there with them when they were told. She wasn't sure how they would take it. His mother hated the fact that he flew. It scared her.

Back at Jenn's house, Jackie asked Jenn to contact Alison. She didn't think she could bring herself to say the words. Jenn called Alison. Eventually Jenn brought the phone to Jackie.

"I'm so sorry, Jackie."

Jackie mumbled something, but then the tears started again.

"I can be on the next plane out," Alison said. "I'll be there by tomorrow night at the latest."

"No, don't come here."

Alison was taken aback by her words. "Why?"

Jackie sniffled and searched for a tissue in her pocket. Jenn held a box in front of her. "I mean, there's no reason. I'll be home soon. I want to come home." She started crying harder, and Jenn took the phone out of her hands.

∽

It had been two days, and Stan's parents must have been contacted by now, but Jackie hadn't heard from them—and didn't expect to. They weren't overly fond of her, and they never associated with her more than they had to for Stan's sake. Jackie supposed the funeral was the last time she would ever see them. She wasn't sure how she felt about that.

The memorial service was scheduled for the end of the week. The captain assigned to assist Jackie had tactfully asked only the necessary questions and stayed out of sight otherwise. Jenn, on the other hand, stayed by her side at all times, and had helped Jackie move into their guest room.

Jackie didn't remember packing, but somehow her clothes were hung in Jenn's wardrobe. As she stared at the clothes, struggling through the mundane task of getting dressed for the day, she noticed she hadn't brought any uniforms with her. Was it her unconscious decision or Jenn's conscious one?

Eventually someone would be assigned to clean out Stan's desk and locker at work and return his things to Jackie. This person would also cull through Stan's personal effects at home, separating government-owned gear from personal possessions. For now, the military was holding on to anything pertaining to flying until after the safety investigation board completed their work. Jackie couldn't have cared less. There was nothing she wanted from the squadron.

Wednesday night as she sat curled up on the couch with a blanket tucked around her, the doorbell rang. She didn't move as Jenn went to answer the door. She heard a deep, familiar voice and looked up.

"Hi, baby," her father said, coming into the living room, followed closely by her mother.

Jackie stood up and ran into his arms, letting the blanket fall. She buried her face in his chest and bawled as her mother rubbed her back.

Having her parents nearby gave her the strength she needed to get through the next few days. The squadron was handling the arrangements for the memorial service. All she had to do was show up.

~

As she entered the chapel with her parents Friday afternoon, Jello and Tina greeted her. Jackie made introductions out of habit, and they all shook hands. Jackie was very quiet, and her mother kept a close eye on her, watching for any signs that this may be too much.

The chapel was full of people milling about, talking quietly. Jackie's mind was numb. She took in her surroundings, but nothing was registering, until she caught movement near the closed casket.

Jackie's heart raced, and blood rushed in her ears. Her mother saw the look on her face and quickly traced her line of sight. There was a young woman in uniform standing with her hand on the wooden box.

Suddenly, Jackie was across the room, grabbing the woman by the arm. She spun her around and growled in her face, "Get your hands off my husband!"

Renee stood in horrified shock. Her eyes were red and puffy. She had been crying, but Jackie felt no sympathy for her. As a matter of fact, she felt nothing but hatred. "How dare you show your face here!" she spat. "Get out of here this instant!" Jackie's face was red with anger, and Renee was even brighter crimson with embarrassment.

Jenn materialized at Jackie's side and gently took her arm. She placed herself strategically between Jackie and Renee.

Renee looked around at the faces staring at her, frozen in place. Jello stepped in to guide Renee toward the exit. The chatter began again in rapid whispers as the uninitiated were filled in on the gossip of Stan and Renee's affair.

Jackie was glad her parents had come to Germany. She didn't realize how much she needed them. Jenn and the other wives were fantastic, providing food and running errands for her, but her parents gave her the strength to return to her house—hers and Stan's.

Her parents had been staying at the house since they arrived, but Jackie still hadn't been able to bring herself to go home. However, it was time. Monday morning, her mom followed her up to her room and helped her pack things for the trip back to the States. They talked a little about people Jackie knew back home. Her mother filled her in on Alison's last visit. They talked about anything but Stan.

Her suitcase almost full, Jackie went to her bedside stand to pick out a book for the plane. When she saw the scrapbook for their trip to Switzerland on the table, she froze. Slowly she picked it up and touched the cover lovingly. Then without warning she heaved it across the room with a scream. It hit the wall with a loud thud and clattered to the floor.

Falling to her knees, she started crying again. Her mom was beside her in an instant. She helped Jackie into bed and pulled the covers over her. Lying beside her, she gathered Jackie in her arms and stroked her hair. They stayed that way until they both fell asleep.

# Chapter 24

The cheerfulness of the flight attendant was grating on Jackie. She closed her eyes and pretended to sleep. Her father tucked the inflight blanket around her shoulders. Jackie smiled in acknowledgement. The attendant was taking drink orders, but she didn't respond. Her mind was still in Germany. Then it switched to Langley Air Force Base and her previous assignment.

She was searching for something, for someone. She was calling out but couldn't hear her own voice. The back door was open, and light was streaming through. Jackie walked toward it, but the door never got any closer. She saw a puddle in the light of the doorway. It was dark and shiny. It drew larger as Jackie walked, but she still wasn't getting closer. The thick liquid reached out toward her, slowly surrounding her feet. She was walking in it now. It was sticky. She stopped walking and bent down.

Jackie started awake; her dad reached over and patted her hand. Settling herself back into the seat, she tried to calm her pounding heart. Sweat broke out across her forehead even as she shivered with cold. Leaning her head back, she gazed out the windows at the clouds. They made her think of Alison.

When they were little and her father was in one of his moods, she and her sister hid in the backyard. Climbing on the roof of the shed to gaze at the sky, Alison told Jackie stories about the castles in the clouds and the people who lived there. Jackie added the description about the food they ate—lots of cookies and cupcakes.

Jackie always thought that someday she would tell her kids the same stories. Her children and Alison's children would play together and make up their own ways to get into trouble. Jackie always assumed her kids would be mischievous like Stan. After all, he had never really grown up. They would be exceedingly handsome with his dazzling smile.

No they wouldn't. Not now.

Jackie stifled a sob. She wouldn't have kids now. Stan had taken that opportunity away from her. First, with his selfishness making her wait so long. Now, by leaving her. She was already in her late thirties. She was at the end of her biological clock. Her chance at motherhood had slipped through her fingers. Her anger flared at Stan. *Damn him!*

The funeral was a closed casket. After a crash bathed in thousands of gallons of burning jet fuel, Jackie doubted there was really anything in the wooden box she had escorted back to the States on the plane. She had provided a flight suit for him to be cremated in, but she was sure this was a symbolic gesture.

Stan's parents were subdued. They hugged her when they saw her, but it was without warmth. Jackie sat in the front row, flanked by her mother on one side and Stan's mother on the other. Her mom held her hand tightly, giving a reassuring squeeze when the pastor spoke words Jackie's mom wanted to emphasize.

Jackie hardly heard the words. She knew people were speaking and saw them move to take their place behind the lectern and then move back to their seats. She watched with a detached silence. She didn't want to cry anymore. She felt cheated.

When she and Stan first met in Korea at Osan Air Base, she was struck by how in love she felt. She thought about Stan all the time. She heard his voice from somewhere in the squadron and made up excuses to be in whatever room he was in. She wasn't fooling anyone. Even her squadron commander knew there was something going on, but he pretended not to notice. Dating wasn't prohibited within the squadron because Jackie and Stan were equal rank and didn't work for each other, but the dynamics of romances within a unit could get messy, so were usually avoided.

When Stan got his orders to leave Korea, Jackie was crushed. She felt he was leaving *her*. He convinced her that he would never leave her; they only had to be apart for a little while.

*Well, he lied*, Jackie thought, staring at the casket. *He did leave me.*

Her father rose and took her elbow. He led her to the front of the room where the casket was displayed with a picture of Stan, a crooked smile on his face as if he had just told a joke. Jackie remembered the day that picture was taken. It was after his finnie flight at Osan—his last flight with the 25th Fighter Squadron "Assam" Dragons. It had been a cold day, but the fire trucks were there anyway and had hosed him down as was the tradition. One of the guys sprayed him head-to-foot with champagne.

She couldn't bring herself to touch the casket. What was the point? She turned and allowed herself to be escorted away, ahead of the crowd.

Back at her parents' house, guests came and went. Jackie understood the cultural requirement to go through this process but didn't feel like participating. To escape the present, she did what she did best—made a mental checklist. She thought about all the things she needed to do, who she had to contact, and what was required to ensure all the paperwork was in order. She would have to get stamps for the thank you cards. Her mom was keeping a book with notes on all the visitors who stopped by.

Soon she would go to Youngstown Air Reserve Base. It wasn't far from her parents' home, and some former squadron mates were going to help her give Stan the sendoff he would really appreciate.

She kept running through things in her head, thinking about the future so she wouldn't think about the past.

Finally, the last person left. "Sweetheart, why don't you go lie down for a while?" her mother prodded.

Jackie nodded and rose from the chair where she had been sitting for what seemed an eternity. She shuffled to her old room and kicked off her shoes. Still fully clothed, she curled up on the bed and closed her eyes. A few minutes later, Alison came into the room, easily recognizable from the sounds she made as she moved about. Jackie felt a blanket being draped over her but was too tired to acknowledge the gesture.

# Chapter 25

It was seventeen-thirty on the east coast of the States when the phone rang. Chaplain Ren Vandensteeg was shutting down his computer before leaving for the night. Everyone else had already gone. "Shaw Base Chapel, Chaplain Vandensteeg," he answered.

"Sir, it's Jackie Austin."

"Jackie?" he was surprised to hear her voice. He hadn't seen her since she left Langley over seven years ago, but Vandensteeg thought of her often. She had been through quite an ordeal and had come out a stronger woman because of it.

"I heard about Stan. I'm sorry for your loss."

She sniffled on the other end of the line. Not wanting to make her uncomfortable, he went on. "Are you in Germany?"

"No," she answered quietly. "I'm in Ohio with Mom and Dad."

"Good. You need to give yourself some time."

He let the silence linger, giving her a chance to say why she had called.

"It's never ending," she whispered.

"What's never ending?"

"This sadness. Why can't I be happy for a change? It seems like anytime I start to pull myself out of the darkness, something bad happens to bring me back down. I mean, I was getting my life on track at Whiteman when some lunatic focused his sights on me."

She paused, and he was sure she was thinking of the loss of her best friend during her first assignment.

"I start to recover, meet Stan, and life is looking good. Then, after I move to Langley, the lunatic turns up again."

Jackie was getting wound up. She didn't open up to many people about what had happened to her as a young lieutenant.

"I thought things would be better now. I thought Stan and I would start a family." She took a deep breath. "He didn't want kids. He strung me along, making me believe there would be time later. That we had no reason to rush into it. Now he's gone, and it's too late. Too late for *us*!" The frustration was palpable in her voice. "I keep thinking, 'Give us one more chance! We'll do better.' But I wake up the next morning, and Stan still isn't here. Crazy, eh?"

The chaplain wished he were with her in person to guide her through this trying time, like he had been at Langley.

"I know this seems impossible right now. But you need to go through the mourning process, and you'll emerge stronger on the other side. It doesn't feel like it now, but things will get better."

"Like things got better after I left Langley?" Her voice was almost mocking.

"Things *did* get better. Think of the good times you had with Stan—the world you got to share. Be thankful for what you had."

There was another period of long silence.

"He was cheating on me, you know."

Vandensteeg shook his head sadly, although Jackie couldn't see. He knew Stan and Jackie wanted different things in life, but he hadn't seen any signs that would indicate infidelity. Of course, he had met them under very unusual circumstances, but he would have thought, having lived through the horror of the attack on Jackie at Langley, they would have been closer than ever.

"I'm so sorry, my friend. You didn't deserve that."

"How can you be so sure? You have to think the best of everyone. You're a holy man."

He smiled at her attempt at humor and took it as a good sign.

"You know, Jackie, you're not the first woman to deal with betrayal. The worst part is you won't get closure on that issue. You'll have to let it go, and it won't be easy."

"You're telling me."

Jackie's personality was peeking through already.

"How long before you go back?" he asked.

"I'm staying through the end of the month. The ORI starts next week, so they won't need me for a while."

"Take your time and don't rush things," he cautioned. "And call me from time to time and let me know how you're doing."

"I will. Thanks for listening."

"Any time, Jackie. You know that."

"Yes, I do. Chaplain, I'm thankful for *you*."

"Give me your number in Germany." He realized Jackie might be too proud to reach out. He would make sure to stay in touch.

She recited the numbers and said she hoped they would see each other soon.

As soon as they hung up, Vandensteeg got down on his knees at his desk and said a prayer for Jackie—a prayer for strength, resilience, and recovery. He knew she would suffer through the distinct stages of grief universal to all those who lose a loved one. He assumed she went through denial and pain right after hearing the news. Now she was definitely angry. But it was a healthy anger that would help the healing process.

He heard the bargaining in her rants. But even then, he knew she was too practical to spend much time in that stage.

He was sure she would cycle in and out of depression, which was the most painful to watch. A bystander needed to be available, making sure she didn't sink so deep into self-absorbed depression that she couldn't climb out. Jackie was fortunate in that regard. Her parents and her sister were loving and supportive. She had her military family close by wherever she was. They would watch over her well.

Chaplain Vandensteeg knew she needed another distraction to get her to the final stage—acceptance. Like her assignment to Korea had been a distraction from the loss of her best friend at Whiteman, something else would come along to occupy her mind and move her onward from this loss. He hoped she would find something quickly, for her sake.

It was a cool, clear day for March; not a cloud in the sky. Jackie sat next to an open field in a lawn chair her dad insisted she bring along. Now she was glad she did. She was surprised how much the rolling hills of Ohio reminded her of Germany. There was no snow on the ground, and rich green patches showed where spring was trying to seize a foothold.

She pulled a quilt around her shoulders to trap in body heat. As she waited, she prayed and tried to listen for God's answer. She felt a warm breeze, as if God Himself had slipped His arms around her, and she knew it would be okay. Relaxing back into the chair, she waited.

Stan's parents weren't here today. Jackie was glad. Although her parents and Alison had offered to join her, she wanted to be alone for this final stage—her final goodbye to Stan.

Stan's parents were upset when Jackie decided to bring his body back to Ohio. They wanted him buried in their hometown, but Jackie knew Stan didn't want to be buried. He hated the thought of someone visiting his grave. He and Jackie had agreed they both wanted to be cremated and have their ashes spread. Worse than having a gravesite, neither wanted to be the ashes on the mantel. Stan's mom didn't believe Jackie was carrying out Stan's wishes. She was sure Jackie was being spiteful and controlling. She and Jackie often didn't see eye-to-eye on things.

Jackie heard the distant sound of thunder although there was no storm. She stood as two dark spots appeared on the horizon. As they grew larger, Jackie felt the familiar tug at her heart. She never wanted to be a pilot, but she loved watching the jets fly and being part of the best Air Force in the world. A-10 Warthogs were her favorite airplane since the first time she saw them fly in Korea. And they were Stan's favorite too. Even though he had switched to the F-16 Viper to take an assignment to Germany, he liked to tell the story about how he got to fly the jet of his boyhood dreams—the Warthog.

The jets flew overhead and rocked their wings. Jackie waved up at them. They circled around, the second trailing behind the first. The next time they passed, the second bird slowed as the pilot opened his speed brakes. A thin cloud wafted out behind the jet.

A tear trickled down Jackie's cheek. Stan would have been pleased that it ended this way. He loved to fly more than anything else. The fact that his real finnie flight was with a Warthog was the right ending.

She said a prayer of thanks for the A-10 pilots out of Willow Grove Air National Guard Base in Pennsylvania who flew in to do Stan this honor.

As the sound of their engines faded away, Jackie packed up her chair. She took a last look around the open field and said goodbye to Stan.

∼

The next two weeks passed quickly. Jackie spent time with her parents doing nothing. They went out to eat, watched television, and went shopping. They let her talk when she wanted to and left her in silence when she didn't want to. They didn't mind when she cried over random events. It was very therapeutic for Jackie.

The Air Force was generous with leave after a death in the family. Jackie had thirty days of leave on the books, and her boss wasn't about to make her rush back when she wasn't ready. He called to check on her but assured her things were going okay and she should take her time.

Alison was able to stay and visit the first week before she had to go back to work. Jackie could tell Alison was avoiding the subject of having children, although Jackie knew very well Alison hoped to get pregnant any day.

Jackie called Chaplain Vandensteeg or he called her about every third day. He also didn't try to force her to cheer up, rather he listened as she talked through her frustration with Stan, his affair, and her wanting to be a mother.

When Jackie expressed guilt that she wasn't at work for the operational readiness inspection, Chaplain Vandensteeg laughed aloud at her. "Really, Jackie? You carry too much on your shoulders. I'm sure you did a great job getting them ready. Let them take the last steps on their own."

"I guess I don't really have an operational job during deployment anyway. I miss it though," she admitted.

"I think you're ready to go back."

Jackie's parents offered to wait with her at the airport, but she wouldn't hear of it. She always hated airport farewells, and it was no different now. She sunk down in a deep cushioned chair and pulled out a book. After reading the same page for the second time without comprehending it, she dropped the book to her lap and looked around.

She watched as an older woman hugged a teenager, presumably her son. He hugged her back but wasn't as reluctant to let go. Probably heading off to college and feeling excited for what lay in wait for him. Jackie continued to stare as the drama unfolded. Now younger brother was hugging older brother in an awkward, too-cool way. Their embrace turned into a noogie contest in which the taller boy had the obvious advantage.

Now it was Dad's turn. The young man tried to offer his hand in a handshake, but the elder pushed past that and took the boy in his arms. They slapped each other on the back a few times, and the man whispered something in his son's ear that made them both laugh.

The mother put her arm around the younger boy's shoulders as the three watched the older son walk toward the security maze. He raised his hand in a friendly wave but didn't look back.

To Jackie, it was like watching a play put on for her benefit. She felt the urge to applaud; the scene was so well scripted.

When she and Stan had talked about having kids, it always turned into a fight. Jackie would bring it up, and he would make excuses and stall. He tried to use Jackie's career as a reason. She didn't push him, knowing he wasn't ready to give up the squadron bars on Friday night and singing drunken fighter songs with his pals. She had decided to wait him out. After all, they had their whole life ahead of them, or so she thought. Her eyes welled with tears.

Before she had a chance to fall into self-pity again, she gathered her belongings. She still had another hour before her flight started boarding, but she needed a change of scenery. Playing voyeur to loving families was not healthy for her right now.

She moved through security in a daze. She showed her military ID and boarding pass to airport security. The guard handed it back to her with a smile. "Thank you for your service."

Jackie mumbled a thanks and lowered her eyes. She knew what she was doing was important, but it all seemed meaningless having buried her husband at the age of thirty-three. She was a widow, but her husband hadn't been killed in battle.

When they called for boarding, she found her seat by the window and stowed her belongings. She made a pillow out of her jacket and leaned against the window. Closing her eyes, she prayed silently no one else would talk to her for the long flight back to Germany.

# Chapter 26

It was early when Jackie arrived at the Frankfurt airport. Business travelers rushed past in their suits while the overhead announcements were repeated in multiple languages. Smoking was still widely accepted in Europe, and the smell permeated Jackie's clothes. She fell in with the river of people flowing to baggage claim.

As she watched the carousel make yet another pass with no sign of her luggage, she felt a hand on her shoulder. She turned into the welcoming embrace of Jenn.

"It's good to see you," her friend said, not letting go. Jim's huge arms encircled them both.

"I'm actually glad to be back," Jackie admitted. "Everyone being so nice to me is draining." She released Jenn and stepped back. "There's my bag."

Jim pushed through the waiting people to grab the black bag from the conveyor belt. He insisted on carrying it and led the women to a waiting car.

"So how are things going at the base?" Jackie asked Jim as they climbed in.

"Getting back into the routine. The jets are flying again. All of them have been inspected, and they didn't find any problems."

"So are they saying it was Stan's fault?" Jackie asked.

"No one has said that."

They sat in silence as Jim navigated the Frankfurt traffic.

"His wingman reported a fire coming from Stan's engine. That's a mechanical issue, not pilot error."

"But . . . ," Jackie prompted. "I hear a 'but' in that sentence."

"They're investigating his actions in response to the inflight emergency."

"Dammit." Jackie let out a long sigh.

Jackie had been home for a few hours when the doorbell rang. Margaret waited patiently on the doorstep. Jackie opened the door, and a delicious smell drifted up from the covered dish Margaret held in both hands.

"Let me get this into the kitchen," Margaret said by way of greeting as she moved passed Jackie and headed toward the back of the house. After setting the steaming dish on the stove and removing her gloves, she gathered Jackie into her arms.

"I've missed you, daughter," Margaret said in her heavily accented English. Jackie had grown to love the sound of the German accent almost as much as German food.

The two women embraced for several minutes. Margaret stroked her hair and whispered, *"Prinzessin, wird es alles gut."* Jackie didn't want to let go. It was such a blessing to have the love of a German mother telling her everything would be okay. With one last squeeze, Jackie finally separated herself from Margaret's soothing arms.

"What did you bring? It smells great."

"You are too skinny! Come, let's eat. I brought you jaegerschnitzel, spaetzle, and brown gravy."

"My favorite! Thank you, Margaret."

Margaret filled glasses with water from the refrigerator and took them to the table as Jackie dished out the food. She carried the plates into the dining room and sat down in her usual seat.

Margaret sat across from her, leaving Stan's chair empty. Jackie's eyes rested there for a moment before she cleared her throat and asked the older woman about her newest granddaughter.

Margaret launched into a story about her latest family visit, and the women forgot themselves for a while, celebrating life rather than dwelling in death.

∼

The light shone through the windows too early for Jackie. She covered her head with a pillow and rolled over, not ready to get out of bed. She wasn't tired, but another morning meant another day of learning to live without Stan.

It was too late. Her mind was already replaying their last argument. Stan had been cheating on her, and she didn't know if she could forgive him. Now she wouldn't even have the chance to try. But she thought they would have worked it out. She wanted to. She wanted the chance.

A quiet noise downstairs caught Jackie's attention. She removed the pillow from her head and rolled to face the door. She listened and heard it again, this time more persistent and louder.

Tossing her covers aside, she headed down the stairs. Through the shaded window, she saw a silhouetted shape. Moving the covering aside, Jackie peeked through the window, where Margaret paced anxiously on the doorstep.

Quickly, Jackie unlocked and opened the door. "What is it? What's wrong?"

"Nothing, nothing," Margaret insisted as she hurried in and closed the door behind her. "I brought you warm brochen from the bakery." She led the way into the kitchen, Jackie on her heels. Margaret opened the refrigerator and pulled out the jam. Jackie filled the pot to make coffee.

They worked in silence as Margaret busied herself getting out plates and silverware. Jackie knew that wasn't a good sign. Margaret always had something to say.

Jackie gave her time to bring up the real reason she was here.

Finally they were seated with fresh coffee, and Jackie spread jam on a piece of still-warm bread. She took a bite and savored the taste. This was a part of Germany she would miss when her tour was over. Nothing was as good as fresh brochen.

Margaret cleared her throat and stirred her coffee again, although Jackie hadn't seen her add anything to it. "Are you going to work today?" she asked.

Jackie shrugged. "I hadn't thought about it. I guess I should go check in." She stared into her coffee mug. "I don't know the correct procedure for this. My boss keeps saying to come back when I'm ready. Will I ever be ready?"

Margaret patted her hand.

"Should I go back now?" Jackie looked at her expectedly. "What's the right thing to do?"

The older lady took Jackie's face in her hands. "Daughter, there isn't a right or wrong. Do what you need to do."

Jackie sighed. "I want to sleep all day," she confessed. "I don't want to face anyone. I don't want anyone to tell me how sorry they are."

"You can hide out for a while," Margaret offered, "but not forever. You need to heal, but the best way to do that is with help from your friends. I'm always here for you, but you also have plenty of friends at the air base that want to help. And they need to heal too. They need your permission to do that."

Jackie knew Margaret was right. It was going to be uncomfortable whenever she went back. Maybe she should get it over with.

"Another day or two won't hurt," Margaret reassured her. "No one is rushing you. I will stay a little longer, so you don't sleep *all* day." They both smiled a little.

"So what got you up so early this morning?" Jackie sipped her now lukewarm coffee.

Margaret fidgeted with her napkin. "The news isn't good today. The locals are not very happy with the Americans."

"Why? What did we do?"

Their eyes met briefly and then Margaret dropped her gaze. "They are upset about the plane crash."

"Upset? What does that mean?"

"They want the base shut down."

Jackie stared at her in disbelief. "This isn't the first plane that's ever gone down. What do they think they're going to solve by shutting down the base?"

"You have to understand. Some are only using this as an excuse to get rid of the Americans. The plane did damage on the ground too. Stan wasn't the only one lost."

Jackie's stomach rolled over. She hadn't thought of anything beyond Stan until now. Obviously the plane came down somewhere. She knew approximately where it happened but never asked for the details. Then she was back in the States, certainly not keeping up with the German news. Now she looked at Margaret, steadying herself for the rest of the story.

"Stan's plane hit on the outskirts of Niersbach in an open field. Pieces of the wreckage traveled . . . ," Margaret broke off, not sure how much to share.

"Go on."

She cleared her throat and continued with a husky voice. "Pieces flew into a nearby cemetery." She spoke haltingly as she tried to pick the most gentle English words. "A woman and her young daughter were planting flowers on a grave. The mother was shielded by the gravestone, but part of the plane struck the young girl. She was killed instantly."

She looked up to see how Jackie was taking the news. Margaret took Jackie's shaking hands into her own. "It wasn't Stan's fault," the older lady assured her. "It was an accident."

"How old was she?" Jackie whispered.

"Seven."

The tears came again. Jackie, who thought she was cried out, now cried for someone she didn't know and for the parents. Losing a child had to be worse than losing a husband.

# Chapter 27

Something was trying to force Jackie from a deep slumber filled with vivid dream fragments. Beside her, his slow and deep breaths lightly caressed her neck and her ear with a low hush. Lying on her side facing the window, her arms held tightly to his arm thrown over her body, holding her firmly. He was snuggly against her back. Their skin joined along their entire length and sensual warmth flooded over her. Another breath rumbled across her neck bringing her a step closer to waking.

The dazzling flash was a fraction of a second ahead of the boom that violently shook the glass in the windowpanes. Jackie bolted up in bed, coming fully awake and stared into the dawning sky with a mixture of surprise and confusion. She tried to catch her breath as another bluish strobe filled the room for an instant. She flinched as a sharp crack rang out a half second later.

It was a rare, morning storm speeding over the neighborhood, the rumbles of thunder already fading, becoming more like the breaths against her neck she recalled from her dream.

Jackie looked over at the still-made side of the bed. She reached out her hand slowly and stroked the surface that Stan once filled. She longed for some evidence of his presence, but the bed was cold and lifeless. In all the mourning she had done for Stan, this was a stunning moment of understanding. The German dawn revealed something profound to her, and it was simple. She loved Stan dearly, but he was forever gone. She was alone in the emptiness.

She looked around their bedroom, expecting things to look different, but they didn't. *How could a person disappear from the face of the earth without leaving a hole?*

A tear rolled across Jackie's nose. She was finally ready to think logically about her last months with Stan. There was more to this process of assimilating, letting go, and moving on. It was time to wrap her head around something in the present and move forward.

The morning sun broke through the clouds as the storm cleared. She lifted her hand to gaze at her wedding ring. The faint sunlight shattered into prisms across the room. Jackie followed the dancing colors with her eyes. The face of her phone illuminated before the first ring and she picked it up.

"Major Austin," she answered, wishing she had cleared her gravelly voice and stuffed up nose. She listened for a second and then swung her legs to sit up straight on the edge of the bed. It was the OSI.

The Air Force Office of Special Investigations was like the FBI for the Air Force. They conducted all felony level investigations relating to criminal, counterintelligence, counterterrorism, espionage, and fraud matters within the Air Force.

"I don't understand. Let's talk now. I have time." Jackie stood up, juggling the phone while she wrapped a robe around her body. She walked down the stairs toward the kitchen.

"First, I want to extend our condolences for the loss of your husband. I'm sure the last few weeks have been difficult. If there's anything we can assist with, please let us know. There are many resources on the base to help in these situations."

The condolence was delivered with a baffling tone of stiff sanctioned babble. The investigator sounded like he was reading from a script. When Jackie failed to respond right away, the investigator jumped into the gap of silence.

"On an official level, we need to talk to you this morning here in our offices, and that needs to be at ten-hundred hours if that's possible for you."

"Okay, I can make ten-hundred. But what do you need to talk about?"

"Ma'am, it's about your husband's accident, and again, we are sorry for your loss. I can't get into any more detail on the phone. So, we'll see you at ten-hundred?"

"Yes, of course."

"Do you need directions, or should we send someone to pick you up?"

"No, I'm good. I'll be there."

She ended the call and leaned against the wall, puzzled by the tone of the investigator. She looked out the window and noticed the morning light remained low. A rumble in the distance warned of another approaching storm cell. Jackie took a deep breath and slowly exhaled. She felt she had taken a step ahead, vowing to refocus her energy on something besides the past. Now the OSI wanted to dredge up the memories again.

Another rumble came with heightened intensity. Jackie walked to the living room's bay window and saw the clouds were ominously dark and moving rapidly toward the base.

Jackie showered, put on her uniform, and drove to the base. Parking her car outside her office, she sat in the silence, bracing herself to face her coworkers.

Eventually she pulled herself out of her car and walked across the parking lot to the building. She didn't remember the door being so heavy.

"Major Austin." Staff Sergeant Ford stood as Jackie approached, and the others followed suit.

Jackie could tell they were uncomfortable. She waved them back to their seats. "Hi, everyone. Thanks for the flowers and the cards. And thank you so much for your concern. I really appreciate that you were thinking of me."

They murmured replies.

"Hey, guys, I know it's going to be tough adjusting, but please don't tiptoe around me. I need to get back to work and try to be normal. Bear with me if I zone out sometimes."

"That's fairly normal," someone quipped.

"Oh, you mean you're used to me zoning out sometimes?" Jackie asked with a dramatic sense of genuine curiosity.

They all laughed, and it broke the tension. Jackie was surprised she could laugh again. "Sergeant Reynolds, can you come to my office and catch me up?"

Jackie was relieved to see there wasn't a pile of papers awaiting her. "Thanks for keeping things going while I was gone," she said once they were seated.

"It's been fairly quiet. The accident investigation—" He cut himself off.

"It's okay. There has to be an accident investigation after any crash. That's no surprise. So, what have you been doing?"

"Well, the investigation has slowed things down a bit. Then it was time for the ORI." Master Sergeant Reynolds gave her the run down on the operational readiness inspection they had completed—and passed with flying colors—in her absence. "The wing commander gave a shout out to you during the debrief. He said that compared to your scenarios, the ORI was a piece of cake."

That made her smile. "I'm glad to hear it. Do you have a copy of the write-ups we got?"

"Already in your inbox, when you're ready for them."

Jackie asked a few follow-up questions, and together they outlined the work for the following week.

"If you need anything, ma'am, you know we're here for you." He stood to leave.

"Thanks. I'm counting on that."

As the door closed, Jackie sank back into her seat. She was proud of herself for getting through the conversation in such an unemotional manner, but now she was drained. Without any enthusiasm, she turned on her computer and waited while all the network security patches were downloaded. Someone had turned off her computer while she was gone, so there was a month's worth of computer updates before she would be allowed to log on to the base network.

While she waited, she glanced around the office, taking in her surroundings. Her eyes fell on the picture someone had taken of her and Stan in Songtan when they were stationed in Korea. They hadn't been married at the time. "Young and in love," as the song went. Stan had his arm around Jackie's shoulder, and she was leaning into him. In those days, they couldn't get close enough. What had happened to them?

The door to the outer office opened, and Mastana walked through the door, jumping when she saw Jackie sitting at her desk. "I'm sorry, Mrs. Austin. I didn't expect to see you." She started to back out the door.

"It's fine, Mastana. Come in. Please." Jackie stood. "How have you been?"

Mastana kept her eyes lowered. "Fine, Mrs. Austin. And you? How are you?"

She wasn't sure how to answer. Mad? Sad? Frustrated? She settled on, "I'm hanging in there. It's good to be back to work." She hadn't thought before she said it, but after it left her lips, she realized it was true. She enjoyed her work—always had. And it felt right to be back.

Mastana stared at her curiously. This wasn't what she had expected, although she knew Mrs. Austin to be a different woman than many of the other Americans she had observed. She felt sorry for this woman who had lost her husband. She knew what that loss felt like, and worse. Suddenly, the vivid images of explosions and weeping and broken bodies that were always in her peripheral vision were now in front of her, unwilling to be pushed aside. For a moment, anger pulsed through her body. Then she pulled herself back into the moment. She had felt what this woman before her was feeling. She saw the pain of her broken heart.

"I am sorry for your loss, Mrs. Austin."

Jackie swallowed a lump in her throat. "Thank you, Mastana." There was an awkward silence. "I guess I have to get used to that," Jackie said with an attempt at a smile, "and I need to think of a more meaningful answer." She picked up another stack of papers.

Mastana backed quietly out of the room.

# Chapter 28

A quick rap on her door brought Jackie's eyes up to her boss filling the door frame. She stood. "Good morning, sir."

"Hi, Jackie. How're you holding up today?" Colonel Harris asked with concern in his voice.

"As well as can be expected, sir."

"Do you have anything pressing going on right now?"

"Just reviewing the objectives for the next few exercises. We need to ensure we cover the areas written up in the inspection."

"Pass that off to Sergeant Reynolds. Let's take a ride."

"Sir?" Jackie's voice implied the question without having to put words to it.

"OSI called this morning. They said they had already notified you. I thought I'd give you a ride."

"That's okay, sir. I can take my car." Jackie started gathering her things.

"I'll wait. I don't mind."

Jackie looked at him suspiciously. It wasn't normal for a colonel to drive for a major. The hairs on the back of her neck stood up. She locked her computer and followed him.

The OSI offices were located on the other side of the base, near the German Politzei. Jackie had only been here once—when she tested for her German driver's license.

Colonel Harris parked in a spot reserved for colonels and above. He held the wooden door open for her and then led the way toward the stairway. The poor lighting and chilly breeze that drifted up from the basement reminded Jackie of a horror movie, and she shuddered.

They walked down a short hallway that opened into a waiting area with a well-worn couch and a government-issued phone even older than the one in Jackie's office. Hanging above the couch were pictures of men in uniform. She didn't recognize any of them so assumed they must be the chain of command for the OSI. It hadn't occurred to her before that OSI had a different chain of command than hers. They must not report to the wing commander. Her imagination immediately kicked into gear, trying to figure how to work them into an exercise.

As she continued her inspection of the space, she took in the counter with bulletproof glass protecting the empty desk and chair behind it.

As they waited, a young airman first class entered tentatively. She was followed closely behind by a senior master sergeant with a fabric diamond sewn between the upper and lower echelons, indicating he was a first sergeant.

Jackie wondered what might have brought this frightened young girl into OSI. The first sergeant didn't seem to be of much comfort. He spent all his time on his Blackberry, barely casting a glance at the frightened woman as she leaned against the wall.

Jackie felt the need to say something encouraging to the airman and stood to approach her when someone said her name.

"Major Austin?"

Two figures stood beside the open door. Jackie quickly took in the young lady who looked as if she were fresh out of college with her forest green skirt and matching suit jacket.

Her white blouse was a nice contrast and was accented by three gold chains around her neck.

The man was perhaps a few years older than Jackie. His hair was silver gray, and he was dressed in a neatly cut suit. Jackie's first guess was that he had been stationed in Korea sometime in the recent past. No one working for the military could afford something that fit that nicely on their salary, unless they had it tailormade in Korea.

"Yes?" she replied. Her boss rose to stand beside her.

"Would you mind following us please?" asked the female. "Sir," she added to Colonel Harris, "you'll need to remain here."

Jackie smiled apologetically at him and followed the man into another room.

"Do you have any electronic devices, pagers, explosives, knives, or sharp objects in your pocket?"

Jackie shook her head.

"Would you mind emptying your pockets and placing all of your belongings in this box?" Jackie felt as if she was going through the airport security and couldn't figure out what all the precautions were for, but she did as she was asked. The young woman used a metal detector to scan Jackie's body.

When she was through, she said, "This way please."

Jackie followed.

They entered a room with three chairs, a cheap wooden table, and a window with privacy glass. Jackie had seen enough TV shows to know that meant someone may be watching on the other side. As her mind took it all in, she noted a closed-circuit TV camera mounted in one corner. For a moment, she was tempted to wave at the camera but resisted.

"I'm Special Agent Christopher Marquette," he said, showing his leather-encased credentials stamped with the words "Air Force Office of Special Investigations" in blue on one side and a shiny golden badge on the other.

A flash of recognition crossed Jackie's face. She had seen this man before.

He gestured at the younger agent next to him. "This is Special Agent Emily Wright." She nodded slightly. "Please have a seat." He pointed to a chair.

After they were all seated, Agent Wright said, "We have a few points needing some clarification."

"Of course." Jackie braced herself, still unsure what information the OSI needed from her.

"First, let me say we are very sorry for your loss," Agent Wright began, staring straight into Jackie's eyes without blinking.

Jackie drew in a breath to respond as she had to a hundred other condolences, but Wright didn't give her a chance.

"Why were you and Major Austin fighting on the Friday night before his aircraft mishap?"

"What?" Jackie blurted in disbelief.

Agent Wright restated her query. "The Friday prior to your husband's mishap, the two of you were fighting. We'd like to understand why."

"If you are implying there's a connection, there's not," Jackie growled, glaring at the agent.

"Then you shouldn't have any problem telling us about it," Agent Wright said calmly, locked onto her glare as intently.

"Next question," Jackie said without blinking.

Agent Wright looked down at her notes. "What was the relationship between your husband and Captain Renee Bennett?"

Jackie bolted to her feet propelling the chair beneath her against the wall. "You've got to be kidding me! What are you actually investigating?"

Agent Marquette spoke in a condescending tone. "Major Austin, if you would please calm down. It's routine—"

"Bullshit!" she spat at him.

Then the light bulb went on. She remembered where she knew him from. He was the asshole she had called out during an exercise when she first arrived at Spangdahlem.

They were in the middle of a scenario, and he tried to flash his badge to get past the security forces airmen so he could leave the base. They had stood their ground, and when he lit into them for doing their job, Jackie stepped in and put him in his place. She had then written him up in her after actions report. She didn't know if anything ever came of it. It was small blip on her radar screen.

Agent Marquette allowed the hint of a smirk. He liked the unexpectedly strong reaction from her. It was obvious he remembered her too, but he wasn't going to admit it. He had been watching her every blink, fidget, and tone since she walked in. He was trying to push her off balance, and she was playing into his hands. She needed to calm down and focus.

He went on. "The OSI investigates all major incidents that involve serious bodily injury or harm to any Air Force member and all major accidents within the Air Force."

"So, yes, we are looking into the circumstances surrounding your husband's death," Agent Wright said as she stood to pick up the fallen chair. She moved it back to the table and motioned Jackie to it. "Major, please sit down."

Jackie's head was spinning, and the thought of talking to the OSI about Stan's relationship with Renee Bennett brought on a wave of queasiness. She sat.

"Major Austin, can we continue?"

"Go ahead." Jackie's mouth was dry.

"So, what was the relationship between your husband and Captain Renee Bennett?"

"I don't know. Why don't you ask *her*?" Jackie said, her voice dripping with sarcasm. She immediately regretted her tone with the agent. She took a deep breath to steady herself.

Agent Wright stared at Jackie for a period of time, and when Jackie said nothing more, turned a page in her notebook. "On Friday afternoon outside your husband's squadron, did you tell someone you would figure out a way to kill your husband?"

"Of course not!" Jackie barked, then caught herself as she remembered the comment she had made to Tina. "I was angry and might have made a smart-ass comment. But that's not the same thing." The question suddenly sunk in. Jackie was taken aback. "What does that have to do with the accident?"

"You tell us," the investigator countered.

"I suppose you think this was *my* fault. That I would sabotage an F-16? My husband's F-16?" Jackie's scoffing tone was mixed with anger and confusion.

"Well, this accident mirrors pretty closely an exercise I recall from," Marquette searched his notes, "this past fall, I believe."

Jackie's face paled. "It's ridiculous you would try to make that connection!"

Agent Marquette barely concealed his delight. His eyes were dancing with sick satisfaction.

"But you did say something about killing your husband," Agent Wright persisted.

When Jackie kept silent, Agent Marquette jumped in. "Why are you not telling us about your husband's affair?"

Jackie jumped to her feet again. "What does that have to do with the accident?"

"You tell us." Marquette quickly followed Jackie to a standing posture.

"This is ridiculous! Don't you have better things to do? I know I do."

"Sit down, Major." His voice was calm. It made Jackie feel foolish, as if she were overreacting. Grudgingly, she sat.

"Major, when did you find out about the affair?" Marquette said in nearly a whisper.

"Really?" Jackie was trying hard to control her emotions and speak more calmly. "This is what you want to talk about? Do you get some sick fun out of digging up dirt?"

He watched her every move.

"Fine, he was getting laid but not by me." Jackie crossed her arms under her chest and stared defiantly at the man.

"When did you discover the affair?" he asked calmly.

Jackie's thoughts were a jumble. When had she really known? Was it only after she walked in on him at the hangar? Or had she known for longer than that? She finally answered grudgingly. "For sure, on Friday."

"Only last week?" Marquette asked in disbelief.

"No, the Friday before the accident . . ." Her voice trailed off.

Agent Wright was about to ask a question, but Marquette raised his hand to stop her. The session had reached a point of transition, and Jackie sensed it. She had essentially corroborated a few key facts. They had gotten what they wanted from her. She had played right into their hands.

Marquette pulled out a pre-drafted sheet and began to read it aloud. "Major Jackie Austin, you have the right to remain silent . . ."

Jackie felt a chill penetrate her like needles as Marquette read the rights advisement. It was surreal.

Unlike the civilian world, rights advisements were given anytime something suspect was discussed. A person didn't have to be under arrest or even suspected of a crime. It was a typical cover-your-ass military move. For all the times she had witnessed a rights advisement, it did little to prepare her for being the target. And even knowing it was fairly common didn't ease the anxiety it brought on.

She was swirling and adrift. The fight in her evaporated.

She struggled to read the paper Marquette asked her to sign to acknowledge she received and understood her rights. She searched the paper to find the line Marquette had read stating her signature did not imply any admission.

"Major Austin, are you willing to continue to talk with us?"

She was shaking now, whether from fear or anger, she wasn't sure.

Marquette continued to observe her every breath. She knew this was his sport, and he was playing his part well. He waited a few moments then tried again with an expression of trained sweetness. "We would like to continue to talk to you if you are willing."

She took a deep breath and looked up. "I want a lawyer," she said quietly and firmly, clearly communicating that the interview was over.

It was a solemn car ride back to the office. Jackie's boss had waited for her and led her out of the building and to his vehicle without asking any questions. Jackie was fighting back the tears she didn't want to spill in front of her superior officer. It seemed weak to her.

When they pulled up in front of their building, Colonel Harris finally broke the silence. "Go home. There's nothing that can't wait until tomorrow."

Jackie nodded without speaking. As she reached for the door handle, he added, "Call me if you need to talk. Or at least talk to someone. Do you want me to have the chaplain get in touch with you?"

She hesitated, then shook her head. She did need to talk, and she knew who she wanted to call.

# Chapter 29

"You aren't talking as much today. What's going on?" Chaplain Vandensteeg asked her.

While she was in the States, they had gotten into a routine of talking a few times a week. Having someone to talk to was important for Jackie's adjustment to her new life without Stan.

"I got called in by the OSI," she said.

He waited for her to continue. When she didn't, he asked, "OSI? What did they want?"

"They think I have something to do with Stan's crash." Her voice was as tight as a piano wire.

Vandensteeg's pen slipped from his hand onto his desk. "You mean the aircraft investigation board thinks someone deliberately caused the accident?"

"Not someone. Me! They're pointing a finger at *me*."

"What are you talking about? How could you have anything to do with a crash?"

"They got word we'd been fighting a lot lately." She sighed. "Some of the wives heard me venting about Stan and his bimbo." Timidly she added, "I might have mentioned being tempted to kill them."

"Oooo." He visualized it vividly. He had ample experience with such things, having counseled other troubled marriages in the privacy of the chaplain's office.

"Of course, I didn't mean it." As an afterthought she added, "Well, maybe I did at the time, but I'd never really do it. It's a figure of speech."

"And I'm sure the OSI agents are used to hearing things like that. Do you think they're going through the drill with anyone close to the accident?"

"But they grilled me! They wanted all the details about the affair and when I found out about it. That's all they cared about. They weren't interested in the crash at all."

"Well, isn't it their job to gather details?" he reasoned. "They need to gather all the facts, even if it's to rule you out. Give it some time."

She didn't respond.

There was no sense pushing the point much further. Jackie wasn't the type to quickly surrender to a wait-and-see approach.

"What are you doing to take care of yourself?" he asked.

"I'm working. They offered to give me more time off, but I don't want it. I'd only sit around thinking. I'd rather be active."

"You know you're eligible for a hardship PCS," he offered. A Permanent Change of Station meant a move from a current assignment to another one. Even though she was on orders to remain in Germany for three years, because of a death in her household, she was entitled to move to a different assignment with fewer memories. As a personnel officer, she would have made the same offer to other grieving families.

"I thought about it, but I really like it here. I like my job and the area. I have lots of friends for support. I don't want to go somewhere new and have to explain my baggage to anyone."

Vandensteeg was glad to hear she had thought it through. Whether she realized it or not, she was on her way to recovery.

"Besides, if I leave, who knows if they will figure this out."

Uh-oh. He knew this side of Jackie; she was like a hungry dog with a bone. "I understand your concern, but don't get in their way."

"He may have been a cheater, but he was my husband. If it wasn't an accident, I want to know what happened."

"Understandably. But let the OSI agents handle this. You should be focused on you right now."

"I am focused on me. I need to know."

He sighed.

"Don't be mad at me," she begged. "I need you to pray for me."

"I've never stopped praying for you." From the time she had entered his office, struggling with her faith, her upbringing, and her stalker situation at Langley Air Force Base, Chaplain Vandensteeg had taken her into his heart. He saw her fight through her inner turmoil and emerge a resilient woman who wouldn't admit defeat. She liked taking matters into her own hands and seeing them through. Few people he met could have pulled off what she did all those years ago.

"Then pray I find the guilty bastard . . . if there is one," she said.

∾

"Hey, you," Jenn said when she opened the door to find Jackie on her porch.

"Hi. Thanks for inviting me over."

"Of course. The kids miss you. Come on in. What can I get you to drink?"

"Nothing, thanks. I'm good." She followed Jenn into the kitchen and took a seat on a nearby stool.

Jenn picked up the knife she had been using to chop celery. "You look thin," she said.

"I don't have much of an appetite," Jackie admitted. "This bullshit with OSI isn't helping matters any."

"It's ridiculous they would think you have anything to do with an airplane crash." Jackie had filled Jenn in on the interview earlier in the day.

"I personally think the lead investigator has a burr under his saddle because we had a previous run-in."

Jenn stopped chopping. "What type of run in?"

Jackie swiped a piece of celery from the cutting board. "It was a year ago at least. He was trying to use his badge to get out of following the rules."

"So you called him on it," Jenn said matter-of-factly.

"Of course. It was the right thing to do!"

"I would expect nothing less from you, Jackie. How's that going to affect this investigation?"

Jackie thought about it. "I'm not sure. If he's worth a shit, he'll get over his personal feelings and move on."

The front door opened and closed. The kids rushed into the kitchen, padding on tiny feet, and attacked her with hugs. She got off her stool and stooped to wrap her arms around them in return.

Jim followed the kids into the kitchen, kissing first his wife and then leaning over to give Jackie a peck on the cheek. "Good to see you."

Jackie smiled broadly. "Thanks. This was what I needed today."

# Chapter 30

Hi, Jackie," Lopass said sheepishly, standing on the front steps of her house.

Jackie's heart melted with sympathy as she took in this downcast pilot. Without saying a word, she hugged him.

Tentatively at first, as if undeserving, Lopass finally relented and hugged her back. Jackie felt his chest heave with restrained sobs but didn't acknowledge them.

Eventually he pulled back and wiped his eyes with the back of his hand. "I don't know what to say," he muttered.

"Neither do I," she admitted with a soft smile. "Come in." She stepped back and allowed him to enter her home. "Would you like some coffee or anything?"

"No, thanks." He stood and looked awkwardly around the room. He had never been here while Stan was alive, and Jackie knew exactly what Lopass was doing. He was trying to get a sense of Stan in his home setting. Jackie sat quietly allowing Lopass to take a moment to connect with his wingman through the shards of Stan's life.

The walls held a skyscape of fighter aircraft in framed photographs, lithographs, and original sketches. A dramatic painting of a Spitfire piercing through gaps in towering storm clouds hung over the sofa. A spectacular model of the A-10

Warthog sat on a mantle shelf. It was slightly banked away from the viewer to reveal an astounding load of weapons.

Lopass's eyes stopped on a bottle of Jeremiah Weed. A grin crept across his face then faded as he picked up the bottle. "You know, you can't drink this stuff warm."

Jackie smiled. Jeremiah Weed was the hallowed sugary bourbon created over a half century ago in some remote still in Nevada. The colder it was served, the easier it was to get down.

"Do not fear. Stan always left one in the freezer, ready at a moment's notice."

Lopass replaced the bottle and put his hands on his hips, taking one last scan around the room. "Mace really did live and breathe flying."

"That he did." Jackie's inner voice continued, *and that's not necessarily a good thing for a marriage.*

He walked over and sat silently on the edge of the couch next to Jackie.

"How are you doing?" Jackie asked, breaking into his thoughts.

"Isn't that my line?" He tried to break the tension.

"I know this has been hard on you too. I can't imagine what you're feeling. Being that close to a crash—," her voice caught, "and knowing it might have been you. I'd rather keep my feet on the ground, thanks."

"We know from the beginning being a fighter pilot means risking our lives every time we step into the jet." He stared at his hands trying to pick his words carefully. He looked up. "We just don't necessarily believe it."

Jackie understood this. Of course fighter pilots think they're invincible. That's how they do their job. If they thought every flight would be their last, they wouldn't be able strap themselves into the ejection seat, close the canopy, and put their faith in tens of thousands of pounds of controlled fire called thrust.

"Are you flying again?"

"I have a sortie tomorrow. My first since the mishap. It's in the local area. They sidelined me until the Safety Investigation Board learned enough to clearly eliminate me as a link in the chain of events leading to the crash." Lopass trailed off.

"The commander had the shrink talk to me to make sure my head was totally in the game, but otherwise, I can spin back up to a normal life." Lopass winced again.

"Are you scared?" She knew it wasn't a fair question, but she was curious.

Lopass met her eyes directly. "Hell, yeah."

She nodded. He was still young so she understood how this might shake his confidence. "Trust in your training," she advised. "You're a good pilot. Stan told me as much." That last part was a white lie, but she didn't see how it could hurt. Lopass had been through enough. He had his whole career ahead of him.

He smiled a crooked smile. "You're full of shit, but I appreciate it."

She smiled. A moment of silence passed.

"Do you mind talking about it?" Jackie asked.

He sighed. "No, but do you really want to?"

"I need to."

He looked at her long and hard. She saw when he finally decided that she was right. Jackie wasn't simply another wife. She was an Air Force officer, and this was part of her life.

"Well, things were crazy on the ground before takeoff. There was a lot of chatter on the radio, and it was hard to concentrate." His face flushed. Then it hit her like a kick in the stomach; the radio chatter was due to the exercise *she* planned.

He wiped his face with his hand as he resigned himself to speak the whole truth. "I made a stupid mistake by setting my radio to the wrong frequency. But when we took off, we were together."

"The takeoff was clean, no surprises." He swallowed hard. "We had just made our turn headed out when I saw a flicker from Mace's jet. Then it exploded. He had this blow torch coming out of his aft engine bay." Lopass instinctively used his hands as an aircraft to replay what he remembered. His left hand was flat and extended in front of his chest, portraying Stan's aircraft climbing in a right-hand bank. His right index finger was pointing outward from Stan's aircraft.

"It was like a rocket flame pointing ninety degrees from his flight path on the left side. Freakin' crazy. I've never seen anything like it!" His sullen demeanor was instantly adrenaline-charged, and his eyes widened at the memory still vividly burning in his mind.

"Fire had burned through the engine bay. It was like a fireworks' fountain coming sideways out of the fuselage forward of the stabilator. Unbelievable! I bet the torch was about the length of a Viper."

Jackie had a perfect picture of it in her mind. Although she didn't have the flying experience to describe the image as Lopass did, she had listened to endless fighter pilot stories and witnessed plenty of hand-flying to clearly understand what he was describing.

"It burned right through one of the fuel cells and bam!" Lopass suddenly realized he was way too loud and panicky and had lost regard for the fact he was in the presence of the widow of the man his left hand represented. He clenched his fist and drew his hands to his chest.

"I'm sorry, Jackie," he said in a much lower, calmer voice. He looked down at the floor, still seeing the image before him through the Plexiglas canopy. "It was so unbelievable."

He raised his eyes to meet hers.

"It's okay, go on." She covered his fist with her hand.

"I chased him the entire time, less than a couple hundred feet behind. At first it was only flames. Then the burner section fell off, and the engine bay was half gone. There were flames and black smoke. It was hard to tell where it was coming from." Lopass shook his head.

"I felt helpless because he wasn't talking, and all I could do was yell for him to eject. I thought he was going to. He told me to pull away." He paused.

Jackie stayed silent and gave him time.

"Jackie, he was headed right for the town east of the base. The plane was toast. The engine was gone, and the fire burned though a lot of shit. The maintenance guys said he would have lost flight controls except for some hard-wired response to the rudder or maybe the trim. I don't know. But I swear I saw the flight path shift. I couldn't believe it! Somehow Mace found a way to roll away from the town. I mean, I was chasing directly behind and overtop of him." He was instinctively using his hands again to portray the two aircraft. "I saw it all. He knew he was going down. I was screaming at him to eject. I thought he did! But instead, he stayed with the plane. He had to be fighting the controls the whole way."

Lopass was reliving the trauma and was rambling from thought to thought. Jackie placed her hand on his sleeve to stop him. "Hey, hey, I get it. He did good."

Lopass was trembling slightly and nodded in affirmation. "He did more than good for all the lives he saved. Only Mace could have done that."

Tears were streaming down Jackie's cheeks, and she didn't bother to brush them away. This sounded like the Stan she had married. He was a cheating shit, but when it had to do with flying, he knew what he was doing.

Lopass looked around the room again, anywhere but at Jackie. She needed time to absorb what he had told her. Yet, she sensed there was more that had kept Lopass sleepless for many nights.

"He told me it was all his fault and then had the cool to tell me to stay safe. He ordered me to stay high and clear. I thought it was because he was going to eject." Lopass reached for Jackie's hands. "But then he didn't."

They fell silent for a minute while Jackie thought about his comment.

"Do you have any idea what the safety investigation is finding?" she asked.

"Not exactly." Lopass shrugged and sat back. "They've kept it all tight. They've only debriefed the top four colonels on base and no one else. Not an official word otherwise."

Jackie sat forward on the edge of her seat. "So, what are you hearing unofficially?"

Lopass smiled weakly at Jackie. She was notoriously in tune with the flying culture, but she wanted to confirm the unofficial reports going around.

"Well, it's clear this was something in the afterburner section of the engine. They call it a burn-through. They pulled all the engines out of the Vipers and went over them with a fine-tooth comb. The maintenance guys said the afterburner section was the only component they were directed to inspect."

"Burn-through?"

"You know the fireworks display I described? It results from a hole in the afterburner section. Normally, the pilot pulls it out of afterburner and no big deal. If you stay in afterburner too long, it can burn through the airframe and all sorts of stuff," Lopass trailed off. "I'll be honest, I don't know why Mace didn't react to all the screaming on the radios. Everyone was yelling at him. By the time he answered, it had burned passed the point of recovery."

Jackie's mind was tumbling through a dozen questions based on what Lopass related. She needed to focus on understanding the cause.

"Can you peel this back for me one layer? What caused the burn-through?"

Lopass shrugged. "I have no idea. That's going to be one of the two big areas the investigation will need to explain. One is the failure mode. How did it fail? The second area will be who. There's always a human action or inaction that in some way resulted in the failure mode."

Jackie nodded in understanding as she picked at her thumbnail, thinking.

Lopass added, "There may be something else, but it's not the safety investigation board looking into it."

"What do you mean?"

"The OSI has talked to a lot of people about the accident. They all have had their rights read to them, so the word's out. It's gotten so bad that the wing commander threatened all the commanders to clamp down on loose lips."

Jackie felt a chill run up her back. Of course, the OSI had done a lot of investigative work in advance of her own interview. She had been out of the country for almost a month. She wished she hadn't said a word to them.

"I've got to get going, Jackie," Lopass said as he stood. "If I hear anything more, I'll let you know."

"Thanks." She stood with him. The last month had taken a toll on him that he would never share with anyone. She wanted to reassure him. "Thanks for being with Stan until the end."

There was a tremendous release on his face when she spoke those words. She was sure he had been harboring some blame for Stan's death, but Jackie didn't blame him.

She cleared her throat. "Thanks for talking to me. Everybody else is walking on eggshells. It's not as if avoiding the subject will make it any less real."

"I wish there was more I could do."

"I know," Jackie replied.

"You can call me anytime." He reached over and squeezed her hand. She smiled weakly.

"Thanks. For now, I need time."

"I mean it; let me know if you need anything. I'll see myself out."

She sank onto the couch as he left the room. The outer door clicked shut behind him. A quiet sob escaped her lips as she replayed the scene Lopass had so vividly described. Then she took a deep breath and calmed herself. She had a lot of details to digest.

# Chapter 31

Thanks for coming over, Jenn," Jackie said as they walked into her living room.

"Of course, honey. What's going on?"

Jackie sighed. "Lopass came by." She knew Jenn would understand instantly.

"How did it go?" Jenn settled into the armchair.

"He's hurting too." Jackie flopped down on the couch and tucked her feet under her.

Neither woman spoke for a moment.

Finally Jackie broke the silence. "I'm glad he came. He told me some things others wouldn't. He explained more of the details."

Jenn sucked in a sharp breath. "Oh, honey, are you sure that's what you needed to hear?"

"Honestly, it's better than what I was imagining. He told me the investigators are looking at the engines as the cause of the fire. He also said the OSI is talking to everybody, asking questions."

"Well, isn't that normal? I mean, there was an accident."

"But if it was an airplane crash caused by mechanical failure, why would OSI talk to so many people? Maintainers and the commander maybe, but why such a wide net? I think something else is going on. They're looking for something, and I want to know what it is."

"Jackie," Jenn's voice had a cautionary note in it. "Don't get in the way of the investigation."

"I want to help."

"They probably won't see it as help. They'll call it interference."

"How can I interfere with them? They have all the resources. I want answers they won't give me."

"Jackie, I know how you are. When you latch on to something, you don't let go. Don't make these people mad. You still have your career to think of."

"But, Jenn, they're focusing on the wrong things! They were quizzing me about the affair, as if that gave me a motive. They're wasting time."

"Just promise me you won't get in their way. You said this Marquette guy already has a problem with you. Don't give him any reason to push harder."

"You know me, Jenn. Would I do something like that?" Jackie asked.

Jenn shook her head ruefully and laughed. "Yes, Jackie, you would do exactly that."

❧

"I need you to get me the tapes."

The crew chief blinked in disbelief. He couldn't be hearing her right.

"No, I'm not crazy," Jackie replied to his unasked question. "There's something more to this story. The Germans are blaming Stan. OSI is blaming me." She looked up quickly and caught the look of pain that flashed across his face.

"No one is blaming you," she assured him. "That's not what I'm looking for." Crew chiefs took great pride in their charge, and each one was precious to them.

He cared enough that he came to her office during his off-duty time to meet with her.

"Couldn't this whole thing have been an accident?" she asked.

He shook his head. "I've been sorting through this over and over. I even pulled all the maintenance records and made copies before handing them over to the investigators. That jet was in good shape. Mace was the first one to fly it after it came back from the depot."

Preventive maintenance inspections were regularly conducted on each aircraft to detect problems before they turned into mishaps. Periodically, every jet was taken apart, examined piece by piece, and put back together again. Due diligence extended the lives of the aircraft.

"The jet had just came out of an extensive phase inspection that lasted over forty-three days. I personally inspected the forms afterward and signed off on its first return flight. It was pristine."

Jackie pressed her fingers against her lips, trying to remember something important. "I think Stan said something about the engines having to go through an additional inspection recently."

"That's because of the accelerated wear from operations in Afghanstan. The depot mandated additional inspections on all engines during phase inspections of the aircraft."

He shook his head. "That's the part that doesn't make sense. If there was abnormal fire coming sideways out of the engine bay, it was most likely engine related." He tried to think it through. "There's a lot of ways an engine could fail. Maybe a turbine blade failed and shot through the fuselage like a bullet."

They got quiet as they pondered the scenario. Jackie shuddered.

Suitor pushed on. "Major Mason was a great guy. Everyone liked him. He always took the time to talk with the crew chiefs—even gave some of the young airmen in supply a look into the cockpit. He told me they should understand why their jobs were important." Suitor paused and swallowed hard. "While I was strapping him in that last time, he was telling me I should make time to get a wife. He said they're worth it."

For a moment, Jackie wondered if Suitor was trying to make her feel better. She looked into his eyes and realized he wasn't capable of telling a lie. "Thanks for that," she whispered.

Her mind turned back to the engine fire. There was something missing from this puzzle, and she needed to figure out what it was. She felt sorry for the crew chief sitting in front of her, knowing the guilt weighed heavily on him but she didn't know enough to set his mind at ease. In her gut, she knew it wasn't his fault, but that wouldn't satisfy him.

She looked around her office with unseeing eyes, searching for her next course of action.

"Do you want to help me?" Jackie asked finally.

"Of course!"

Jackie smiled at the fact that he agreed before he even knew what she really wanted. That showed the dedication that was standard for the ground crews that kept the jets flying.

"I want to figure out who did this to Stan."

"What do you mean?"

"Well, let's assume it wasn't mechanical—the jet was in perfect shape with extra inspections on the engine. And it wasn't a pilot error—I mean, a pilot couldn't cause an engine fire, right? So, there has to be another explanation. Let's hypothesize a few possibilities."

Jackie was vintage-Jackie, pacing the office and thinking aloud.

"Perhaps someone wanted to take Stan out. Or maybe it wasn't Stan specifically. Maybe it was the jet, and he was the unlucky one."

"But it's the aircraft accident investigation's job to figure it out. They've collected all the facts."

Jackie knew the board was made up of pilots, maintainers, and other subject matter experts for the jet. "They're concentrating on how the jet went down, which is vital. We need to figure out who wanted it to go down. That is, if we're troubled by a perfect jet flown by an excellent pilot crashing in a field."

Jackie supposed that the Accident Investigation Board had already revealed that the "mishap" was not an accident; that's why the OSI had been called in. They investigated criminal intent. She didn't want to put her trust in the lead asshole.

She knew she had stabbed at the heart of this tremendously talented airman.

"I don't have access to the cockpit recordings, but I do have access to a whole lot of other stuff. Where do we start?" he asked.

Jackie shared with him the indications Lopass had given her.

He looked around the office. "Can I have a piece of paper?"

She retrieved a notebook from the bookshelf and handed it to him. He pulled a pen from his pocket and started scribbling furiously. Jackie wasn't sure what she had said to spark that much writing, but she let him go. When he looked up, he asked, "Were the flames orange or yellow?"

"I'm not sure. He didn't say, but I can ask him."

Senior Airman Suitor ripped a page from the notebook and handed it to her. She grabbed a pencil out of the drawer and jotted herself a note.

"While you're at it, I have a few more questions for him."

They talked more and brainstormed theories. Jackie had some ideas because she had done research for her exercise scenarios, but she was amazed at the technical knowledge of this crew chief. He couldn't have been in the Air Force more than six years, yet he was responsible for a multi-million-dollar aircraft. And he talked about it like it was his baby. The pride was evident in his voice.

"Let's lay out the timeline." Jackie reached for another piece of paper. She drew a horizontal line through the middle of the page. On the right end of the line she wrote "Monday."

"The jet flew on Friday," Senior Airman Suitor offered.

On the left end she wrote Friday. "What time?"

"It landed at eleven-thirty. Airman First Class Green and I worked on it until about fifteen-hundred."

Jackie added the notations to the chart. "What hangar were you in?"

"Eight. Sherman was right outside on his jet after we left. He said he stayed until about fifteen-thirty."

"Maybe we should mark where all the F-16s were. That will help us determine if it was this particular jet they were after or any jet."

"That is if there is a 'they,'" he added cautiously.

"We'll have to proceed on that assumption for now," Jackie said.

Suitor took a note. "I can get the layout of the ramp over the weekend before the crash from the maintenance logs."

He looked up quickly. "Wait! I remember seeing a security forces' car outside one of the hangars as we were leaving the maintenance bay for the day. I don't know which one because it was down the ramp. It was either HAS five or six. We were in a hurry, so I didn't pay much attention, but we can probably check the blotter to see what that was about."

Jackie felt her face get hot at the memory. He must be referring to when the cops responded to Stan's crushed car. "I know what that was," she admitted. "Good thought though. We can look at blotter entries for the rest of the weekend." She jotted down a note to contact her friend in the security forces squadron.

"What's behind the hangars?" Jackie asked.

Suitor stared off into the distance, trying to visualize the set up. "Behind hangars four through nine, there's woods. The fuels area is behind one through three."

"How deep are the woods before the fence?"

"Maybe two-hundred yards. Enough to dampen the noise from the flight line a bit, but in the winter, you can see the fence."

"Was there any maintenance over the weekend?"

The questions and conjectures went on for hours.

By the time Suitor left, Jackie was exhausted but energized at the same time. She was glad to finally be making headway toward getting answers. At least where the crash was concerned. There were some questions the airman wouldn't be able to answer for her. Only Stan could give her the closure she needed. She would never know why he chose Bennett over her.

# Chapter 32

Jackie and Margaret walked around the square in the middle of town.

"Are you feeling all right now?" Margaret asked her.

"Yes, I think so." Jackie wasn't sure what right would be from now on. She had to reset her expectations to match her new reality.

"Do you want to talk about it?"

"I feel guilty sometimes, you know? Like when I get caught up at work and realize I haven't called to tell Stan I'll be late. Then it hits me again that I don't have to answer to anyone anymore. There's a split second where I feel relieved. Then I feel guilty."

Margaret put her arm around Jackie's shoulders as they walked. "It's okay to move on with your life. It doesn't mean you are forgetting Stan. It means you are healing. He would want that."

Jackie sighed. "Why do you think he didn't want me anymore?"

"Don't make his failings about you, child," Margaret admonished. "Stan was still immature in many ways, but he did love you. I think it was himself he had trouble loving."

Jackie looked at her sideways. "How does that make sense?"

"Generally, strong women hold things inside things and try to discover what will make them better. Men are more concerned with how others see them and need constant reassurance from others as to their self-worth."

"So I wasn't giving him enough reassurance?"

"There you go again, taking on the blame. You were there for your husband. I think he was jealous of your success and sought comfort elsewhere. That's not your fault," Margaret said.

Jackie walked in silence, trying to embrace the counsel her friend had given her.

~

The next morning, Jackie called Captain Brad Brody. "Brad, I need a favor."

"Good to hear from you too."

"Sorry. How are you, Brad?"

"Fine. Thanks for asking. And you?"

"Fine. Now I need a favor."

Jackie heard the smile in his voice. "Whatever you need, Queen Jackie."

"Can you get me copies of the police blotters for the two weeks prior to Stan's crash?"

The silence that followed wasn't reassuring.

"Why do you want them?" he asked.

"Curious, that's all."

"Nice try. What are you up to, Jackie?"

She sighed. "I'm doing a little research."

"That's not for you to be doing. If you have an idea, let the OSI agents know about it."

"They won't listen to me. Hell, they think I had something to do with it," she replied in disgust.

"That's not true. They have to look at all angles. It's their job."

"Does that mean you aren't going to help me?"

After a short pause, he replied, "I'll email you copy, but if you find anything, at least let me know. I can tell the agents myself."

"Thanks, Brad. I owe you."

"I've heard that before."

Jackie replied with a sarcastic, "Ha, ha," and hung up. She hoped Suitor was able to get the information he was supposed to be gathering.

When the email arrived from Brad, Jackie anxiously opened it. She started with the last day and worked her way back. She noted Brad had not sent anything after the initial call of an aircraft emergency.

It was all pretty routine. The exercise responses were noted in a different color to distinguish them from real world responses. They kept them in the same log to track where their units were at all times.

As she read over the report from Friday night about a vehicle incident near HAS 5, her face got hot. Running into his car was a childish thing to do, but she would probably do the same thing again. Oh, what she would give to have the chance to work it out with Stan. She didn't know if it was better or worse that they had been fighting right before he died. Would it hurt more had they been on good terms? She couldn't hurt any more than she did now.

As her thoughts digressed, she kept reading. Then she caught herself. Did she reread the same thing twice? She paged up over the last few entries. No, it was there twice. A patrol responded to an intrusion alarm in Sector Romeo along the fence line. Nothing found.

She continued to read from where she left off. There it was again—an intrusion alarm in Sector Romeo. No unusual activity discovered. She printed off the pages, grabbed a highlighter from her desk, and looked specifically for the entries having to do with false alarms. After a half an hour, she had highlighted seven in a two-week period. They happened on different shifts, at different times of the day. At first, they were at various locations around the base. The last three were all in the same basic location—Sector Romeo off of Vandenberg Avenue in the housing area.

Jackie looked up at the clock. It was getting late, but she wanted to see what was going on at that fence line. She grabbed her hat and headed out the door.

As she drove by the fence line slowly for the second time, she tried to figure out the best way to approach it. She didn't see anything of interest from her car and decided to get out and walk. Turning around, she found a small parking area at the edge of the field meant for guests of people living in base housing.

Jackie was thankful she was wearing ABUs today because the boots were much better for trudging through the grass. Although the wing commander was a stickler for ensuring the grass was always cut to regulation height, this area seemed to be more like an open field than someone's yard. The grass was up to her shins, and the soft dirt underneath would have been a mess to clean off the black military pumps she wore with her blues.

Making her way to the back fence, she was careful not to touch anything and chance setting off another alarm. The sun was going down quickly now, and she wished she brought a flashlight. She walked the length of the fence, inspecting the top and bottom of each section for any signs of tampering but didn't see anything special.

Suddenly lights blinded her, and she put her hands up instinctively to cover her eyes. Through her fingers, she saw the blue flashing lights of a police car. *Really?* she thought in disgust.

Two figures approached her cautiously. To her, they were only silhouettes in the headlights blinding her. "Major?" one said.

Jackie walked toward them. "What's up?" she asked as innocently as she could muster. As she got closer, she recognized the staff sergeant and senior airman, but didn't recall their names.

"What are you doing out here?"

"Walking."

When it was clear she wasn't going to add anything, the staff sergeant asked, "May I see an ID?"

Jackie pulled it from her right breast pocket and handed it to him.

He studied the picture and looked closely at Jackie, then handed it back. "Do you live in base housing?"

"No."

"Then why walk here?"

"Why not?" She wasn't going to be helpful; she had tried that with OSI, and it hadn't gotten her anywhere. "Why are you here?"

"We got a call of suspicious activity, so came by to check it out."

"I wouldn't call walking suspicious. Maybe your caller was bored and wanted to stir up trouble."

"We've had—," the senior airman started to say before the staff sergeant elbowed him to stifle his remark.

"I suggest you find someplace else to walk," the staff sergeant said.

"I'll consider it. This spot's a little boring anyway, wouldn't you say?"

They looked at her in silence.

"I mean, why have this field here anyway?" Jackie gestured to the open area as if she were truly pondering the question. The airman's eyes dart over her left shoulder.

Deliberately, she turned to her right and walked back to the fence.

"Major? Where are you going?"

"Walking." With that, she continued along the fence line, away from the area the senior airman had pointed out with his eyes.

# Chapter 33

The phone rang, and Jackie knew before she answered it who it would be.

"IG, Major Austin," she said.

"Jackie, what the hell are you doing?" Brad Brody snapped.

"What are you talking about?"

"Don't play with me, Jackie. Your name's in the blotter. What were you doing sneaking around base housing last night?"

"I wasn't sneaking. I was walking."

"Bullshit. You found something. What is it?"

She hesitated but, in the end, decided Brad was on her side. "Can you come by my office?"

"I'll be there in ten minutes." He hung up without another word.

Jackie was staring into space when Brad walked in. She had given up all pretense of trying to get work done today.

"Want some coffee?" she asked.

"Had mine, thanks." He sank into the chair across from her desk. "Well?"

She pushed the papers toward him. He picked them up and quickly scanned them, focusing on the areas she highlighted.

"So?" He dropped them back on the desk.

"Isn't it strange to have so many false calls to the same area?"

"Not if the alarm system is going out.

"Is it?"

"I don't know. I'd have to look into it."

"Would you please?" she asked.

He sighed. "I asked you to tell me if you found anything. Not go snooping around on your own."

"I didn't find anything. I wanted to see where that area of the fence was. As far as I can tell, it isn't anything special. It's deep in base housing. My guess is it's an open field for kids to play ball in or something."

"Then why the suspicion?" he asked.

"There were alarms going off all over the base. Then they narrowed down to that particular area."

"So? Alarms go off all the time. Most of the time they're nothing."

"What if that was the idea?"

"I don't follow."

"What if someone wanted you to *think* it was no big deal, but it really was?"

"You said it's an open field. Who wants to break in there? And even if someone did get on base, it's pretty far from anything important. I mean, I guess someone could do home invasions, but military folks aren't exactly known for having a lot of money."

"I haven't figured that out yet," she admitted. She sat back in her chair and stared at the ceiling in concentration. "Maybe it was a distraction."

This time Jackie approached the fence line from the outside. It took longer to find the right spot because she didn't have coordinates corresponding to the German street names. When she thought she was close enough, she found a place to park and grabbed her flashlight. It was dusk, but she didn't know how dark it would be in the tree line growing along the outer side of the fence.

As she pushed low hanging branches out of her way, she thought through her encounter with the security forces the night before. She was sure the airman had almost said they had been having a series of false alarms lately, but the staff sergeant cut him off before he could.

She reached the edge of the trees but remained within their protective cover while she walked along the fence line toward the spot she suspected held the airman's interest. There. Was the fence darker in that spot or was it her imagination? She stepped closer and squatted down to inspect the area. Definitely different. She risked turning on the flashlight but kept the beam pointed downward. The fence had been mended. Welded, if she had to guess. She traced the mended portions. It looked as if the fence had been cut from the ground to Jackie's knees in a half arc. Looking closely, she saw where the metal was slightly bowed, as if it had been pulled back.

A car approached, so Jackie clicked off her flashlight. Staying close to the ground, she held her breath as the car went by. When it was out of sight, she stood and slipped back into the trees. *I didn't see anything about a breach in the security fence in the blotter,* she thought.

～

I don't see what the big deal is," Senior Airman Suitor said. "It's about as far from the flight line as you can get." He stared at the map Jackie had placed in front of him.

Jackie looked up sharply. "You're right! It *is* as far as you could get." She studied the map and then pointed at a spot near HAS 8. "This is where Stan's jet was parked the night before the accident." She placed her finger on the spot in base housing that had drawn all the false alarms. "This is where the alarms were going off. That would pull the security forces off their usual routes."

Because of the many exercises she had scripted, Jackie knew the basics of how the security forces were trained to respond and shift to cover areas. "What if the intent was to pull forces *away* from the flight line?"

Suitor thought about it. "I suppose. But why all the false alarms?"

Jackie was thinking about how she tested various players in her exercise scenarios. She typically devised situations that timed responses and threw in ambiguous events to see how forces reacted. The transparent goal was measuring response time. However, in one exercise, she was stunned that a fire rescue crew went directly to the smoke of a coincidental grass fire rather than direct to the coordinates they were given. It was amazing how easy it was to distract a team under intense pressure.

Jackie looked through Suitor as an idea formulated in her mind. "Let's assume all of these alarms were to distract. Let's *assume* it was an opportunity to test reaction times. Let's walk through it." She was pacing now and talking with her hands.

He nodded. "Okay. I'll go along with you. So, you're saying this last alarm on Sunday was the day someone messed with the jet?" He was warming up to the idea. "But wait a minute." He was running through the scenario in his mind's eye. "One person couldn't be setting off the alarm *and* tampering with the airplane. There had to be more than one, don't you think?"

"You're right!" She was also seeing the picture unfold before her. "But how did the person get on the flight line?"

"I'm sure the OSI has already checked with the guards posted at the entrances to the flight line to see who came and went that weekend," Suitor offered.

"Sure, but do you think the guards really remembered all the names? It's not like they write them down. And that's assuming the person had a line badge. What if they didn't? How else could they get on?"

They huddled over the map for an hour, focusing on the fence surrounding the flight line.

"Are these fences alarmed too?" Jackie asked.

"I would think these are," he said, pointed to the line bordering the civilian countryside. "But why would we alarm the fences within the base?"

Jackie knew she'd have to ask Brad for help . . . again.

# Chapter 34

The next day, Brad knocked on the door of Jackie's home. She opened the door to welcome him. "Thanks for coming over."

He nodded to Senior Airman Suitor who looked up from the papers he was examining on the dining room table in front of him. "Nice to be invited to the secret club."

"It isn't quite like that," Jackie said. "But I told you before, I can't stand by and let things happen to me. I need to figure it out for myself, before I get charged for killing my husband."

Brad rolled his eyes and followed her into the dining room. "I'm kidding. I told you I'd help. What are you up to?"

"Airman Suitor was the crew chief for Stan's jet." The men shook hands.

"I remember meeting you last summer," Brad said. "You helped out with the jet tour when my parents came to visit. They still talk about it."

"I'm glad they liked it," Suitor said.

Jackie gestured to the piles of papers and maps. "Airman Suitor has some ideas about what could have caused the fire Lopass reported seeing. We're guessing though, because the accident investigators won't tell us anything."

"Of course not. They have to finish first. What makes you think you can figure it out without all the details?"

"Lopass described how the fire shot out of the engine before the crash. He said it was blasting sideways like a blow torch. Airman Suitor read an article about burn-throughs; the indications were the same. Apparently, that's the unofficial guess within the maintenance community as to the cause of the crash."

"Although we have an idea what might have caused the fire, that isn't the mystery we're on to right now. We're concentrating on who had the opportunity to get to the jets. Hopefully that will lead us to why," Suitor explained.

"You're assuming it was intentional then?" He raised his eyebrows at Jackie.

"Well, I certainly don't think it was carelessness."

Brad shook his head. "Okay, I'll go down this rabbit hole with you. What do you have so far?"

"Remember my trip to base housing?" Jackie asked.

"Of course. You did make the blotter, after all."

"Well, I went back the next night—"

"Jackie!" Brad interrupted her. "What the hell! I told you—"

"Just listen," she shot back. "Did you know the fence had been cut?" She watched his face. He didn't show anything but disbelief.

"No way. That would have been reported."

"But it wasn't—reported, I mean. I looked through the blotters you gave me."

"Maybe it was older than the blotters I sent you," he argued.

"The mends to the fence were pretty new. No time to rust or even discolor."

"Why would anyone cover up someone cutting the fence? Don't you think someone sneaking onto the base would be a big deal?"

Jackie pulled out the printed copies of the blotter he had sent her. "Look at this." She rifled through the pages until she found what she was looking for. "See the response times? On this one, it took about six minutes for the patrol to respond to the alarm."

"That's normal," Brad said.

"Yes, and it's consistent with the previous alarm responses, until this one," she pointed at the page. "The patrol took over twenty-five minutes to respond."

Brad looked over the page. "But there were other things going on. Look, a disturbance at the Class Six store. And here's a report of a traffic incident by the back gate."

"I didn't say there wasn't a good reason for the delay. But then look at the next time the alarm went off." Jackie took the pages from him and flipped back a few. "Less than two minutes to respond. And before you say anything else, there was also an alarm at the commissary at the same time. But this time, the patrol's priority was an alarm that was repeatedly going off. Why? If they thought it was a faulty alarm, why rush?"

Brad looked baffled.

Suitor jumped in to explain. "We were thinking the patrols were starting to assume the alarm was faulty, and so when they had to prioritize, they put the outer fence at the bottom. When they finally responded and saw the cuts in the fence, they figured they screwed up."

"Rather than telling anyone, they decided to fix it on their own. But next time, they jumped on it when the alarm went off," Jackie finished for him.

"I'm not sure . . . ," Brad wrestled with the idea in his head.

"Don't think like a captain," Jackie suggested. "Think like a young airman who made a mistake that didn't hurt anybody. Would they tell on themselves and not get another chance, or cover it up and swear to do better next time? The way they probably saw it, nothing was hurt. Notice it was the same guys who responded to both incidents."

She and Suitor kept quiet as the security forces captain mulled it over. It would be hard to find fault in his own guys.

After a few minutes, she said, "But that's not what we're really getting at anyway."

He gave her a confused look.

"We don't think anyone was really trying to sneak on the base," Suitor said.

"Why cut the fence then?"

"To get the effect they got—the patrols to respond even faster the next time," Jackie explained. "The last time the outer fence went off was the Sunday night before Stan's crash. I'll bet it hasn't gone off since."

Brad shook his head. "You aren't making sense. If they weren't trying to get on base, what does that have to do with the crash?"

"What if the alarm was a distraction to pull the patrols' attention from the flight line to allow someone else to sneak onto the flight line and sabotage the jet?"

"That's a lot of guessing," he objected.

"But it's a theory," Jackie persisted. "What we can't figure out is where they would have crossed to get on the flight line to begin with."

"You're assuming the person snuck onto the flight line. What if they simply walked on?" Brad asked.

"What do you mean?"

"The flight line is guarded with alarms too. Crossing the red line would be tough. There are cameras feeding directly to the station."

The red lines were painted on the ground outlining an area a person could not enter without a line badge. Obviously, that was only a reminder and not a physical barrier, but as Brad said, the cameras and patrol would catch anyone who crossed where they weren't supposed to.

"So are you saying that a member of our Air Force would do this?"

"I didn't say it was one of ours," he corrected. "Jackie, we're in a foreign country. There are foreign nationals all over the base. We have to hire a certain number as part of the SOFA agreement."

She hadn't thought of that. One thing the Status of Forces Agreement did was ensure the locals received a fair number of jobs so the U.S. wasn't putting people out of work. "I thought that only applied to office workers and cleaning crews."

"You're a closet snob, Jackie. We're in Germany. You've heard about German engineering, trains, clocks, and beer. The German nationals are quite capable of working anywhere on the base," Brad said.

Jackie blushed in embarrassment. It *was* a snobbish thought.

"Did I mention beer?" Brad grabbed his parched throat.

"Okay, okay. I get the hint." A moment later, Jackie returned from the kitchen with two beers. The men gratefully accepted them.

"What workers would have a line badge?" she asked, continuing their train of thought.

"Runway repair, the guys who cut the grass, folks who do maintenance on the buildings," Suitor said.

"Do any work on jets?"

"No, we see to our own planes. But some do work in fuels."

Jackie thought about this. "If these people could get on the flight line at any time, why would they need a distraction?"

"We don't do runway repair or cut grass in the middle of the night," Suitor said.

"Someone could have gotten onto the flight line earlier for his day job, and then hung out until it got dark."

"No one would think twice about someone they saw every day going through the checkpoint."

"Where would a person hide until dark?"

"You'd be surprised at the number of places I've found people napping," Suitor said. "Behind storage barrels, under tarps. Hell, I even found one guy sleeping in a jet!"

"Okay. Let's assume a guy got on the flight line during the day and hid out until dark. When the time was right, his buddy triggered the alarm, causing the security forces to shift their patrols."

Suitor picked up her train of thought. "He slips out of hiding and runs to the jet—probably any jet. I doubt it mattered which one."

"The engine had been checked recently," Jackie said. "It wouldn't have had a burn-through for no reason. Someone had to have tampered with the engine. I can't see that being an accident."

Brad nodded. "Okay, so you think someone damaged the jet intentionally. Why?"

"I don't know," Jackie said exasperated, throwing her hands in the air. She turned on her heels and started to pace the room. "We're Americans. Is that enough?"

"It could be an act of terrorism," Suitor said.

"On one plane?" Brad asked.

"One that they succeeded on. All the jets were checked after the crash. They did send another one back for overhaul when they found weird markings inside the engine, but no actual holes. What if the plan was to do more, but they were interrupted?" Suitor said.

"Terrorists usually go for something big, don't they?" Jackie speculated. "And then they take credit for the attack."

"Taking down an F-16 right under the nose of the U.S. military is a pretty big deal," Suitor said.

"And it did delay flying longer than usual," Brad agreed.

"That's because once they found markings on the second jet, they were taking no chances, and everything was checked twice," Suitor said.

"But Lopass said if Stan had pulled the engine out of afterburner in time, the fire would have gone out, and it could have returned to base." Jackie cringed as she realized she just pointed the finger at Stan for taking the wrong action in an emergency. She held back the tears that threatened to fall.

"What if it wasn't terrorism but only loss of confidence?" Brad asked.

"What do you mean?" Suitor said.

"Well, exposing a weakness in the design that can be so easily exploited, maybe it's an embarrassment to the U.S. Trying to show our military isn't as undefeatable as we seem."

They all let that idea sink in.

Jackie sighed. All this talk seemed unreal to her. She wanted to go back to her quiet life of fighting with Stan over whether or not to have a baby—not dealing with terrorists. Suddenly she felt very tired. "Guys, thanks for coming over. I need some time to think."

"Jackie, we need to take this to OSI," Brad said.

She looked from him to Suitor, then she nodded. "I know. But can I have a little more time? I don't think we have enough yet for them to take us seriously. Brad, will you check the blotters again? See if the alarms stopped after the crash."

"Sure, first thing in the morning. I hope you're wrong about my guys though. That's a huge mistake to cover up."

"I know. That's another reason not to talk to OSI unless we're sure."

Suitor walked to the door. "Ma'am, thanks for letting me help on this. I don't know if it'll come to anything, but it's better than sitting in the dorms doing nothing."

"You're a great help," Jackie assured him. "I'm glad you agreed to work with me."

They shook hands as Jackie opened the door for him. Brad followed Suitor out into the night air. It was clean and fresh. Somewhere there was a wood fire burning, and the smell floated on a breeze.

"No more snooping around," Brad told Jackie as he shook her hand. "We don't know what this is about, but we don't need another casualty."

Jackie smiled faintly. "Yes, sir." She closed the door gently behind them.

As the men made their way to their cars, Brad stopped. Suitor turned to face him.

"I didn't want to bring it up in front of Major Austin," Brad said, "but did you know Major Mason was having an affair?"

"No shit!" he said in disbelief, before he caught himself. "I mean, sir, that sucks. Does Major Austin know?"

"She didn't find out until recently. It was one blow on top of another."

"Who was it, if I may ask?"

Brad thought about it for a minute. He probably shouldn't tell a maintainer one of *his* superiors was involved in wrongdoing, but he decided Suitor would find out soon enough. And if Jackie trusted him to help with her personal investigation, he needed all the facts.

"Captain Bennett."

"No shit!" Suitor said again.

Brad chuckled at his reaction. "Yeah, so be careful what you say around her."

"Yes, sir. Around both of them," Suitor reassured him.

# Chapter 35

Dammit, Jackie, you were right," Brad said without even identifying himself on the phone first. "The alarms stopped after the crash. At least the ones fitting the pattern. There will always be some type of nuisance alarms. Animals set them off, high winds blowing things against the fence, that sort of thing. But I looked for the locations that seemed to be targeted and nothing since that night."

Jackie rested her head in her free hand. She wanted to be right, but at the same time, she wanted this to be over. And now she knew it wasn't. There was more to this story, and she needed to get to the bottom of it.

"And I also took a walk around base housing," he continued. "It does look like the fence was cut and repaired. I called in the guys who responded to the alarms we discussed." There was heaviness in his voice.

"Are they going to get in trouble?" she asked.

"Hell, yeah! What a stupid thing to do. Even if they didn't have anything to do with the airplane crash, you don't cover up a potential break-in to the base, even if you think it's kids making mischief. That's security one-oh-one."

"What did they say?"

"They had stopped at the Base Exchange for some coffee when the alarm went off. It had been a repeat nuisance alarm, so they finished their break before going to check it out. When they got there and saw it was cut, they panicked. The airman wanted to call it in, but his partner didn't want to get caught loafing on the job. He already has that reputation." Brad was mad and disappointed. She didn't envy him.

He went on. "They at least did a security check. They found evidence of footprints in the heavy mud outside the gate, but no signs that anyone got through. The cut in the fence was bowed as if pulled on but not bent back as if someone crawled through, and there was no mud or footprints inside the fence. They decided to fix the fence themselves and keep it a secret." He sighed.

"Jackie, I'm sorry this happened, but I really think they're stupid, not criminal."

"Oh, I know," she reassured him. "I'm sorry you have to go through disciplining your own guys. Let me know how it goes."

"Yeah, this sucks. I'll be in touch."

She hung up the phone and sat staring at her computer screen trying to decide her next move.

Senior Airman Suitor quickly combed through a database of F-16 accident reports going back decades. From what Lieutenant Lopass Mitchell described, Suitor needed to focus on anything related to an afterburner burn-through.

Most of the occurrences resulted in relatively minor damage. As a result, they were reported in very concise safety reports. That made most of the reading fly by.

However, a number resulted in a complete loss of the aircraft, and in at least one case, the pilot didn't survive. These reports were called Class A investigations and had extensive data and analysis leading to detailed explanations of the failure mode. He printed whatever he could from the database and set those aside in file folders to read in detail.

Suitor stretched and glanced at his watch. He had time to get in a few more files before he needed to head out. His workspace was strewn with technical manuals and diagrams used to educated himself on burn-throughs. It seemed like a daunting task, but Major Austin was counting on him.

He walked to the refrigerator in the break room at the back of the hangar. Grabbing a soda from the stash there, he deposited fifty cents in the "honor system" cash box resting in the butter dish opening in the door.

Kicking the door closed with his foot, he popped the top on the can. On second thought, he turned back to the table next to the fridge, grabbed a candy bar, and tossed another dollar in the cash box, not bothering with the change. It was going to be a long night.

He went back to his desk and sighed. The stack with the smaller safety reports was considerably taller than the Class A investigation stack, but that did little to ease the feeling of despondency that overtook him at the thought of reading about the many damaged and destroyed airframes and the loss of an aviator's life. Pushing the taller stack to the side to give himself more room, Suitor armed himself with a fresh notebook and a pencil and began reading the first accident investigation.

Two hours later, he grabbed the third file in his queue. A name caught his eye, and he had to look twice to make sure he wasn't seeing things. "Maintenance Subject Matter Expert: Captain Renee Bennett," he read. *What are the chances?* Quickly scanning the report, key words jumped out at him. Afterburner burn-through, airframe fire, brought the plane down, pilot ejected unharmed.

He went back to the beginning of the printout and began again, taking notes as he went, like with the first two reports.

He didn't want to jump to any conclusions, but it was quite an interesting coincidence.

As Jackie read through the files on her desks, her mind kept drifting back to what she had learned from Suitor. She was more convinced it hadn't been an accident, but she wasn't buying terrorist either. It was *one* airplane. Why something so small? The idea behind terrorism was to strike fear into the hearts of many. Even if they had made it to a few more planes, that still seemed a bit subdued compared to grandiose acts of terrorism like the Mumbai train bombings or even Benghazi. Terrorists always want to take credit after the fact, and there was nothing in the news about possible terrorist involvement or even that the plane had been tampered with.

She needed to walk through the actions as if it were a scenario she scripted. What is the first thing that happens when a plane is lost? The fleet is grounded. Okay, then what? An investigation.

"Wait a minute," she mumbled. "Backup." Typing frantically into her computer. She pulled up newspaper articles about past accident investigations to see how long planes were typically grounded.

What if that was the objective? Ground the planes. Who would that benefit? Jackie was struggling to follow the thread to a logical conclusion. She needed more intel—literally. And she knew who to visit.

Captain Paige Parker was the intelligence officer for the 81st Fighter Squadron. She was extremely bright and had won Wing Junior Officer of the Quarter a number of times over the last few years. She had also dated one of the pilots from Stan's squadron, which is how Jackie got to know her well.

Instead of calling, Jackie decided to go straight to the squadron. It would be easier to talk in person than try to explain what she needed over an unclassified phone line. When she got to the checkpoint to enter the flight line, she reached into the center console for her line badge. It wasn't there.

"Dammit!" With everything that had happened, she never found her line badge. She pulled up to the shed where the security forces airman was standing and rolled down her window.

"I don't have my line badge with me. Would you mind calling Captain Parker in intel for the eighty-first and tell her Major Austin is out here? She'll come get me."

"You'll need to park over there." The airman gestured to a parking area behind her left shoulder.

"Thanks." Jackie backed up and parked the car. She put on her hat and stood outside to wait for Paige.

It didn't take long for Paige to arrive at the gate. "Thanks, Airman Snow. Appreciate you calling me."

Airman Snow saluted the captain as she spoke. "No problem, ma'am. Glad I could help."

Jackie met Paige at the red line, and Paige escorted her toward the building. When they were out of sight of the guard, Paige stopped Jackie and gave her a hug. "How are you?"

She returned the hug gratefully. "I have my moments," Jackie admitted. "Some days are better than others."

"You should have called. I would have come to your office."

"Thanks, but I really needed to get out. Besides, what I want to discuss may be better handled in the vault."

Paige raised one eyebrow but didn't continue that line of questioning while they walked. "It was a nice service for Stan. I'm sure the burial was tough though."

"It was a cremation actually. Yeah, we did it in Ohio. The A-10s from Willow Grove spread his ashes for me."

"That's cool. Stan would have appreciated that."

Jackie smiled slightly. "It was a beautiful flying day too."

They walked in silence the rest of the way. Captain Parker led Jackie into the vault where her desk was located in a back corner.

"Don't you get tired of no windows?" Jackie asked.

"Most the time I'm so busy, I don't notice." She pulled a chair up to her desk so Jackie could sit. "So what's this about?"

Jackie sighed. "I need to know what types of missions our wing is involved in right now that were hampered by the F-16s being grounded."

Paige looked at her suspiciously. "That's a weird question. And one I'm not sure I want to answer."

"Well, I know about our deployment schedule and the rotations. But is there anything that I wouldn't know about?"

"If you *wouldn't* know about it, there would be a reason, and I sure as hell wouldn't tell you. Jackie, we're friends, but because we're friends, I don't think you should be asking me these questions."

Jackie leaned forward and rested her elbows on her knees. Her head slumped forward, and she thought about the best way to redirect.

"Paige, I know Stan's crash wasn't an accident. OSI thinks I might have had something to do with it because of his affair with Bennett."

Paige cringed at Jackie's matter-of-fact announcement. They read each other's reaction in an instant. It was obvious Paige already knew about Stan and Bennett, and it was obvious Jackie knew that Paige knew. There was no need to patronize each other. Paige broke the pregnant pause between them. "I can see why you wanted to damage him, but not an airplane."

Jackie gave a slight chuckle. "At last, someone who understands me." She sat back. "From the maintenance reports on the jet, it seems to me someone must have intentionally tampered with the engine."

"How did you get the maintenance reports?"

"The crew chief wants to solve this mystery as much as I do."

Before Paige had a chance to admonish her, Jackie kept talking. "I got to thinking, what good does it do to take down one plane? Seems petty in the big scheme of things. Senior Airman Suitor theorized that perhaps the intent was to take out a few planes, but the person got interrupted."

"So now you're wondering what happens when you take down a few planes?"

Jackie nodded. "Obviously the jets were grounded. How long did this one last? I was gone part of the time."

"Two weeks until everything was back to normal. They had a wing stand-down for two days for all the air crew and maintainers. Then, a few days later, they decided all the jets needed to be inspected. Something related to the mishap. That took a while. I'm not really sure what they were looking for. I heard they were focused on engines."

"And did we miss anything important during that window?"

"Now we're back into the 'I'm not talking' part," Paige said. "But even if we were supposed to be somewhere at a certain time, the Air Force would send someone else. It's not like we're the only F-16s on the continent."

"Yes, but did they only ground our planes?"

"At first it was only the ones at Spang. Then, rumor was they found some damage, so headquarters ordered inspections for all F-16s within the theater as a precaution. Those checks weren't as disabling as the inspections here, so they were actually flying full up. We were the only ones down hard, and like I said, it only took a few weeks to get them all flying again."

Jackie noted Lopass was right about how, in the clamp down on information, everyone was still picking up clues.

"So what am I missing? I know Stan was on a cross country training mission, but was there anything else going on? You know, maybe someone wanted to delay or stop the wing. Maybe there was a breach of comm security, and someone knew something. Maybe Stan was unlucky and got in the way." Jackie's face turned sullen.

Paige hesitated again. She was weighing what to share or not. Jackie had a top secret security clearance, but she didn't have the need to know. *Or did she?*

Finally Paige gave in. "I can't give you the details, but I can tell you, yes, we had to pull out of a mission, and they tagged another unit. The Air Force didn't miss a beat. But, Jackie, Stan was also part of the mission. He wasn't on a simple cross-country trip."

# Chapter 36

Thank you for bringing this to our attention," Agent Emily Wright said.

"Do you understand the significance?" Brad asked. "Can you tell if the cause of this crash was the same as the one in this old investigation?"

"We'll have our experts look it over."

"Will you let me know?"

"I can't discuss an ongoing investigation."

"But now you have reason to look at Renee Bennett. She has flight line access and the know-how to pull this off."

"We haven't closed the door on any leads so far. We'll follow up on everything." Wright was paging through the summary and casually looked up at Brad. "If you pick up on anything out of the ordinary on Major Austin, I'd appreciate a call, day or night."

He searched for a reaction, realizing she was only mildly interested in the information he presented. "Yeah, sure. I'll keep my feelers out."

Brad left the OSI agent's office more frustrated than when he went in. His mind was in a fog. Wright asked him to scout out Jackie but didn't ask for the same on Bennett. They definitely had a bias among their suspects.

When Senior Airman Suitor had brought him this information, Brad was sure it was a slam dunk against Bennett, and it would deflect OSI's determination to pin the accident on Jackie. Now, he was convinced they would need to find something very striking to refocus their sights on other possibilities.

He hadn't mentioned his visit to OSI to Jackie or Suitor because he didn't want anyone to think Jackie had put him up to it. This way she could honestly say she didn't know anything about it if they asked.

Now it didn't matter. He and Suitor had better link up with Jackie and think this through again. Bennett had the means, if not a motive.

~

Mastana went about her routine. She didn't mind working. She certainly didn't mind the money they paid. But she was disgusted to be around the uniforms on the air base. There were too many memories. The wound was still raw, and every time the airplanes flew overhead, she cringed.

Her husband said it was important for her to work, and so she forced herself to be around the Americans.

If she were being honest with herself, what bothered her more than the memories was that she was finding it hard to hold on to the resentment that had been her life-force for years. She was starting to see the Americans as friendly and quite generous. They worked very hard and long hours, but they took the time to talk to her and even pitched in to help her with doors and emptying trash.

She had expected to be treated disrespectfully, but here in Germany, she saw them differently. Not as the enemy who had killed her first husband and son, but as people who also experienced loss—like Mrs. Austin. Mastana read the pain on her face, and her heart tightened. She shared that pain. She knew the nightmares Mrs. Austin must be experiencing, but she couldn't bring herself to speak. They were from different worlds. They weren't friends but both had lost loved ones.

Mastana found herself softening, and she couldn't afford that. She got in and out of the offices quickly when people were around. She didn't meet their eyes and didn't speak unless spoken to, and then as little as possible. Nonetheless, the Americans always greeted her by name as if she were one of them.

When the offices were empty, she lingered longer. She didn't snoop so much as take the time to look around. Her eyes sought out the photographs displayed. She took note of the placement of objects on the desk and analyzed the priority people placed on things. She thought it ridiculous when she saw pictures of dogs and cats displayed as if they were family members. How could people put such a high value on an animal?

She noticed the photographs on Mrs. Austin's desk kept moving. Months earlier, she had a beautifully framed photo of her and her young man, leaning in close and smiling broadly for the camera. Days before the accident, it had been pushed haphazardly aside to make room for files and papers to litter her usually neat desk. The Monday morning of the accident, Mastana had noted the photo was face down on her desk. At first, she had assumed this was an American custom dealing with death. Then she realized Mrs. Austin had not been back in the office since the accident, so it must have been done before. Now that Mrs. Austin was back to work, the picture stood again, but now it was behind her desk on the credenza. Mastana surmised it was so Mrs. Austin didn't have to see it every time she sat down.

She was still curious about the face-down stage but would never ask. It wasn't her place. She wondered what it would be like to lose Aashna. Hers was an arranged marriage, mostly to allow her to stay in Germany and give her some standing in their community. She didn't love her husband, but she did respect what he had done for her. He didn't have to marry a widow. Yes, he was harsh to her, but she was thankful to him even if she would never grieve his passing as she had with her first husband. She would never love anyone the way she had grown to love her first husband. Her thoughts were haunted by the memories of him and their son. It hurt so much.

Mastana's eyes swept the office one last time to see if she missed anything. She backed her cart into the hallway and continued on her way.

As Jackie walked through the commissary filling her cart, she felt melancholy. She caught herself adding Stan's favorite snacks to her basket and then putting them back on the shelves. Ready to give up on this pretense of getting back to normal, she decided to leave the cart where it was and walk out. She'd come back another day.

That's when the two ladies approached, pushing their own shopping carts.

"Honey, we miss you," Tina said as she wrapped her arms around Jackie.

"We want you to keep coming to our wives' luncheons," Nancy added, with a hand on Jackie's shoulder. She caught herself too late on the word 'wives' and looked down, embarrassed.

"I miss you all too," Jackie said, although actually she had been avoiding the squadron wives. She knew when they looked at her, they were thinking they were glad it wasn't their husband; Jackie didn't blame them.

She also knew that for weeks, Stan's affair with that Bennett-bitch fed the gossip troughs of the Officers' Spouses' Club, which was currently a membership of all wives. She couldn't stand to look them in the face, knowing they had speculated about some of her most embarrassing moments.

"Is there anything we can do for you?" Tina asked.

*Bring Stan back*, she thought. Aloud she said, "No, I'm fine. I need time to adjust; that's all."

"I get it," Nancy said. "Well, if you need anything, make sure you call. I don't know if it helps or not, but maybe you should know."

Jackie braced herself for what was coming. Nancy had a lust for gathering gossip and then being the first to spread it. Her lips were never idle, and it was all about feeding her self-esteem. Over many years, Nancy had abandoned her filter of sensitivity and discretion, so it was in character for her to be incredibly blunt and rude in public.

Tina was horrified, and she gave Jackie a look that begged forgiveness and communicated she was not part of this.

Tina grabbed Nancy's arm above the elbow and squeezed.

Ignoring her, Nancy went on, "I hear Renee Bennett had moved on from Stan. She was in someone else's bed."

"Well, of course," Jackie said. "I didn't expect her to mourn long."

"No, I mean *before* the crash," Nancy quickly put in.

When Jackie didn't say anything, Nancy continued. "Susan told me . . . or was it Sheila? Doesn't matter." She waved her hand dismissively. "She told me Bennett was with some high-ranking guy now. And it started over a month ago. Susan's husband overheard Renee telling Stan; she thinks it was to try to make him jealous."

Nancy was so caught up in her gossip, she didn't notice the color drain from Jackie's face.

*Stan really had ended it with Bennett?* Jackie hadn't believed him. He was still a shit for having an affair to begin with, but maybe he hadn't given up on them altogether.

Tina came to Jackie's rescue. "Nancy, can we get off this topic? Jackie doesn't need more drama right now."

Nancy finally took note of the look on Jackie's face. "Oh, I'm sorry, honey. I didn't mean to go on like that. I thought you'd like to know."

Jackie nodded. She did want to know. But now she needed time to process the information. "It's fine, really. Thanks for telling me. I need to get going. I have to . . ." She hesitated as she tried to think of an excuse, but nothing came to mind. ". . . be somewhere," she finished lamely. Without unloading her shopping cart, she walked up the aisle to the front of the commissary, leaving the two ladies staring after her.

# Chapter 37

Nancy can be such a twit," Jenn said. Jackie had filled her in on her encounter at the commissary. The ladies were sitting in Jenn's kitchen drinking coffee. The sound of laser fire and explosions from the living room served as a backdrop to their conversation.

"She doesn't spend a lot of time thinking before she talks, that's for sure," Jackie agreed.

"What are you going to do about it?"

"I'm going to ask Bennett."

"Are you sure that's a good idea? You almost ripped her head off last time you saw her," Jenn reminded her.

"And I still might." Jackie shook her head. "No, I'm more in control of those feelings now. I want to know if Stan really broke it off with her though."

"Does it matter?"

"To me it does. I'd like to think he hadn't given up."

"What if you find out it isn't true? What if he hadn't ended it? Then how will you feel?"

Jackie thought about it. "Like shit probably. But it can't be any worse than I feel now. Now I'm assuming he was a cheating bastard. Maybe it'll be easier to forgive him if I knew he was trying to do the right thing." She stared out the window as she continued speaking. "Until I talked to Paige, I thought Stan refused to cancel his training mission because he was going to see Bennett. Now I know that he *couldn't* cancel because it wasn't a routine mission."

"Why didn't he tell you that?" Jenn asked.

"Because it was classified at the time. He wasn't allowed to tell me."

Jenn sipped her coffee. "Do you want me to go with you to see Bennett?"

Jackie shook her head. "No, I'll be fine. And I promise not to hurt her—much."

~

"What are you doing here?" Renee Bennett asked.

"Can I come in?" Jackie said.

Bennett shrugged and stepped aside. Jackie entered her small apartment and looked around. She couldn't help but wonder how often Stan had stopped here and told Jackie he had to work late.

As if reading her mind, Bennett said, "Mace has never been here." She led the way into the sitting area and gestured toward the couch. "I'd offer you something to drink, but I assume this isn't a social call."

Jackie sat on the edge of the couch and didn't relax. "Is it true that you and Stan had stopped seeing each other before the accident?"

Bennett looked at her with hard eyes, and Jackie didn't see any sympathy there. In their talks, Chaplain Vandensteeg tried to explain that Bennett was probably jealous of Jackie. Jackie had everything Bennett had ever wanted. She had a career, close friends, and a husband. Well, *had* a husband. His death probably wouldn't lessen her extreme jealousy of Jackie's life. Jackie tried to keep that in mind as she waited.

"What is it you want to hear?" Bennett said. "That Mace was coming back to you? How would I know?" She sank into the chair across from Jackie.

"I heard—"

"Rumors are shit," Bennett cut her off. "People love to tell rumors because it's entertaining. They don't care what effect it has on people."

Jackie heard a slight slur in Bennett's speech she hadn't picked up on before. "I'm here because I don't want to listen to the rumors. I've come straight to the source."

"Mace was a prick." Her words were hostile, but Jackie sensed the shakiness behind them was telling of a deeper emotion. "We had something special, you know. Something he couldn't share with you. You were always too serious, no spontaneity. You should work on that." She got up and walked toward the kitchen.

Jackie sat quietly, seething.

Bennett returned with a beer in hand. She waved it in front of her as she spoke. "For you, work was the end result. For me, it's a means to an end. That's why Mace and I complimented each other so well. Our workday ended together, and we forgot about it for a while. I hear you always brought yours home with you. Not a smart move." She took a swig from the beer bottle.

Bennett laughed a quick, derisive laugh. "You know, he thought if he was promoted, you'd love him again. I told him you didn't care about his promotion, as long as *you* were promoted."

Jackie was shaking with fury now. She didn't know if it was because Bennett knew more about her husband's psyche than she did, or because Stan was stupid enough to think her love was based on his promotion potential.

Taking a calming breath, Jackie said, "What you had couldn't have been all that special if you moved on so quickly after the accident. I hear you're already in someone else's bed."

Bennett shook her finger as if Jackie were a naughty child. "Now what did I tell you about rumors?"

"You know they're saying you killed Stan because he broke up with you."

"That's bullshit and you know it! You saw us together that Friday night. I think *you* killed him because you were pissed he didn't want you anymore."

Jackie stood. "I feel sorry for you, Renee. At this rate, you aren't going to get anywhere with your career *or* your love life."

"You bitch!" Beer sloshed onto the rug as Bennett stabbed at her with her beer bottle. "How dare you judge me? If you hadn't noticed, your fairytale life is falling apart before your eyes."

Jackie walked out without another word. Bennett may be right. Her life was falling apart, but she refused to sink as low as Renee Bennett.

# Chapter 38

Thanks for coming over, sir," Special Agent Chris Marquette said, motioning to a seat across from a small rectangular table.

Colonel Harris sat, and Agent Marquette took the seat facing him. Wright was in her usual position perpendicular to Marquette and Harris. They had played these parts many times. Wright's responsibility was to watch and document Harris's responses. From the beginning, the stodgy, plodding formality of the interview had Harris close to the boiling point. Marquette felt that was a plus from his point of view.

"Okay, folks, can we hold off on the bright light and rubber hoses for a minute?" Harris cut off Marquette as he began reading the first words of a prepared script for investigative interviews of material witnesses.

Marquette was startled by the colonel's interruption but looked up at Harris calmly. Marquette had the experience to know anything can happen in an interview and keeping control was his job. *Plan B*, he thought.

Harris pressed on. "Tell me what's going on. What gives you the right to suspend Major Austin's security clearance?"

Marquette perked up. "Colonel, we need to ask you a few questions about Major Austin, but I'll go ahead and respond to that inquiry and any others you may have." Marquette would get his way eventually. It wasn't a bad idea to keep the colonel happy, especially if the colonel wasn't the target of the investigation. In the big picture, it kept the alpha male a friend of OSI, which had unlimited value down the road.

"Colonel, let me first say that what we talk about cannot be discussed further with anyone using any manner of communication." This was part of his introductory script, and he would normally pause and sternly demand, "Do you understand?" In this case Marquette spoke almost apologetically and added gently, "I hope you understand this, sir."

"Of course, of course," Harris acknowledged, nodding.

"Thanks for understanding, Colonel," Marquette smiled. Without Harris even picking up on it, Marquette initialed on his script, noting the required statement and acknowledgement.

"To answer your question about her security clearance, we have credible evidence potentially linking Major Austin to the aircraft accident in which Major Mason was killed, so it's standard procedure to suspend access to classified material and secured areas. That's all."

"What evidence?"

Marquette assessed that the colonel was going to challenge each statement, so he used a tactic of giving him a bite at a time.

"Her line badge was found in a hangar near where the jet was parked."

"Why is that surprising? She has a line badge. She has access to that area. So it fell off at some point. Big deal."

"You're right, Colonel, but I'm curious. Being in her chain of command, you know her well, right?"

"Indeed I do."

"How would the major normally respond to something like a lost line badge?"

Harris jumped at the chance to be a cheerleader for Jackie. "She's meticulous in everything she does. Responsible. She knows the rules and the risk and would take care of it as soon as possible."

"Well, that's been puzzling me." Marquette placed a check mark on the paper in front of him. "She's really a great officer by the look of her records, so you know, it troubles me she would fail to report the lost badge for over a month." Marquette needed to put some doubt in Harris's mind about his star employee. He calmly awaited a response.

Harris shrugged. "She's had a hell of a month with her husband's death. You should probably cut her some slack."

"Well, I'm hoping you can help us do that, sir."

"What are you saying?"

"Sir, we know she had her line badge the Friday before the crash. She was seen on the flight line talking to some of the maintainers. And we found it in the HAS Monday morning. That means she lost it sometime that weekend."

"Okay. But that still doesn't mean she had anything to do with the accident."

"Colonel, it simply puts her in the vicinity during the time we suspect the aircraft was tampered with," Marquette said meekly, as if it was simply a notion of his. "I guess it's not uncommon for someone in the IG to be doing some type of IG work in an aircraft shelter on a—" Marquette paused and pretended to search his papers. "—on a Friday afternoon."

He acted as though he finally discovered the fact he was searching for. "Here it is. Actually, sometime after seventeen-hundred hours." Marquette looked up. "The guard remembers seeing her come through the checkpoint. The squadrons had finished early, so there wasn't much traffic at that time of day. He knew her because he had worked on the exercise team for her in the past. He saw her drive toward the shelters."

Marquette looked back down and shrugged. "Seems late to me on a half-day Friday, don't you think? No one else was working."

"Well, yeah. I can't imagine what she would be doing there that late." Harris looked down at the table for a moment. "That's a waste of cold beer at the club." He looked up with a grin on his face, expecting a response.

Both Marquette and Wright laughed heartily. Way too heartily. Marquette had a sense of having lured a twelve-point buck into his sights. The colonel had suddenly relaxed a bit and was treating them much more casually.

Marquette glanced down at his interview plan. "Let me make sure I answer all your questions, sir. We also know she and her husband had been fighting . . . ," another pause for emphasis, "a lot. And, it was kind of out of character for Major Austin."

"What do you mean?" Harris asked.

"Well, sir, I don't know what you observed, but the fighting was often in public forums."

"I hadn't heard that. That's not like Jackie." Harris leaned back in his chair.

Marquette placed another checkmark unobserved on his sheet. Wright made a quick note on her pad of paper that lay in her lap out of Harris's sight.

"All married couples fight," Harris reasoned. "That's no reason to take down an aircraft. Hell, if that's all you got, my wife would be in a lot of trouble." He grinned again, and Wright chuckled loudly, but Marquette was stone-faced and locked onto the colonel's eyes.

"Sir, your wife wasn't fighting with the now-deceased Major Mason."

The look on Harris's face showed that the tone of rebuke had hit home.

Marquette returned to his amiable demeanor as he searched through his papers. "As the IG, you get the blotter each morning, right?" It was a dumb question used to set up the next objective. "Darn, Agent Wright, can you get me a copy of that thing?"

"Right away," Wright bolted up, having no idea where she would find a copy of the blotter entry she knew Marquette had right in front of him.

"Never mind, Agent Wright," he said before Wright reached the door. "I found a copy right here." He turned the sheet so Harris could read it across from him. "This was the blotter entry I'm scratching my head about."

"Oh yeah, Austin's fender bender. I did read this." Harris then added forcefully in another round of cheerleading for Jackie, "And the major informed me all about it promptly and responsibly by email."

Marquette was several steps ahead, knowing the blotter was a very concise summary of the event, and maybe the major's report to her boss was just as abbreviated. "So, she told you all about it." Marquette pushed several photos in front of Harris as Wright carefully waited to assess the response.

"Shit!" Harris exclaimed as he examined the damage to the passenger side of a car. "This is more than a fender bender! Are you sure this is the same event?"

"Ah, positive. Absolutely. I assume she painted the picture for you, Colonel."

"Whoa, not exactly." Harris was still looking at the pictures. Marquette waited a moment to play his next card, but to his delight, Harris saved him the trouble.

"How the heck do you get this much damage in a parking lot?"

"Sounds like she might not have been straightforward with you about the accident. It actually took place on the flight line."

"The flight line? I didn't get all the details, I suppose."

Marquette made another checkmark on his paper.

"Well, sir, that's why I'm so confused by all this. Especially that she didn't wait for the cops to come. I guess she drove home.

She was asked by the security forces commander to come by and make a statement, but she never made it in. Can't imagine what her car looked like as she drove off the base . . . " Marquette trailed off, having dangled the image in Harris's mind.

"When did this happen?"

Marquette answered in a punctuated tone, "The Friday night before the accident . . . of all coincidences."

"Well, Austin obviously spared me some of the details," Harris noted at half-volume.

Marquette felt he had Harris on the verge of dropping his persistent advocacy for the major.

"Any chance you recognize the car she hit?"

Harris picked up a picture. A second later, his face illuminated with surprise. Marquette maintained his air of innocent ignorance that begged 'do tell.'

"Damn, that's Mace's red Mustang."

"Mace?"

"Mace is her husband." Harris stared at the photo. "Was her husband."

"Oh, I see." Marquette nodded. "I'm sure Major Austin explained that coincidence."

Harris looked at Marquette baffled.

"I wonder if Major Mason was in the car when she crashed into him. Don't you, sir?" Marquette was tapping his finger on the photo. "Kinda looks violent, doesn't it?"

Harris was speechless.

Marquette drew a deep breath as Wright rolled her eyes.

"So, Major Austin T-boned her husband's car on the flight line after witnesses said she had a recent public confrontation with her husband. Then she drives her car—which looks like who knows what—away from the accident scene." Marquette shook his head. "Then, as you said, she promptly reported it to you in an email that weekend but left out a few teeny weenie details, including that it was her husband she slammed into—and I mean slammed."

He took another exaggerated breath. "And then Major Mason's F-16 is sabotaged outside the same hangar where we found Major Austin's line badge after the accident."

"Sabotaged?" Harris's head snapped up.

"That's the working theory." Marquette continued softly, "Then a few days later, Major Mason crashed and burned. Maybe Major Austin didn't get enough satisfaction taking her anger out on his car. So to answer your question, that's kind of why we needed to suspend her security clearance. I hope you understand, sir."

Agent Wright struggled to keep from grinning.

Harris sat silently, eventually nodding.

The two men stared at each other for a time. Finally, the agent broke eye contact. "Sir, I understand you're frustrated. By all accounts, Major Austin is a very capable officer. She's served you well, and she's served her country well. But she is human. She had access; she had opportunity. We placed her at the scene in proximity to the sabotage. She had plenty of holes in her alibi over the weekend where she could have gone back to the base. We know she was in the HAS sometime between Friday afternoon and Monday morning. She is known to come and go at all hours. Most importantly, she and Major Mason appear to not be able to control their anger in public, and this photo looks a bit violent to me. Don't you think, Colonel?" Marquette was tapping his finger again on the crushed in driver's side of Stan's Mustang.

Harris huffed and pursed his lips. "It's not enough to believe Austin would cross the line."

Marquette snapped his fingers like he just added two and two. "Sir, I don't know Major Austin, but I'm thinking she has a short fuse and explodes at people all the time." He picked up a crash photo and slowly fanned it across his face.

"No, no, not Jackie. She's as steady and cool as they come. She may be tenacious but not explosive. Once she makes a decision, she's on the scent. No turning back. I've never seen her blow up. No, not Austin."

"And you know her well, right?"

"You bet."

"I know I'm not getting to all the questions you have, but could I ask you to look at this?" Marquette was nodding to induce Harris to nod in agreement. Wright handed Marquette a clear plastic sleeve. Inside was a green 5x7 inch card. It was stained across the top and a quarter from the bottom was burned away. However, the handwritten print was clearly legible. Harris examined it for a moment and then froze.

"What is this, Colonel?"

As a pilot himself, Harris recognized the form right away. "This is a mission card," he trailed off.

"Which mission? Can you tell?"

"It says right here it was Major Mason's on the day of the crash." Harris indicated the writing on the top line.

"When do you think he filled it out?"

Harris responded in a monotone, "Sometime between Friday and Monday most likely."

Harris was staring at the huge letters scrawled over the card that read "GO TO HELL!!!"

"Who do you think angrily carved that onto the card, Colonel?" Marquette leaned across the table on his elbows.

"It could be anyone."

"Major Austin?"

"Maybe. It's block writing. How can anyone tell?"

"Okay, then let's go with who would have had access to the card."

"Anyone in the squadron, I suppose," Colonel Harris answered.

"And Major Austin."

"I suppose, if he took it home for some reason."

"Actually, he did take it home. His scheduled wingman told us they prepped for the mission on Thursday, and he saw Major Mason place his flight bag in his car Thursday night as they left the squadron." Marquette spoke matter-of-factly as he sat back in his chair. "I don't think anyone in the squadron had the opportunity to see the mission card, let alone write on it."

Harris started to say something, but Marquette jumped in to keep him pinned down on the mat.

"We also have her fingerprints on the card. I suppose the coincidences are adding up, don't you think, Colonel?"

Harris slumped back in his chair as he processed all he had been told. There was so much he hadn't understood before coming into the office to defend Jackie.

"Can I answer any more of your questions, Colonel?"

Wright burst out a snort she caught and converted into a faked coughing fit. Marquette had achieved all the things he needed from the planned interview. Except one.

"No, thanks. This is all a bit surprising."

"Colonel, maybe you think you know her well, but you only know what you see. Seems to me she's been hiding a lot of things from you. Wouldn't you say?"

Harris eyes flared but bit back his first reaction. Instead he simply acknowledged with, "Maybe so."

That was enough for Marquette.

"Sir, I want to make sure you understand why we need to suspend her clearance." Marquette played his part until the end.

"Sure, I get it." A security clearance was the least of Jackie's problems right now.

"You know, I think in a roundabout way we got the information we needed. We really shouldn't waste any more of your time, sir."

"Oh." Harris seemed surprised and stood up. "Well, thanks."

"You bet, sir. We'll let you know if we need to talk to you later."

After Harris left the building, Agent Wright kept watch through the blinds from Marquette's ground floor office.

"Is he still there?" Marquette sat at his desk to make additional notes from the interview.

"Going on five minutes since he got in his car."

"Is he on the phone?"

"Nope, just sitting there. What do you think he's doing?"

Marquette looked up. "He's either realizing he did more harm to his favorite major than good, and he's angry at himself or . . ." He got up to take a peek. "He's thinking she totally fooled him, and he's pissed at her."

"Either way, he's an angry colonel," Wright said.

# Chapter 39

As Jackie approached her office, she noticed the cleaning cart in the doorway. She pushed it gently aside and slipped past.

"Good morning," she called out.

The woman dusting the bookcases froze.

"Mastana? Are you okay?" Jackie asked.

The woman came back to life and busied herself finishing the shelf. Without turning, she said, "Mrs. Austin, I will be gone right away."

"Don't rush off on my account." Jackie put the papers she was carrying on her desk and turned on the computer. While she waited for it to boot up, she watched Mastana. The woman was careful not to look directly in Jackie's direction.

"Mastana?" Jackie repeated with a measure of softness. "Is something wrong?"

The young woman stood straighter. Jackie sensed her internal struggle. Slowly Mastana turned toward Jackie.

Jackie saw yellow and purple marks on Mastana's face. There was a cut above her left eye that should have received stitches.

Jackie rushed around the desk and put her hands on Mastana's upper arms. "Mastana! What happened? Who did this to you?" The woman stiffened under her touch, and Jackie quickly dropped her hands.

"I'm sorry. I don't mean to overstep, but please, let me help you."

"I'm fine," Mastana said. She tried to move around Jackie to leave the room.

Jackie positioned herself between Mastana and the doorway. "What's going on? Why won't you tell me?"

"There is nothing to tell. This is not your concern."

Jackie shook her head. She wasn't sure how to connect with this woman from a culture so foreign to hers. She said a quick, silent prayer, asking for the right words to be heard.

She tried again. "I know we're from different worlds. But we're both women—strong women. And we have to respect ourselves or no one else will."

The woman's eyes softened slightly. Maybe Jackie was getting through. She jotted a number on the back of her business card and slipped it into Mastana's hand before she had a chance to run away.

~

*How does this woman see into me?* Mastana asked herself as she pushed her cart down the hall. *We are nothing alike.* Then she saw the falsehood in her words.

They were alike. They had both lost loved ones. They were both struggling to keep moving every day. Mrs. Austin's pain was still very new. She wondered how long the pain would feel like hot steel against her breast. Was it there when she awoke in the morning and still burning as she fell into an exhausted sleep as it was for Mastana?

And did she feel guilty when she laughed? When, for a moment, she forgot about the past, about the pain—when she caught herself planning for the future? She hoped not. She hoped Mrs. Austin would be able to let the dead rest and allow herself a future.

But she knew it wouldn't happen as long as Mrs. Austin continued to dwell on the crash. Mastana had seen the papers on the desk when Mrs. Austin was away from the office. Mastana knew she was constantly searching for answers. She had even heard her crying sometimes from behind the closed door. At those times, Mastana had quietly walked away, choosing to come back at a later time to empty the trash.

What would happen if she discovered the truth? Would it help or hurt her more? Mastana suffered that pain. She didn't wish it on anyone, not even her enemies. Allah said we should forgive. He holds the right for revenge. That was a lesson she had learned, but her husband had not.

Aashna was quiet by nature, and Mastana liked that side of him. But the men he had fallen in with were bad influences. They weren't faithful and righteous as Mastana's first husband had been. They had convinced Aashna the Qur'an did not *actually* say alcohol was bad. As a matter of fact, in chapter two, they pointed out, it says alcohol also contains some benefit; they left out the remainder of the passage that further states the evil is greater than the good.

This gang of misfits Aashna elected to hang his hat with were not true followers of Islam. They twisted the words of Muhammad to meet their needs. They stressed that alcohol was fine, as long as they did not pray while intoxicated.

Mastana knew this was errant logic, but her husband was lonely in this land, and his selection of friends was slim. The more time he spent with the weak ones, the more he was excluded from the true believers. They shunned those who didn't hold true to the teachings of Muhammad.

When Aashna was with his friends, his mouth would not close. The spirits took over his brain, and he spouted nonsense he read in the papers. He railed against the Americans—the very ones who gave him money to live. He did not see the irony in his hateful words toward them.

Or maybe he did, and it made him even angrier.

His compatriots made things worse. The Afghan refugees who had settled in this region in Germany had sought each other out like magnets. They gathered often, in one or another's home. They spread their evil words about infidels.

When Aashna was in a quiet mood and not susceptible to their suggestions, they plied him with drink. The more he drank, the more vocal he became, soon talking like one of them. Because he had been in Germany most of his life, his accent was heavy with German sounds. The men took great pleasure in mocking his speech and teasing him that he was not a real Afghan. Mastana knew it hurt him. He wasn't in his home country during the worst of the fighting, and he didn't have the grounds to boast that he was a freedom fighter.

It was during these visits that Mastana tried to make herself disappear. She took long walks or sat outside the house. Her husband yelled for her, but she pretended she did not hear. This might also be a sin because she was supposed to submit to her husband. Mastana did not believe Allah meant it to be this way. The evil one entered her husband along with the drink, and she no longer considered him her husband, one to whom she should submit. Allah would judge her when she met Him face-to-face.

When the men harassed Aashna for taking American money, he defended himself by saying he was positioning himself for when he could serve Allah for a greater purpose. He countered the men's snide comments by accusing them of falling asleep and not being ready to do what needed to be done when the time was right.

He bragged about his access to the base. The stupid infidels were so trusting that anyone could go anywhere if they filled out the right paperwork. And he was in a position where he easily listened to the men talking. He said he was gathering intelligence and biding his time to make his move.

That thought made Mastana shudder. Were the Americans that naive? Was it that simple? She had access to many buildings. She remembered how easy it was for her to slip into their hangars and remove things with no one catching her.

She had done that to avoid punishment. Her husband had insisted on proof of her loyalty to him over her American employers. She had been very frightened, but she did as she was told. Her husband was the master of the household, and she must obey him.

He had been so happy with her that night. The tool she presented as proof of her commitment was casually cast aside as of no importance. She realized it wasn't anything special, only a test, and she had passed. He had made love to her gently like he had done when they first married—before he had begun hanging around this set of friends who perverted his mind and filled him with evil thoughts.

The next day, she overheard him bragging to his friends about his dutiful wife and how well trained she was. She felt she should have been happy with his praise. Instead, she felt ashamed.

The American women she encountered on the base worked side-by-side with the men. They dressed the same, held the same ranks, and even did the same jobs. Mrs. Austin even had men who *worked for her*. Mastana wondered what that would be like.

And here was this woman, fresh with the grief of losing her own husband, worried about a woman who cleaned her office. Why did she bother? What difference did Mastana's battered face and bruised ego mean to her?

Mastana thought about other women in her neighborhood who she had seen covering their faces for days at a time. She assumed they had done something especially bad that deserved the wrath of their husbands. It wasn't that uncommon.

She tried to recall an American woman with bruises on her face. She couldn't. On the back of the stalls in the restrooms on base, she had seen posters with a picture of a crying woman, along with a phone number to call if a woman needed help.

She pushed her hair out of her eyes and winced as her fingers touched the bruises on her cheekbone.

She pulled out the card Mrs. Austin had given her. She turned it over to see what she had written on the back. It was a number. The same number from the posters. Maybe it wasn't only for Americans.

# Chapter 40

Jackie and Brad sat at a table in the food court waiting for Senior Airman Suitor. It was the end of the lunch rush, and there were plenty of empty tables. They had found a spot in the back, away from the other diners. When Suitor came through the doors, they waved him over.

"Grab some food," Jackie told him. "We'll wait for you."

He sat. "No, thanks. I'll get chow to go when we're done. I told some of the guys I would bring back something for them," Suitor explained. "Besides, I have an update for you. Did you hear that Captain Bennett has been relieved from duty pending results of an investigation?"

That caught Jackie off guard.

She hadn't thought about it, but it made sense. Bennett was in charge of all flight line maintenance for the squadron F-16s, and she had access to everything. Jackie was slightly relieved to hear not everyone was focusing only on her.

"She's working at the maintenance group pushing paper and is none too happy about it."

Jackie really didn't give a shit whether or not the wench was happy, but she kept that thought to herself.

"Well, I also have something to report." Turning to Suitor, she said, "First, if you haven't heard it through the grapevine, yes, I do know Stan was having an affair with Bennett."

Suitor did his best to act sincerely surprised.

"Nice try, but I can't imagine that scuttlebutt isn't already all over the maintenance group."

Suitor smiled apologetically.

"It's okay. Thanks for trying." She smiled back. "Anyway, the wives' network tells me Stan had dumped her, and she had already moved on before the crash."

"Are you shitting me?" Brad said. "Then she had means *and* a motive!"

"Of course, she denied it," Jackie said.

"You talked to her about it?" Brad asked incredulously.

"And you didn't rip her face off?" Suitor added.

"She wasn't very forthright. She said they were still an item. I did catch them together at the hangar that Friday."

A light bulb went on in Suitor's head. "Oh! Was that your car at the hangar with the cops?"

"It was Stan's. What was left of it after I, ah . . . bumped into it."

Brad rolled his eyes. "I don't want to hear this." He plugged his ears and mumbled, "na na na na na. . ."

"Okay, okay." Jackie stopped him.

He looked at his watch. "I'm sorry to cut this short. I have a briefing to go to. Is there anything else I'm supposed to be looking into right now?"

"It would be interesting to know what the OSI knows," Jackie said.

Brad wrestled with himself for minute before he decided. "They're gunning for you, Jackie."

"I figured as much. I seemed to have pissed off the lead investigator."

"Not a good idea when you're under investigation," Suitor offered.

"Oh, it was well before that. He's a bit of an asshole."

"Now what are you going to do?" Brad asked.

She tried to stay upbeat. "Guess we'll have to show them the error of their ways."

~

In decades past, the room would have been filled with cigarette smoke and ashtrays overflowing with snuffed out cigarette butts. Tonight, in their federally mandated, no-smoking facility, Agent Marquette and Agent George Ramirez impatiently awaited a fresh pot of coffee to get them through another couple hours. And they were expecting Agent Wright to return.

"We need to press and get on with this," Marquette said. "We have enough evidence against both officers to warrant a comprehensive search warrant, but everyone is pushing back. This is typical of senior leadership when high-performing and well-liked officers are suspected of something major—like murder." He squatted down to see if the slow drip of the brew had accumulated enough to allow him to refill his cup. "If these two women were enlisted rather than officers, one of them would already be hanging."

"Isn't that the truth." Ramirez didn't look up from copies of interviews stacked in front of him.

"I want to get to their personal email and texts before they go mucking around with it." Marquette decided he would steal a cup at half pot level.

"Agreed. Hey, have you ever seen women go after each other when they're pissed? Seems like they always find a reason to blame it on the guy."

Ramirez looked up at Marquette to see him grinning for the first time in a couple days. "You know, you're exactly right. Say a guy steals a guy's truck. He might go shoot the guy who stole the truck, but he'd never shoot the truck."

Ramirez let out a laugh. "Brilliant observation. And if a guy steals a guy's girl, the guy goes after the guy."

"Exactly." Marquette snapped his fingers. "But if a girl steals another girl's guy—"

"They both shoot the guy!" they said in unison.

Marquette sat on the table and held his hot coffee with both hands. Suddenly, the banter was not as entertaining. Marquette had run across two love triangles in his career, and both involved murder/suicide. "Okay, I'm tired of jackin' around with this case. We gotta move."

"What's the play, Chris?"

"Let's get both ladies back and show our hand a bit. Maybe the lawyers will give us some leash if they think it helps their case. I want some inconsistency in statements to open another hole. Maybe that gets us a warrant, and we get GPS data, texts, email, everything."

"Copy, I'm with you." Ramirez affirmed by clinking his coffee mug to Marquette's.

They jumped as Wright bolted through the doorway, out of breath. "We got prints in HAS eight where Mason's jet was parked from Friday until it launched on Monday."

"All right! Tell me it's Major Jackie Austin!" Marquette punched an undercut into an imaginary gut. He deflated when he looked up at Wright's stone face.

"We found both their fingerprints—Bennett and Austin."

# Chapter 41

It was a standard set up like any interview, except Agent Ramirez had taken the caps off the front legs of the chair of the interviewee. It was only about an inch difference, but Ramirez had seen the tactic long, long ago in a 1940s movie.

In the movie, it included shaving off one of the chair legs to make it wobble, and the idea stuck with him for years. Of course, he wasn't about to saw the leg off a government-issued chair, but over his years of investigative work, he believed an inch of mismatched height with both the interviewer and the table created enough discomfort. It interfered with the intense concentration required to maintain a façade of lies. This was the strategy for both interviews scheduled today—inconsistencies and accidental revelations.

Marquette arrived bristling with energy.

"You're looking pretty refreshed for a guy running on a few hours of sleep," Ramirez said.

"Are you kidding? I love this stuff! I can't wait to get into the ring of competition and manipulate my opponent." He clapped his hands together. Marquette was an extremely charismatic soul to those he met for the first time. "If there's a weakness to exploit, I'll find it."

As they filled their coffee cups in the break room, Marquette shared his interrogation techniques with Ramirez.

"All you have to do is establish trust and openness. For the vast majority of U.S. citizens and a few categories of undocumented immigrants, there are a few interest areas to focus on. You just profile the person's interests during the introductory niceties. For men, it's sports, hunting and fishing, car restoration, and microbreweries."

"You throw a ball like your seven-year-old daughter! No way you'd be caught baiting a hook or changing your own motor oil. And what do you know about beer? You only drink blended scotch . . . a lot of it."

Marquette laughed. "You're right, my friend, but they don't know that. I learned the most effective icebreaker technique during my first assignment. You memorize the largest cities in all fifty states and three key things about each state. Ask your mark where they're from, then followed the answer with another question. 'How far is that from Denver?' It's a very simple tactic, but when the target is under extreme pressure, simple things have an effect."

Ramirez shook his head in disbelief.

"Now for the ladies, you have to take a different route. In high school, I worked part time in my mother's dress shop in Elisabeth, New Jersey. She taught me to compliment the way a woman made her dress look great, not the other way around. Unfortunately, in the military, that's not a great opening with the uniforms. But I didn't suffered the endless hours of chatter that occurred in Mom's shop and learn nothing."

Marquette looked at his watch. "Are we ready, amigo?"

"She should be here in fifteen." Ramirez had purposefully scheduled Renee Bennett's interview at 0630. He loved the early hour play because the subject was most likely not going to sleep well the night before, was more likely to skip breakfast, and was probably going to feel miserable during the interview.

Agent Wright walked into the break room to find the coffee pot completely empty. "Curse you," she said.

Ramirez got to his feet. "No cursing allowed, Emily. I confess. It was me. You get ready for Captain Bennett. I'll make more coffee."

"How's that a good thing?"

"You don't like my coffee?"

Marquette interrupted. "Okay, crew, let's get moving. Emily, you hold her for about twenty minutes. If her counsel starts asking about the delay, bring her in. Otherwise, let her cook."

"Yes, sir."

"And, George, make some of your crappy coffee."

$\sim$

Sitting next to her appointed Area Defense Counsel, Captain Bennett hunched over with her arms crossed, eyes closed. Her stomach was sour, and she wished she hadn't finished the second bottle of wine the night before. There was no reason why such an early appointment should be delayed. It couldn't be good. Her lawyer seemed oblivious and scanned a year-old magazine.

Agent Wright burst into the waiting area, startling them both. She greeted them, asked for IDs, and invited them to bypass the metal detector.

*Now they're in a hurry,* Bennett thought.

They followed her into the interview room and took their assigned seats. With equal abruptness, Marquette entered, and Bennett and her military lawyer stood out of habit. Marquette reached out his hand, and Major Scott Hartwick obliged with a firm and warm handshake. In contrast, Bennett offered up a cold, clammy fish.

"Please, please sit down." Marquette gestured toward the chairs. They all took their seats.

Marquette continued to address the lawyer without looking up, instead, making a fuss over placing his papers in stacks. "Major Hartwick, I think we've run into each other before. We may have overlapped at McConnell not too long ago."

"Really? When were you there?"

"You remember the horrendous tornado that ripped through the off-base housing area? That was ugly."

Hartwick jumped on the shared memory. "I was fortunate. It missed my house. Sure made a mess of the yard though. I lost a lot of trees in that storm."

Bennett noted Marquette didn't actually say they overlapped, rather that they *may* have overlapped. Then he didn't answer the direct question about the timing. She would have to watch this Marquette guy closely. He was up to something. It wasn't hard to memorize the military biographies for all the Area Defense Councils on base. It was a good parlor trick to get the lawyer talking, and it seemed to be working. Bennett sat back, frustrated with the chit chat.

"Of course, it was nothing like the legendary tornado that hit McConnell in 1991," Marquette added.

"Oh yeah, you can't spend more than five minutes in a bar in Wichita without someone talking about Andover 1991."

"You from that area?"

"Yep, I'm Kansas-born and raised."

Marquette smacked his lips. "The thing I love the most about Kansas is the barbeque." He pointed his index finger up at the ceiling to make a point. "A hundred days, a hundred ways. Food heaven!" he quoted from a barbeque commercial.

That got Hartwick rambling about his family's secret recipes for the next couple of minutes.

Bennett's head was swimming from the strangeness of it all, but she sat in silence.

"So, let's get to it, shall we?" Marquette clapped his hands and smiled.

Hartwick elbowed Renee like he had everything perfectly set. She rolled her eyes.

Marquette dramatically fumbled with a compact recorder and placed it on the table between them. "There you go."

Hartwick nodded in approval of the perfunctory detail.

"We've already read Captain Bennett her rights in the previous interview, so I need to state that for the tape. We have agreed to meet again, and Captain Bennett has her counsel present, Major Scott Hartwick. Agent Emily Wright is also in the room. I, Agent Christopher Marquette, am conducting the interview. Do we all understand?" Everyone nodded in agreement. "Can we get some verbals on the record?" Marquette smiled and pointed at the recorder.

Hartwick leaned into the recorder and said, "Yes, we do."

Marquette winked at Hartwick and started his battle plan. Shifting his demeanor, Marquette went on the attack. "We know about the affair between Captain Bennett and Major Stan Mason. I need to ask a few questions—"

"Wait!" Hartwick looked from Marquette to Bennett and back again. The agent had gone from a buddy shooting the shit to attack dog with the click of the tape recorder button.

"I have a few follow-up questions about their affair," Marquette said.

Renee's survival instincts boiled up. She slipped a hand onto Hartwick's thigh, out of sight under the table to give him assurance. She faced the agent. "Yes, there was a brief error in judgement. What do you want to know?"

Hartwick's clenched jaw made it obvious he was caught off guard. Bennett now needed to control both men in the room.

"Well, Captain, we want to hear your side about the affair. That's all." Marquette cast his eyes at the table.

Bennett paused to consider her response. "We had an alcohol-induced moment."

"How big was that moment?" Marquette continued to look down at the table with disinterest.

"Not big."

"What's big?"

"She already told you; it wasn't a big deal," Hartwick jumped in.

Marquette ignored him. "How many times did you have sex, and were there any plans made for the future between you?"

She pulled her hand back and crossed her arms defensively across her chest.

"We know you had an expectation that Major Mason would leave his wife for you." Marquette's comment didn't affect her, but it hit her lawyer hard.

She smiled sweetly. "He might have wanted to, but I wasn't that serious about him."

"Really?" Marquette feigned astonishment poorly and wrote something in his notebook.

"Why does that surprise you?" Bennett asked coyly, playing his game.

"Well, we heard he was stringing you along. That he was the one who didn't want anything serious, but you were stalking him."

"Stalking?" she asked incredulously. *That was a new one.* Then she caught herself. "He was lying, as all men tend to do in his situation."

Marquette labored to suppress a grin. "All men? Are there a lot of men?"

Hartwick perked up, but she put her hand back on his thigh and squeezed to silence him before he had a chance to stop her from continuing.

She leaned in toward Marquette. "I'm single, sir, and who I bed, I bed. There's no crime there."

Marquette's face showed surprise at her boldness, but he quickly pressed ahead. "In the military, bedding a married man is indeed a crime—"

"But the real crime is when a man betrays a woman's commitment to him. Right?" Agent Wright cut in from her place leaning against the wall.

Marquette turned slowly to look at Wright but didn't say anything.

Bennett looked at this new player in the game and sized her up. "He didn't know the meaning of the word commitment," she said. "He was cheating on his wife, after all."

"I don't know why you put up with him as long as you did," Wright said.

"He was fun during TDYs." Bennett felt Hartwick's leg muscles tighten under her hand. Maybe she had made a mistake asking him to represent her. This was going to add another complication.

"It must have really ruffled your feathers when he decided to call it quits. Did he find someone else?"

"I told you, he was crazy about me. Couldn't get enough." *These people were stupid if they thought Mace had passed me over for another woman. He was a confused little boy who couldn't handle what he had.* The pulse in Bennett's neck was throbbing fast.

"How was it you got sidelined? I understand he was off to meet another woman when he found himself . . . dead," Wright said.

Bennett's eyes opened wide and she had to keep her jaw from dropping at the suggestion, then she collected herself, tugging on her uniform blouse to straighten it. "He thought because he wore government-issued pajamas called a flight suit that he could take whatever he wanted." That's what she needed to do—turn the tables. She was a victim here. A victim of the

Air Force flying club that prized their prima donnas. He came on to her!

Wright shook her head in sympathy. Pushing herself away from the wall, she pulled out a chair at the table and plopped down across from Bennett. "Guys like that run this damn Air Force, and they wonder why it's a mess," she said in disgust.

*Finally, someone who understands*, Bennett thought. "Bag wearers think they have all the answers. To hell with us support officers! What do we know? *We* don't play god every time we go to work. They're so used to doing it in the jet, they forget when they come down to Earth that they are the same assholes they were when they took off!"

"And they never have to suffer the consequences!" Wright's voice rose in volume to match Bennett's.

"Never! Pilots don't have consequences," Bennett said sarcastically. "They can get away with anything!"

"At least Mason won't get away with it!" Wright said with a conspiratorial grin.

"Damn straight!" Bennett hit the table with her hand.

"He deserved to be killed," Marquette said forcefully, jumping back into the conversation. He slapped the table next to Bennett's hand.

"Yes, he did!" she barked, slapping her hand on top of Marquette's. While holding his stare, she applied pressure through her fingertips and lightly drew her thumb up the side of his palm to join her fingers.

Marquette froze.

This invasion of his personal space was disconcerting and distinctly sensual. Marquette focused on controlling his response. Never had any subject of an interview made a physical connection with him like this. Never a touch. There

255

were a score of incidents where he was attacked in rage, but this was totally different. He leaned back in his seat and slipped his hand from under hers.

Wright was oblivious to the electricity at the table. "I wouldn't let him get away with treating me like that. How about you?"

"Because I could sabotage his jet if I wanted, you think I would roast his ass?" She continued to focus on Marquette as she answered Wright's question. There was defiance behind her eyes. "Ice pick in the heart during sex would be a lot easier to explain, you know, a crime of passion. Isn't that what it's called?"

Marquette thought this interview had a bizarre quality he struggled to overcome. "You're saying it's more likely you'd screw a guy then kill him, rather than sabotage his jet? Doesn't give me much comfort." He looked pointedly at the lawyer.

Bennett's cool demeanor cracked slightly when Marquette broke their eye contact. She flung herself back into her seat with a huff.

Marquette watched the lawyer process the implication. When nothing was said, he continued. "The way I see it, Mason finished with you and cast you aside. On to the next. So you decided revenge was in order."

Bennett placed both hands on the table and leaned in to put her face close to Marquette's. "I can screw anyone I want whenever I want. My revenge is cutting them off when *I'm* done. No man is worth the time it would take to kill him. So, go screw yourself, Secret Agent Man!"

Hartwick had finally regained his control. "Stop! This is over; this is over!" He pushed the recorder across the table into Marquette's lap and pulled Bennett to her feet. "We're out of here." They stumbled toward the door as Wright moved to block their exit.

Marquette extended his hand to Hartwick. "Amigo, I'm sorry; this evidently surprised you."

Bennett lunged at Marquette and slapped his outstretched hand away. "Get stuffed!"

Hartwick grabbed Bennett in a bear hug from behind as Wright stepped calmly between her and Marquette. The lawyer faced Bennett toward the door, and she melted into a compliant exit.

～

Ramirez had watched the action from behind the two-way mirror and was still having a hard time controlling his laughter as he replayed bits of the interview in his head.

"Come check this out," he said to Wright as he stared at the cameras monitoring the parking lot

Wright joined Ramirez. They watched as Bennett and her lawyer exited the building. His gestures were those of a man lied to and betrayed. He grabbed her arm and spun her to face him.

She attempted to stroke him affectionately, but he batted her hands away. She then appeared to plead with him with more physical contact, but he seemed to respond in anger. Suddenly, she morphed from cowering dog to an attacking wolf. She had him backed against a car and was poking into his chest. Wright and Ramirez jolted when she suddenly slapped Hartwick across the face with a force that nearly knocked him to his knees.

Marquette was numbly writing notes from their interview. "What are they doing?"

"This is not a typical attorney-client relationship," Ramirez said with a smirk, still gazing out the window.

Wright rolled her eyes. "She's a black widow, if you ask me."

"Black widow?" Marquette asked.

"Really?" Wright gave Marquette a puzzled look. "She was diddling with him the entire time. Don't tell me you missed that?"

Marquette was genuinely baffled. "Diddling?"

Ramirez and Wright glanced at each other, and then looked at Marquette. After several seconds, they realized he was serious. They both burst out laughing. For the first time ever, it was the flawless master who missed some key nuggets of an interview.

"Chris, she was stroking his leg under the table. Our suspect is moving on to an interesting relationship with her attorney," Ramirez said.

Marquette dropped his head into his hands. "A black widow and a scorned wife?" He rubbed his eyes. "We're no closer than we were before."

"Yeah, but it's getting a whole lot more interesting, don't you think, Emily?" Ramirez looked at the monitor again to see Bennett drive away.

Wright shrugged her shoulders. "Whatever."

Marquette continued to rub his eyes. "Well, crew, my money's on the scorned wife, no matter how evil the black widow appears."

"Me too," Wright offered. "What's your bet, George?"

Ramirez was still watching the lawyer sitting in his car. "Before I bet, can we wait to see if Bennett's attorney turns up dead?"

# Chapter 42

The day had been long enough for Jackie. The OSI game was as transparent as her first visit. Make her wait. Put her off balance.

She suppressed a gaping, extended yawn as she glanced around the gloomy room. It had been a long day, and she was ready to go home. Her counsel, Captain Randy Richardson, elbowed her and with a grin asked, "Let me guess, cops and robbers bored you as a kid?"

She let out a laugh, realizing her yawn could be interpreted as boredom on the threshold of another interrogation. It was really lack of sleep from the stress she was under.

Captain Richardson was a fair-haired, young superstar in the Air Force Judge Advocate General community. He was also well known across the base as being a serial volunteer, enthusiastically engaged in every do-good initiative from planting trees to remodeling safe-house hostels for German teens. Jackie knew him by his reputation but only recently got to know his mettle as a lawyer after he was assigned to her as Area Defense Counsel.

During their first consultation, Jackie had data dumped a lot on Richardson concerning her own covert investigation. She had been prepared for the worst response from him and had expected him to keep her in check with an admonishment to back off and "trust the system." To her pleasant surprise, he took a completely different tack.

"Until someone restricts where we can go, we are free to gather information and use it to your benefit. We'll do whatever we can for your protection and, if necessary, your defense," Richardson said. "But there are a few red lines we will *not* cross under any circumstances." He explained them in great detail and then, apologetically, asked her to repeat them back in her own words.

She obliged. "We will not lie. We will not hedge or deceive or spin the truth. We will not break any laws."

Captain Richardson nodded his approval.

At that point, Jackie felt comfortable enough to let him know about the others who were helping her. She added some details she had skimmed over initially in order to protect her cohorts.

Richardson was exceedingly impressed by Jackie's determined effort, and he reasoned she had enough material to begin strategically filtering it into the hands of the OSI. Marquette and company would be obligated to follow up on it all. "In essence, we steer their investigative activity similar to how they try to steer an interrogation."

It was Richardson's idea to allow Brad to be their messenger, feeding information to the OSI they wanted them to have. He had already brought Renee Bennett into their lineup of suspects, and he had all the credibility of a law enforcement colleague offering assistance.

"OSI wants to talk to you again, and I think it's a good idea," Richardson had advised. "It might give us some insight as to the direction of their investigation. You can respond when you want to or decline if we think the line is threatening."

In the end, she had agreed.

Now, as they waited in the interview room for the questioning to start, her lawyer reminded her to stick to the plan. "Only talk if I think it's safe, and don't lie." He looked at her sideways. "Get up for a minute."

Jackie stood, and Richardson turned her chair over. He grinned as he removed the end caps from the back two legs of the chair and righted it. He placed them on the table, and they took their seats again.

Captain Richardson gave her a wink as Marquette burst into the room. Wright and Ramirez flanked Marquette and, in perfect precision, took chairs directly across from Richardson and Jackie. "This is not going to be friendly," Richardson whispered to her.

Marquette wasted no time. He placed a recorder in the middle of the table and turned it on. Quickly he summarized for the record that Jackie had been advised of her rights and returned with her counsel voluntarily. He listed the people in the room and began.

He spoke to Captain Richardson in a monotone, forceful voice. "Major Austin has been up to some interesting after-hours activities that are impacting our investigation. Have you had an opportunity to explain to her the penalty for obstructing an OSI investigation?"

This was an unexpected kick-off to the meeting. Richardson stalled with a question. "Can you explain why that would be necessary?"

Marquette ignored Richardson and turned to Jackie. "Are you trying to obstruct our investigation, Major Austin?"

"Don't answer that question, Major Austin," Richardson said firmly, maintaining his poise. "Agent Marquette, we are here to help you with your investigation, not obstruct it. So, we need you to keep your questions relevant to the facts and evidence—"

Marquette cut him off. "Fact . . . Major Austin's marriage was in shambles. Fact . . . Major Austin learned her husband was having an affair with Captain Renee Bennett. Fact . . . they

261

had an explosive and public argument. Fact . . . witnesses say she said she wanted to kill him. Fact . . . she ran her car into Major Mason's car." He paused for effect. "All this right before the crash."

Jackie was reeling at the incriminating grenades he was tossing at her. Each time Marquette said "fact," he took a document from Agent Wright and dropped it onto the table in front of Agent Ramirez to immediately retrieve and restack. It was the first time she had heard all the pieces assembled, and she suppressed an impulse to scream and justify herself on each so-called fact.

In contrast, Captain Richardson loved the treasure trove of information he was gaining. He had no intention of interrupting, lest he inadvertently sidetrack Marquette from completing his well-rehearsed theatrics.

The hail of gunfire culminated with Marquette saying to Jackie, "And, Major, we got your fingerprints in the HAS where your husband's jet was parked that weekend. You know, the weekend before he crashed." His voice trailed off in a near whisper.

The barrage overwhelmed Jackie. Her mind was flooded with a vivid image of Stan and Bennett together in the hangar. She felt a swirl of pain, anger, and fear. Worst of all, she was grasping the case against her.

Captain Richardson read her face and stepped into the gap. He calmly asked, "Agent Marquette, we don't know what or where you've been fingerprinting. Is there something specific you would like to discuss?"

Marquette ignored his question. Keeping his eyes locked on the lawyer, he slid a plastic bag across to Jackie. "Is that your handwriting, Major?"

Jackie recognized the artifact immediately. It was Stan's green line-up card with her message scrawled across it. Until this moment, she had completely forgotten about it. "Yes," she whispered as nausea wilted her.

Richardson realized his client had unnecessarily given Marquette something he needed. "Stop!" He pushed the card back to Marquette. "Look, if you want to discuss pieces of evidence, then officially give us the evidence. We'll examine it and give you a statement. How's that? Otherwise, we're done here."

Marquette returned to where he began. "It's not uncommon for a perpetrator to try to interfere with witnesses, documentation, and all sorts of evidence. Can you explain why Major Austin is stealing maintenance documentation? Why is she seeking, clearly confidential information, from the safety investigation?" He leaned into Jackie. "Major Austin, are you trying to cover something up?"

"What?" Jackie asked with disbelief.

Captain Richardson raised a palm to stop Marquette. "I'm sure I didn't hear you accuse Major Austin of wrongdoing without solid evidence," he said sarcastically. "You must have her confused with someone else. You better get your facts straight."

Marquette snapped. "You better be telling Major Austin that an obstruction charge tacks on another five years and fifty-thousand dollars!"

"Major Austin hasn't done anything to tack onto," Captain Richardson scoffed.

Jackie was electrified with the realization of the case OSI was building against her. An intense motivation welled up in her. Her only thought was to get out of the room and back to solving the mystery. Taking slow, calming breaths, she controlled her expression. She listened passively as the back and forth between Marquette and Richardson degenerated into a stalemate. She then reached over and placed her hand on Captain Richardson's arm to interrupt him mid-sentence. "We're done."

He nodded and turned to finish his sentence to Marquette.

Jackie clawed her fingernails into his sleeve and cut him off. "No, we are completely done here. Let's go." To the surprise of the agents, Jackie stood up and headed for the door.

Ramirez jumped ahead and stood between Jackie and the door. Captain Richardson was clumsily moving the chairs to catch up to Jackie as Marquette was saying something about not being finished.

Jackie glowered at Ramirez and stiffened. "Get out of my way, Agent Ramirez, or you will need to tack on an assault charge. I said we are done."

If Ramirez had any intention of calling her challenge, it wilted in the heat of Jackie's glare. He slowly reached for the doorknob and opened it, allowing her to pass with Richardson in tow.

Somewhere behind her, Agent Wright was saying something about them coming back to review a summary of the discussion, but Jackie rushed quickly out of the building without looking back.

She paused under the light of a streetlamp. "We weren't actually given any restrictions, right?"

"You mean working with Brody and Suitor?"

"Yep."

"I didn't hear them say stop," Captain Richardson confirmed with a devilish grin that abruptly faded. "What I did hear is you need to hurry up. I think they could clamp you down at any moment."

# Chapter 43

Her husband had visitors again. When they began their anti-American talk, Mastana slipped outside. Their loud voices raged through the open window, teasing her husband for taking orders from the Americans, for bowing to American ways.

He protested, saying he was only using the Americans; his employment was only a way to get close to them. Mastana didn't wander off. She wanted to know what he was referring to.

"You idiots!" Aashna said. "When I gave you one simple job to do, you failed me."

"You gave us menial tasks. Nothing important," the men protested.

"I asked you to do simple things, keeping with your abilities," he chastised them. "You couldn't even trigger a few alarms when you were told."

"What good comes from harassing the Americans in this way? It's an irritant, nothing more. We cut the fence before. So what?"

"That was only a test! I needed to see how long it would take the Americans to react," Aashna explained, trying to hold back his temper.

"Do not be mistaken. I do not mind messing with the Americans, but it bores us. We found other things more entertaining to occupy our time."

"Fools! If you had done your task and triggered the alarms as instructed, it would have given me time to complete my work."

"You mean drive that stupid van without getting a ticket?" one man said in a mocking voice.

"Poke fun as you will. Allah knows I was doing my part toward defeating the infidels. You did not do your part. The security cars returned to their duties too quickly. I had only climbed into the second jet when they returned. I barely escaped undetected."

The other men laughed. "Aashna, you are nothing but a braggart. You talk big, but we see no reason to believe you had a plan. You are taking credit for Allah's will on the Americans."

"Allah used my hands!" he shouted. He hurried from the room and returned moments later holding something in his fist. "This is the tool that brought down that plane! Something so small against something so large. A modern-day David and Goliath!"

"That is a simple tool found in any hardware store. Why should we believe you?" the mocking man asked.

"A tool like this may be purchased anywhere, but it was not! This was taken from the Americans. I thought it fitting that their own tool be the cause of their destruction."

Mastana's heart skipped a beat. The tool she had taken from the hangar? Is this what her husband was referring to? What did it have to do with the accident?

"Sometimes it pays to be unassuming. The men talk and are careless of their surroundings. I heard about a flaw in their airplane design, and I took advantage of it."

"What flaw?"

"The skin of the engine is thin. It doesn't take much to cause damage," Aashna said.

"If the Americans know about this weakness, they must have a solution," one of the men said dismissively.

"That's why it was important for me to get to more than one engine and more than one plane, you imbecile!" Aashna spat. "Hit them hard before they have time to react. They can put out a fire in one engine, but not in ten or twenty!"

The men should have taken Aashna more seriously. He was a very smart man—a very dangerous man.

After they left, Mastana crept back in the house. The room was a disaster with glasses and food containers scattered about the tables and floor. These men were pigs. She was disgusted with her husband for his talk and association with these small-minded swine. She tripped over something, and a glass beer bottle skittered across the floor. It was American beer, she noted.

"What?" Her husband startled from his position on his favorite recliner.

"It is me," Mastana responded.

"Hmpf." He grunted and dropped back into his slouching repose.

"Aashna, you were only telling tales when you talked about the plane, were you not?"

Eyes still closed, he waved his hand in her direction dismissively.

"Aashna, this is important. Did you have something to do with the airplane crash?"

His anger flared. "Woman! It is not your place to question me!"

She jumped at his harsh response. It scared her. "Aashna?"

"Just because you cater to the infidel trash does not mean I should," he spit. "What is one plane to them? It should have been more!"

267

Mastana was stunned at the revelation. This was a crime. This was murder. She was grasping the implications of what Aashna just confessed. She thought of the carnage in her own village and whispered, "Even one death is too much."

Aashna bellowed at her. "There can never be enough dead Americans. They all will be slaughtered!"

Mastana's head was throbbing, and she screamed, "You are not the man I married! You are a murderer!"

Mastana didn't see the blow coming. Her head snapped back and light exploded behind her eyes. The second blow, this one a backhand, sent her toppling over the low table in front of the couch. She smacked the back of her head on the wooden arm of the chair and landed in a heap.

Feeling his form looming over her, she slowly opened her quickly swelling eyes. "You do not get in my way. Afghanstan is my country. One jet was a down payment only. Next time I will bring down more!"

He kicked her as he moved past and down the hall.

She laid motionless. Afraid to move, afraid to absorb what she had heard.

# Chapter 44

Jackie was exhausted. She wondered if this was how she would feel for the rest of her life, going from event to event without enthusiasm, looking forward to nothing. She knew from her weekly chats with Chaplain Vandensteeg that her feelings were straight out of a textbook. He assured her continuously she would eventually snap out of it, but she had to give herself time to mourn. She felt she *was* mourning. As a matter of fact, it felt like unending mourning. She wanted to be past this stage and on to the next.

In the meantime, she went to work every day and did her job. Having her security clearance suspended didn't affect her IG work much, only limiting her access to certain locations on base. Still, the only thing that sparked her interest was her ruminations over Stan's accident. Not over his death. That still made her cry. But when she tried to unravel the mystery surrounding the crash, she felt her mind was working again. Although she tried to look at the problem from every angle, she knew she was missing something.

It kept her up late at night, which was why she was so exhausted every morning.

She flipped the lights on in her office and tossed her hat on the credenza behind her desk. She collapsed into her chair and stared at the stacks of paperwork on her desk. She was unmotivated to get started but forced herself to focus.

As she picked up the reports from her team's last round of staff assistance visits, she noticed a newspaper under the folders. She wondered if it had gotten mixed in by mistake when someone turned in their reports. Then she noted it was a German paper. She pushed the reports aside and looked closer.

Her German wasn't very strong, but she didn't have to be able to read it to understand the topic. The photo accompanying the article was the crash site near the cemetery. The blackened grass and broken headstones made for a creepy picture, more so because of the black and white, granular quality of the photograph.

When she unfolded the paper to translate the German words, something fell onto the floor at her feet. Jackie picked up the thin, metal object. It was heavy and solid, about ten inches long, with a slightly enlarged, flat end on top. The bottom thinned out to a point. She had seen a tool like this in her father's woodshop when she was little. She had no idea why it would be folded into this newspaper. She set it on her desk and turned her attention back to the article.

This was definitely about Stan's accident, but the paper was over a week old. Why would someone leave this on her desk?

She couldn't read it, but she thought she knew who could. She gathered up the paper, stuffing the metal tool in the cargo pocket of her ABUs.

&#x223D;

Nothing has changed, Jackie," Paige said as she walked Jackie from the entry control point back to her building. Jackie had not been allowed to replace her line badge, pending investigation. "I still can't tell you anything."

"It's not about that," Jackie reassured her.

They walked in silence the rest of the way. Instead of turning into the vault where her desk waited, Paige led her down another hallway into an extra office.

Jackie didn't take offense. She knew people were being cautious around her now more than ever. Without pretense, she flattened the foreign newspaper on the table in front of the officer. "Can you read this?"

Paige picked it up to get a better look, and the picture of the crash site leapt out at her.

After a few minutes, Paige looked intently at Jackie. "Where did you get this?"

"Someone left it in my office. What does it say?"

Paige shook her head. "I don't know if this is some kind of sick joke or not, but you should let Brad know."

"Why would Brad care?" Jackie thought her friend was being overprotective, suggesting she get the cops involved over someone leaving newspapers in her office.

"It's about the crash. Some of the German locals are saying American pilots can't be trusted." She scanned the paper for the highlights. "They are calling for the German government to kick the U.S. bases off German soil. I'm sorry, Jackie," she said quietly, looking directly at her. "They say they have a source that claims the crash was pilot error."

Jackie was shaking. Quickly Paige got to her feet and put her arm around Jackie's shoulder. She eased her into a chair.

Taking both hands in hers, she knelt in front of Jackie. "Are you okay?"

Jackie blinked back the tears. "This is bullshit! Stan was a great pilot. If he could have avoided this, he would have."

"I agree with you. Everyone on base agrees with you."

"Then who's this source claiming it was pilot error?"

"It doesn't matter. It's sensationalism. It sells papers. You know there are those in the German community who want the

Americans gone. Don't let that get to you. The real question we need to answer right now is why someone put this on your desk."

Jackie crossed her legs and felt a sharp jab in her thigh. She quickly sat up and pulled the metal rod from her pocket.

"What's that?" Paige asked.

"Don't know. It fell out of the newspaper."

Paige examined the instrument for a moment and then gave Jackie a puzzled look. She held the object in one hand and reached for the newspaper with the other. "You say someone wrapped this thing up in a newspaper article about the accident?" Before Jackie could nod, Paige continued. "And then someone went into your office after you left last night and placed it on your desk?"

Jackie nodded. "Yes."

"Way too weird, girl. I'm calling Brad."

When Jackie finished recounting her discovery for Brad, the three of them sat in silence trying to discern the meaning.

Ever the professional cop, Brad used a piece of paper from the copy machine to take the metal rod from her hand and look it over. "Let's go for a walk, ladies."

He got up and the two women followed him out of the building. They didn't speak as they walked toward the maintenance hangar.

"Has anyone seen Senior Airman Suitor?" Brad called out as they crossed the threshold, not giving anyone the chance to acknowledge their presence.

A young man jumped to his feet and pointed toward a back office. "Back there, sir."

"Thank you." Brad led the way toward the back.

Senior Airman Suitor appeared in the doorway of the small room. "Sir, ma'ams." He acknowledged them all with a head nod. "Is there something I can do for you?"

"Can we talk in there?" Brad gestured.

Suitor stepped back and gestured for them to enter. He had removed his ABU shirt in the heat of the hangar and now reached for where it hung on the back of the chair. As he slipped it on, the four crowded into the small space, and Paige closed the door.

"Show him, Brad," Jackie said.

Brad handed him the metal rod still wrapped in the paper Brad had used when he took it from Jackie.

Suitor took the paper and unwrapped the metal rod. Understanding he was meant to avoid touching the object directly, he only used the tip of his finger to determine if it was sharp. "It's a scribe. What's the big deal?"

"Scribe?" Brad asked.

"Well, it's a kind of awl." Suitor pretended to hold it with one hand while making a motion with the other like he was working with the tool. "This one is used in metal shops to scribe steel." He looked up and assessed he needed to explain further. "It's used to make a groove on hard metal surfaces." His audience was now nodding in clear understanding.

"See how sharp this is at the point? Sometimes, if the metal is thin enough, a maintainer can bang with a hammer one time and poke a hole for fasteners and whatever."

Jackie quickly filled him in on the newspaper left on her desk and told him the tool was wrapped inside it.

"That's strange," Suitor said. "I swear this was the type of tool that went missing from one of the HASs a few months back. We all had to do a toolkit inventory. What a pain in the ass."

Suitor looked more closely at the metal piece in his hand. "This could have done it!" He delicately tapped his finger on the tip of the scribe again as if estimating its sharpness. "It's the right size. It's sharp enough."

Paige was confused. "What are you talking about?"

Suitor explained. "The jet had what's called an afterburner burn-through. It happens if there's a hole in the afterburner section. It's a known failure mode in the F-16. That's why all the engines were pulled, and the afterburner sections were very carefully inspected. The rumor is that the safety investigation found some punctures in an area of the afterburner that hadn't burned."

"What does that have to do with the engine catching fire?" Paige asked.

"We won't know exactly what happened until the safety board finishes, but I researched some similar accident reports going back decades. It's really not that complicated."

He stood up and grabbed a marker for the dry erase board. "The afterburner section is like a tin can without a top or bottom. When the pilot wants maximum thrust, he selects afterburner on the throttle, and fuel sprays directly into the hot air flowing through the burner can." Suitor drew a diagram on the board as he spoke.

"That gives a huge increase in thrust, but it really uses up the fuel fast, so pilots only use it when they need to."

"Like on takeoff," Jackie added for Paige's benefit.

"Right, and according to the previous accident reports, if there's damage to the burner, the additional fuel used during thrust can cause the fire to burn through the engine."

He paused and saw Paige was intently waiting for more. She asked, "Would you be able to look into the engine before flying and see the damage? I've seen the pilots do their walk arounds before they start, and they always stop to look into the tailpipe."

"Excellent point, Captain," Suitor said. "Here's what's truly amazing about the big-brained engineers who designed this thing."

He turned back to the board and sketched as he talked. "The burner can is made of some strong stuff, but when it's fired up, the temperature is so high, it can burn the metal on contact."

He grabbed another color of marker for his next point. "So, the fire never actually touches the metal because the burner wall is designed to have a very small insulating layer of air." He drew an arrow to a fresh section of the white board and sketched away with more precision.

"If you look at the skin of a burner can, it's filled with perfectly designed and manufactured holes that aerodynamically produce this really thin layer of air."

Paige was starting to get the picture, but this wasn't exactly answering her question. "Okay, before you get too far into the rocket science, I still don't understand why the pilot wouldn't notice the damage."

Suitor drew a cutaway of the skin of the burner can. "This stuff is about microns of precision. In one accident, they postulated that a millimeter of imperfection disrupted the insulating blanket of air, causing that tiny defect in the metal to burn away. When the metal burned, it created more disruption, causing more burning. Finally, the super-high-pressure fire in the burner can escaped right out a huge hole!"

"Like a blow torch," Jackie said in a monotone, recalling Lopass's firsthand description.

Suitor created a red scrabble of ink over the entire collection of sketches to emphasize the catastrophic outcome.

Paige was getting it. "No one's really going to pick up on the tiny bit of damage it takes."

Suitor was proud to have enlightened her. "Yes, ma'am."

Jackie turned quiet and cold in order to only think of the physics and not of the man sitting in the cockpit a mere twenty feet from the damage Suitor illustrated. She looked down at the table. "So, this thing, the scribe is—"

"The murder weapon," Brad said. The room fell quiet as they all thought through the implications of the discovery.

Paige broke the silence. "I can't picture it."

Suitor picked up a pencil to represent the tool and carried it to the white board. He placed it as if it were on the inside of the burner can pointing outward.

"All you need to do is jump up in the burner can, put this thing into one of the holes, and tap, tap." He showed the tool now piercing the wall of the burner can sketch.

"It flares the hole out, and it's not perfect anymore. It's going to burn right there when the pilot selects afterburner."

He moved the tool several times along his sketch and at each stop he said, "Tap, tap."

Brad asked, "How long would it take to do this if it was something deliberate?"

Suitor thought for a moment, then reached for the waste basket. "Well, time me."

He inverted the waste basket and placed it by the table. "First, you need a step ladder or bucket to get into the burner. It's about this high." He motioned at mid-chest.

"You step up and crawl into the can." They all moved back a step as Suitor stepped on the waste basket and then climbed onto the tabletop on his hands and knees. He took the pencil and pretended to use a mallet to tap the scribe through the imagined skin of the can in six or seven places. He then stepped on the waste basket and jumped down to the floor.

"What did that take?"

No one had actually timed it, but Brad said, "Damn, that was less than a minute."

There was another long silence as they pensively digested the feasibility that a shop tool like this was capable of bringing down a Viper.

"Okay." Paige cleared her voice. "I've got to ask a really stupid question."

"Isn't that your job as an intel weenie?" Brad said.

Paige shoved him and challenged, "Okay, jerk. Maybe *you* can answer my question. If the pilot stops using the afterburner, does it stop burning?"

Brad surrendered with a shrug.

They turned to Suitor for some insight, and he was in deep thought gazing into the distance. "That's a really good question. I have no idea."

Paige made a face at Brad.

Suitor walked over to a shelf and slid out a thick technical manual. He sat at the table flipping through the table of contents.

"This is the pilot's F-16 manual, and in this section, you have emergency procedures. It has a section on afterburner burn-through." He paused to find the exact line. "Throttle out of afterburner." He scanned the two pages.

"Evidently, that's it. You turn the afterburner off, and the fire stops. Then you land as soon as possible. That's it."

Paige and Brad were also reading the section over Suitor's shoulder, but Jackie stayed seated at the far end of the table staring down at the floor.

Again, Paige spoke without thinking. "So why on earth didn't Stan do that?"

The heads of the two men jerked up to see Jackie's reaction, and Paige was horrified at her insensitivity. "I'm so sorry, Jackie." Paige put a hand on her shoulder.

Jackie had everything Lopass reported swirling in her head. She knew exactly why Stan failed to react to a very simple, but potentially deadly, emergency. He was completely distracted, and she knew she had been the main ingredient in Stan's distraction.

*He was tired and angry like he gets when wingmen make mistakes—when he makes mistakes. He wasn't hearing all the warnings on the radios.* Lopass expressed his frustration that Stan either had radio problems or turned things off in the endless chatter.

Jackie struggled not to tear up. She patted Paige's arm. "Let's table all that and get back to how the damage occurred." Paige gave her one more squeeze and sat on the table, dangling her feet over the edge.

"Or, who inflicted the damage," Brad suggested.

"It could still be Captain Bennett. She would know what it takes to cause damage on the inside of an engine. A hammer and scribe aren't hard to wield," Suitor said.

Jackie wasn't convinced. As much as she hated Bennett for her affair with Stan, she didn't see her capable of crashing an airplane over a breakup.

"But who left the newspaper? She wouldn't do it. Someone else must know about it," Jackie said.

"Maybe another boyfriend?" Suitor suggested.

"Why come to me?" Jackie asked. "If someone had evidence, he should take it to the authorities. Maybe this is a sick joke, as Paige said."

"Who else has access to your office?" Brad asked.

"Almost anyone in the building," Jackie said. "The files are under lock and key, but there's nothing in the office that's worth locking up. Only at night when I go home. Throughout the day, it's unlocked."

"Do you think one of your well-intentioned exercise writers was bucking for that free lunch you give out for new ideas?" Brad asked.

"I don't think any of them would be stupid enough to use Stan's accident as a starting point. Besides, they would have left me a note explaining their idea or talked to me in person. It's a competition for them. They wouldn't want anyone to poach their ideas."

Paige hadn't been in on their past speculation and was trying to catch up. "You think because Mace ended it with her, Bennett could have killed him?"

"Are you *assuming* he ended it?" Jackie asked. "I've heard rumors, but I did see them together that Friday night."

"Sorry, Jackie. I thought you knew, or I would have told you sooner." Paige gathered her thoughts. "The grapevine is that after the last deployment, Bennett went on the prowl again. The guys in the squadron were steering clear of her, so she stopped hanging out at the squadron bar. The Friday night before the accident, she showed up, drunker than a skunk. She started making a scene, egging Mace on. He wasn't rising to the bait though. She stormed out. He followed her. I think he was worried she was going to try driving like that. I didn't think much of it until now."

Jackie's face paled. Stan had tried to tell her it was a misunderstanding. He had tried to explain, but she hadn't listened.

# Chapter 45

Aashna had been puttering around in the carport. With no warning, he rushed inside, tearing cupboards open in the kitchen, looking for something. Leaving drawers wide open with contents strewn across the floor, he rushed from room to room.

Mastana's heart sunk. She knew what he was looking for. It was the tool she had taken from the air base. What were the chances? But what was done, was done.

"What are you searching for?" she asked helpfully, following him into the bedroom.

"Get out of my way!" he spat.

"I am only trying to help, Aashna."

"You can help by keeping silent!" He shoved her roughly aside.

Stumbling, she hit the wooden footboard of their bed. Seething in anger, he grabbed at her to make her stand. She slipped from his grasp.

This time, he clasped her shoulders and drove his knee into her lower chest. The crunch like a tree branch being folded in half reverberated in her ears and took her breath away. She slid to the ground, unable to breathe. He left her there.

The outside door slammed. When the sound of the car engine died away in the distance, she slowly worked herself into a sitting position. The pain was sharp, and she knew it was more broken ribs. It had happened before. The doctors would do nothing but tell her to be more careful.

Another sharp pain. Mastana tried to catch her breath, but she couldn't get enough air. The panic started to overtake her. She worked hard to control her emotions, thinking of the songs she used to sing to her son when he was small and scared.

Lowering herself back to the floor, she found a position where she breathed easier. When her heartbeat slowed to a more normal rhythm, she gently slid herself toward the bedside stand. After what seemed like agonizing hours, she reached the table. While lying on the floor, she couldn't reach the top of the table, but the white cloth she had knit so carefully to keep the lamp from marring the wood hung over the edge.

Careful not to jar her ribs more than necessary, she reached up and clasped the laced edge with her fingertips. She pulled until another stab of pain like hot steel pierced her side. She recoiled and pulled her hand back. Fabric trapped in her fist, the cloth was pulled from the tabletop, bringing the lamp and her phone toppling onto Mastana's motionless form.

She lay gasping for breath. The thought of passing out and being found by Aashna in her vulnerable state gave her the strength to continue. She seized the phone now within her reach and dialed the emergency number.

D o you think we should share this with the OSI?" Jackie asked Captain Richardson as they sat in his office. Brad was with them, ready to play his part in whatever was decided.

"Go over the conversation with me one more time," he said.

Against Brad's advice, Jackie had gone to see Bennett again on her own. As luck would have it, Bennett had recently finished her second interview with the OSI and was feeling a little nervous about the outcome. Jackie played on that and pressured her until Bennett had given her an alibi for the weekend before the crash.

"When I talked to Bennett, she admitted she had been with Colonel Carpenter the weekend before the crash," Jackie said.

"The maintenance group commander?" Richardson confirmed.

"Yep. Makes it even worse since she's in his chain of command."

"Now they're both in trouble. Adultery is bad enough. Add potential for preferential treatment and it's a slam dunk," Brad said.

"Did she say she was with him the *whole* weekend? Never snuck out to get coffee or to run home for any reason?" Richardson asked, taking notes this time.

"She didn't get that specific. She said his wife and kids were out of town, and they spent an unplanned weekend together."

"Did you confront him with this information?" asked Richardson.

Brad shook his head in disbelief. He knew the answer before she spoke. Jackie ignored him. "Of course. How else would I know if she was telling the truth?"

"Did he corroborate her story?"

"No, but the way he was acting, I know there's something to it. He was very nervous and defensive, but he didn't get angry at me. I think if he were truly innocent, he would have been threatening me with all sorts of things. I think he was more interested in convincing me, so I'd stop asking questions. He had heard about Stan and Bennett but not until after the accident. I think he knows his fling with Bennett is about to become his worst nightmare."

"Is this something OSI needs to know about?" Brad asked the lawyer.

"No. It's still hearsay. Besides, we don't want anything to help clear a suspect other than Major Austin. It'll be up to Bennett's lawyer to explain her alibi, if it comes down to that."

"What do you want me to do?" Brad asked.

"I don't think we want to mention the damage might have been done with a scribe because we certainly don't want them to know you have one in your possession, no matter how you came by it. I have it tucked away for now in the safe. We don't know for sure that it's connected with the case, so we aren't withholding evidence."

"What about the fact that the case Bennett worked on found the damage was done accidently by a maintainer?" Jackie offered.

"They should have already figured that out if they read the report Captain Brody pointed them to. It does show Captain Bennett knew how it could be done, but it also showed them how *easily* it could be done."

He consulted his notes. "You should take them a copy of the police report about the accident between Mason and Austin."

"But don't they already have that?" Jackie asked.

"Yes, but Captain Brody doesn't know they have it." He turned to Brad. "They said they wanted your help. Tell them you were looking into some things and came across the report and thought they should have it. Did you bring me a copy?"

"Yep." Brad handed Richardson a folder.

Richardson took a minute to look it over. "Major Mason told the cops who responded that Major Austin put the car in reverse instead of in drive by accident. He said the two of you," he said nodding to Jackie, "were talking. He was standing outside the car, and you were sitting in the driver's seat. When you went to leave, you didn't realize you were in reverse when you hit the gas."

"So they had no reason to insinuate I was trying to kill him!" Jackie said.

"Of course they didn't think you were trying to kill him. They wanted you to react. You did fine," Richardson assured her.

To Brad, he said, "When you're over there, see what else they're considering. Offer to get them whatever they need so we can see what they're looking for. So far, they really don't have anything."

~

Jackie sat in her living room, racking her brain over the details she knew about the crash. Her research was depressing her. She got up and poured a glass of wine. She still couldn't figure out why Stan was targeted. Or even why the F-16? Why Spangdahlem? What was important about this place?

Taking her wine glass back to the couch, she sat cross-legged and opened her laptop. She had committed all the facts she and the others had gathered to a document. Stan used to tease her about being organized. Her life hadn't seemed organized lately though. It started falling apart months ago, culminating on that horrible morning.

Everything had gone wrong. She had been fighting with Stan. She had left her line badge at home—or lost it, as it turns out. Stan's wingman had come down with the flu or something, so Stan was late taking off. She had learned this later when his scheduled wingman confessed to Jackie that he felt guilty about his role, however small, in the chaos of the morning.

The exercise she had written and planned had thrown fuel on the fire, giving everyone more distractions to deal with. Of course, that hadn't caused the crash. It was only one more factor in the mess of the day.

Maybe it was the end result of Murphy's Law.

Jackie sat up straighter. "When things seem overwhelming complicated, break them down into smaller pieces." Her dad had taught her that when he was going over case files. Her father had been a cop after serving a short time in the military. Jackie loved to listen to him talk aloud to himself as he sorted through notes and graphs. Her mother didn't approve and would shoo Jackie away from her dad's work area whenever she caught her listening.

Someone was trying to tell her something with the newspaper and the scribe. What other information was available, no matter how seemingly insignificant? Focus on the small bits. Start with the newspaper.

It was German paper anyone could get their hands on.

It was left on Jackie's desk, specifically for her to find. Why her? Because it had to do with Stan? Why not take it to the OSI? Why would the OSI care about a German newspaper? Maybe because what the paper is saying is true? It was Stan's fault?

What does the scribe have to do with it? If it was the tool, or similar to the tool, that damaged the jet, Stan wouldn't have done it. No one would think he would damage the plane and then climb into the cockpit. That made no sense.

So what was the point of leaving the scribe and the newspaper on the desk *together*? Perhaps simply to tie the scribe to the crash. Just leaving the metal rod on her desk wouldn't have meant a thing to Jackie. She certainly wouldn't have connected it to the crash. So that must be it. The newspaper was purely to link the scribe and the crash.

Okay, she felt like she was getting somewhere.

The phone rang. She felt around the couch for where it had fallen. She found it between the cushions and answered it on the fourth ring.

"Hello?"

"May I speak to Major Austin?" a voice thick with a German accent asked.

"Speaking."

"Major Austin, I am Frau Becker from Sankt Elisabeth Krankenhaus in Wittlich. I didn't know who else to call. We have a female patient here who is badly injured but won't provide me any information. She had your card with her things."

Jackie searched her mind for the name of a female airman she had given her card to recently. "Is she active duty?" Jackie asked.

"I don't believe so. I think she works on the American air base though."

The light bulb went on for Jackie. Mastana! "Give me the address. I'll come right over."

The nurse passed the information to Jackie, and she scribbled it down. She ran to the bathroom and brushed her teeth, trying to get the smell of the wine from her breath. Slipping on her shoes, she was out the door in under five minutes.

# Chapter 46

Jackie approached the hospital room with dread. She didn't know what she expected to see, but assumed it had to be pretty bad for the hospital to call her.

As she got closer, a male voice, not speaking English or German, sounded loudly from a hospital room. There was a pause as if he were waiting for an answer, then more yelling. Jackie couldn't understand the foreign tongue but caught a few English words—*F-16, hangar, flight line.* What was going on here? She peeked around the doorframe to catch a glimpse of Mastana. She looked frail and scared in her hospital gown, surrounded by monitors and connected to an IV drip.

Mastana glanced up in time to catch Jackie duck her head back. There was momentary silence before Mastana's raised voice spoke quickly in the foreign language.

Jackie heard a slap and quiet cry of alarm. Giving up all pretense of stealth, she stormed into the room. Mastana held her hand to her cheek, and her eyes were wide in surprise when Jackie rushed around the corner.

"*Wer bist du?*" the man yelled at Jackie in German. He must not have remembered their one brief encounter.

Her eyes were fixed on Mastana, searching for signs of further harm.

Switching to English, he asked again more forcefully, "Who are you, and why are you in my wife's room?"

Jackie redirected her attention to Mastana's husband and tried to stand tall with confidence. "I know Mastana from work. I heard she was here and wanted to check on her."

The man turned angrily to the woman in the bed and barked questions at her Jackie didn't understand.

"No, I did not," she answered in English for Jackie's benefit. "I do not know why she knows I am here. I told no one."

Jackie interjected. "I have another friend down the hall I was checking on. She recognized Mastana so I thought I would check on her too." She approached the bed and put her hand on Mastana's arm. Aashna moved protectively closer to the bedside.

"How are you feeling?"

"I am fine. Thank you, Mrs. Austin. I fell. Nothing to be concerned about."

"I know how that is." Jackie played along. "I can be so clumsy."

A look of relief washed over Mastana's face. "Thank you for coming."

"Take care of yourself. Nice to see you again," she said to Aashna.

As she walked away from the room, more angry whispers followed her. Her blood was boiling with anger, but she didn't know how to help.

Jackie went back to her car and sat behind the wheel. She wasn't sure what she should do next. The hospital door flew open, and a man stormed out. Jackie acted instinctively, starting her engine and waiting until he climbed into his car. She then slipped her car into gear and followed Mastana's husband.

The roads in Wittlich were lined with cars parked along both sides and plenty of traffic. It was easy to follow him without being noticed. Eventually her luck ran out, and they left the city heading toward Minderlittgen. The road was straight and not crowded. At the rate he was moving, Jackie didn't think he was taking time to look in his rearview mirror. And even if he did, the sun was low in the sky, and her headlights were on. He wouldn't be able to see past the glowing eyes of the car.

He slowed slightly as he entered another village, then made a quick right. By the time Jackie got to the corner and made the turn, his beat-up Fiat was parked on the side of the road, but its driver was nowhere in sight. Jackie pulled her car into a spot three houses before the apartment. She lowered her window a few inches and shut off the engine.

It was a nice night for April—not too hot, not chilly. Jackie sat listening to the crickets and distant music playing as she tried to decide what to do. She didn't really have a plan.

The sun was gone from the sky completely now. A door slammed, and a Mastana's husband stalked down the sidewalk and approached the Fiat. Without glancing around, he got into the car and sped away.

Without thinking, Jackie slipped out of her car and locked the door. She walked casually toward the house, glancing nonchalantly around for any neighbor who might be out enjoying the night air. It was quiet except for the occasional dog barking. Even the music had ceased. She reached the front door and knocked with confidence. She didn't expect an answer but was making a show of it.

After waiting what she felt was an appropriate amount of time, she glanced around one last time, put her hand on the knob, and turned it. It was very common to leave doors unlocked in Germany. A habit she could never quite get into. She walked through the front as if she were expected and this was the most natural thing in the world.

The lights in the front room were off, but a glow came from the back of the house. She headed that way and nearly tripped over an upturned chair protruding into the walkway.

She left the chair where it was and watched her step more carefully after that. As she looked around the room, she saw other signs of disarray, broken glass, and knocked over lamps. She shuddered when she thought of Mastana lying battered in the hospital bed.

Entering the kitchen, she glanced around. A diagram was spread out on the table. It took her a while to get her mind wrapped around why it looked so familiar. With sudden realization, she spotted the large rectangles laid out in a row like she and Senior Airman Suitor had done with the hangars when they were trying to figure out the parking of the jets. She leaned in to look closer. There were handwritten notes around the edges and arrows going different ways. The notations looked like times, but before she could study it closer, a car door slammed.

Her eyes searched for an escape. The backdoor was blocked with garbage bags. She couldn't get through without moving the bags, and there was no way to put them back so her visit would go undetected.

She moved rapidly to the only other door. Yanking it open, she slipped inside and pulled it closed behind her. It was a small pantry but there was plenty of room for her to hide if she crouched below the hanging baskets holding various vegetables. Lowering herself to her knees, she reached up with her right hand to stop the swaying of a basket she bumped with her head.

She worked to quiet her breathing and slow her heart.

Angry voices of multiple men shattered the silence as they came through the front door. One cried out loudly, and Jackie suspected he had tripped on the same chair she had discovered. Wood slid across the floor as he kicked it out of his way.

Again, Jackie couldn't make out the language the men spoke. She remembered Mastana saying her husband was

Pashtun and assumed it was his language. It sounded rough and guttural to Jackie's untrained ears.

Her heart thumped wildly. She shifted her weight and tried to push herself farther back into the pantry in case someone decided to open the door. She felt a vibration from her hip and realized with panic that her cell phone was still turned on. The men were so loud she was sure they hadn't heard the vibration, but a ringing phone would be much louder.

As quickly as she dared, she worked the phone free from the holder on her belt. She immediately punched in the password and turned the volume all the way down. She wasn't willing to shut the phone off all together. She may need it to call for help if things got any worse. She pressed the phone against her chest to eliminate the glow from the screen.

By this time, the men had made their way into the kitchen. The refrigerator door opened and closed. The click of caps hitting the floor was distinct as many bottles were opened. The talk subsided as the men guzzled their first mouthful.

Jackie flinched when something tapped the bottom of the pantry door where she hid. Looking out through the downward-angled slats of the door, she saw a bottle cap teetering to a stop on the other side.

The talk started again. Although Jackie didn't understand the words, the tone of the voices was clearly angry. That gave her an idea. She held her cell phone away from her chest only enough for her to peek at the screen. She blocked the light with her hands and her body as much as possible as she searched the menu for the right button. Then she placed the phone on the floor, using the bottom of the door to block the illumination from the screen. She held her breath and prayed.

The men's voices were growing louder, and Jackie was getting more and more frightened. There was no telling what would happen if she were caught here. Anger and testosterone were a horrible combination.

The heated voices reached a crescendo, punctuated by the sound of a body hitting a wall and the shuffle of many feet as men jumped in to break up a fight before it had a chance to get out of control.

The voices faded as the men headed toward the front room. There were a few more hurled exchanges, then the front door opened and slammed shut. Someone was still walking about the kitchen. The relative quiet was more disconcerting for Jackie then the brash voices.

A loud crash caused her to jump, and she hit her head on the basket again. Quickly she grabbed it to stop its movement. She was sure her heart could be heard now. When things quieted down again, she glanced through the slats and saw shards of bottles and the large map that was once on the table now on the floor against the kitchen wall. Because of the angle of the slats, Jackie couldn't see up, but she imagined Aashna pacing the kitchen in frustration as she listened to his heavy breathing.

The refrigerator opened again. Aashna yelled a curse and slammed the door. His curses continued as his voice faded to the front, and that door was also slammed.

Jackie counted to ten, trying to decide if it was safe to move. She gathered her phone and noticed the battery was almost dead. Carefully she pushed open the door an inch at a time. When it was quiet in the house, she crawled to the opening.

As she pushed herself to her feet, her hand knocked over a stack of rolled up tubes of paper leaning in the corner of the pantry. They looked to be about the same size as the diagram on the table. Hastily, she unrolled one. It was very similar and definitely of the base. With two hands working furiously, she rolled it up. She gathered the other rolls into her arms and started to work her way out of the closet.

On second thought, she replaced all but one roll, the one she had opened. From this many, one missing would probably go unnoticed. Having them all disappear would be suspicious.

She backed out of the pantry and closed the door. The men had left the lights on, allowing Jackie to easily navigate her way to the front door. She peeked through the glass beside the door, trying to make out any shapes lingering in the darkness. The Fiat was gone, and there were a number of empty spots on the street.

She waited a moment longer, took a deep breath, and opened the door enough to sneak through. She tried to remain calm as she walked directly to her car, not bothering to follow the sidewalk.

Her heart was pounding in her chest and a rise of panic welled within her. She didn't want to use the clicker and draw more attention with the flashing lights and small beep that accompanied the door latch being released. Her hands were shaking, and she dropped the keys as she fumbled to find the keyhole in the dark. Crying inwardly with frustration, she fell to her knees, feeling around desperately under the car with her right hand while she gripped the rolled tube in her left.

Something sharped pierced her palm, and she pulled it back quickly. Red ooze sprang from the gash in her skin. "Dammit!" She resisted the urge to wipe her hand on her jeans and stooped lower. Searching with her eyes this time, she saw light from a nearby streetlamp reflecting off the metal key ring Stan had gotten her from one of his many trips.

She snatched it as beams from headlights arched across the buildings behind her and a car turned in her direction. She averted her face and stood up quickly. This time, she was able to unlock the door on the first try.

Inside, she jammed the keys in the ignition, smearing blood on the steering wheel and gear shift. She put the car in reverse and backed up a few feet, watching the old Fiat parallel park only two spaces in front of where she sat.

Keeping her head down, she put the car in drive and pulled out as quickly as she dared. Aashna's figure moved toward the walkway carrying a six-pack of something in his left hand.

It wasn't until she was miles away from Mastana's house that she made herself pull over to stop the trembling in her hands. She wrapped her bleeding hand in fast food napkins which littered her car. One after the other quickly soaked through. She knew that probably meant stitches.

Gingerly, she put the car in gear and pointed it toward Spangdahlem.

# Chapter 47

It was late when Jackie got home from the military hospital. As she suspected, she received five stitches. They had given her mild pain relievers for the first twenty-four hours and told her to take it easy. She flexed her right hand and winced at the pain. They had numbed her hand during the stitching, but the feeling was starting to return. After struggling to open the prescription bottle with her uninjured left hand, she successfully extracted two pills, popped them in her mouth, and washed them down with a bottle of cold water from her refrigerator.

While she waited for the medication to take effect, she sat down on the couch where she had left her laptop in her hurry to get to Mastana in the hospital. She let her mind wander back to everything she had discovered. Now she had to add in the base map she had found at Mastana's house.

Why would Mastana, or more likely her husband, have maps of the U.S. airfield? Could there be a connection between his anger and Stan's accident? Or was she reaching?

Jackie knew it was a long shot but decided to see if there was anything to her hunch. Mastana said she and Aashna were from the Kandahar province in Afghanstan originally, but Mastana always seemed reluctant to talk about it.

Quickly she opened her laptop and did an internet search of the region, going back many years. There were plenty of old news articles. Many were about the good things the NATO forces were doing in Afghanstan. There were lots of pictures of soldiers with children.

Some of the left-wing newspapers ran nothing but negative articles. Jackie was surprised to see stories about villages that had been destroyed during American air raids—men, women, and children dead. The Afghan government railed against the Americans for the unnecessary violence brought upon innocents.

As with most things in the news, Jackie tried to take it with a grain of salt. Everyone makes mistakes, but she didn't believe the U.S. government would launch a strike against an entire village of innocents—not since the Vietnam days. During her time deployed for Operation ALLIED FORCE in support of Kosovo, Jackie had seen U.S. leaders turn strikes away from obvious enemy targets "just in case" there might be an innocent nearby. They had become so afraid of making an error that Jackie saw it as a sign of weakness. War was never pretty, and neither side had a sure-fire way of never making mistakes. But Jackie knew the Americans went out of their way to make the best decisions possible.

She would have to ask Mastana if she had lost her village. Maybe that's why Mastana said she had nothing to go back to. *Could it have been at the hands of the Americans?* The thought made Jackie shudder.

*Would something like that drive a need for vengeance? Was that what the sabotage of the jet was about?* Maybe Suitor was right and more jets were targeted, but the plans had been foiled. Maybe it wasn't Mastana necessarily, but any Afghans living in Germany who might have experienced some of the same heartbreak.

Was Mastana capable of doing something so terrible to Stan? Jackie hoped not. The woman might be hurting, but her eyes seemed too kind to exact vengeance on someone else. But something was going on. Jackie had to figure out what.

She did a search on Afghanstan and pulled up a site called "Afghanstan Online." She scanned through the webpage. It stated that since the fall of the Taliban, the cultural position of women has improved greatly, although they are still forced into marriages and often denied a basic education.

One sentence was highlighted inside a black border. "One in every three Afghan women experience physical, psychological, or sexual violence." Another article declared that attempted suicide for women and girls ages fifteen to forty was on the rise. Jackie thought about how sad those facts were. She was pretty sure Mastana fit into the violence statistic but hoped she wasn't part of the latter one. She would have to try again to talk to her.

In her many Air Command and Staff College classes, Jackie had learned radical groups typically targeted the poor, weak, or oppressed. Those who felt they had nothing to lose—or something to prove.

She did a search on Taliban, grateful she was on her personal computer rather than at work. The last thing she needed was the computer geeks sniffing out the word "jihad" on her search engines.

The main hits for Taliban were connected to recruiting. Jackie was disgusted as she scoured through the articles—men preying on young orphans and refugees and turning them into suicide bombers. It was horrible. They searched out the displaced, even the ones now living outside Afghanistan and Pakistan. They used the survivors' guilt many Afghans felt about having fled their homeland. They even recruited in mosques.

The internet offered a platform for reaching even more Islamic radicals than before. And it fueled them with ideas on how to seek revenge against infidels.

Jackie couldn't bring herself to watch the videos posted on YouTube. Reading about the people drawn to the cause depressed her. Many articles pointed out that for these people, there is always a feeling of alienation and of not being understood, a feeling of being shut out, and a search for recognition. She shuddered. That description fit so many people. Even Renee Bennett.

Isn't that why she acted the way she did? Constantly searching for a man to give her completeness? Still, Jackie didn't suspect her of turning to the Taliban for fulfillment. She was a slut, not a martyr.

But what about Mastana? Did she have a reason for revenge? Jackie hated to think that about her. Where did the physical violence fit in? Maybe Mastana was being forced to do things against her will. That fit more with the little Jackie knew and felt about her.

Jackie was sure Mastana knew more than she was letting on. Could that be why she was in the hospital? Jackie had tried to talk to her about the bruises on her face and was sure her husband was responsible, but Mastana wouldn't discuss it. Typical battered wife syndrome. She had known Mastana since Jackie first started working in the IG's office. She had never picked up on the signs before. Was this a new thing or had she been that unobservant? If it was new, why now?

She felt she was on to something.

What if Mastana was the one who had left the scribe on her desk? She had access to Jackie's office. She was a regular around the office, and Jackie hadn't thought much about her being there.

How could she test her theory? She wasn't sure how to proceed and didn't want to bring it up to the guys. They would think she was grasping at straws. Suitor and Brad still had their sights set on Bennett. Jackie wasn't feeling it though. She knew women in lust did some pretty stupid things, but she couldn't believe Bennett really cared *that* much for Stan. He wasn't her first and, apparently, wasn't her last. Jackie didn't see her doing something so drastic for revenge.

No, Jackie felt there was something bigger at play here. She wasn't making the leap to some grand plan to thwart a U.S. mission on foreign soil—her brainstorming with Paige had talked her out of that. But there was something more.

～

The next morning, Jackie called the office and told them she wasn't feeling well and wouldn't be coming in. Master Sergeant Reynolds assured her he would hold down the fort.

Jackie took a quick shower, careful not to get her stitches wet. Getting dressed was challenging as she favored her right hand. She would have to learn to be more ambidextrous.

Dressed in civilian clothes, she headed back to the Krankenhaus where she suspected Mastana was still recuperating. As she drove into the parking lot, she looked around for any sign of Aashna's car. It was still early, and Jackie hoped she could talk to Mastana before her husband recovered from his latest drinking binge.

The woman looked so helpless and frail under the white sheets. Her eyes were closed, and a tube under her nose helped her breathe. Jackie took a deep breath herself. She was shaking slightly as she approached the bed.

Mastana's eyes flickered a moment before opening fully. Her face registered first confusion, then recognition, and then fear as her eyes darted about the room.

"He's not here," Jackie answered the unspoken question.

Mastana relaxed slightly. "I told you I am fine. You must leave now."

"Mastana, I know your husband did this to you."

She started to deny it, and Jackie cut her off. "Don't bother. I also know he's done a lot worse." Jackie pulled her cell phone from her pocket.

Mastana's eyes rested on the phone, trying to understand Jackie's next move.

"He killed my husband," Jackie said coldly.

"He did not!" Mastana stated with as much defiance as she could muster in her condition. It wasn't very convincing.

Jackie remained silent. *Wind the clock*, she reminded herself. Now more than ever, she needed to slow herself down to ensure she didn't do or say the wrong thing.

"Why would he want to do such a thing? What did Stan ever do to him?" Jackie asked.

"What makes you think it was about your husband?" Mastana snapped.

Jackie was taken aback by the change in Mastana's demeanor. She didn't want to believe this battered woman could be involved.

"So he did do it! If it wasn't about Stan, why take out a plane? What's your husband planning?"

"What difference does it make? One man?" Mastana's face was red with anger. "You Americans kill indiscriminately. Killing from above like cowards! No care as to who gets hurt in the process."

"What are you talking about? Who got hurt? When?"

"Innocent people! Those were *my* people. My family!" Mastana tried to sit up, and the motion caused her to wince in pain.

"Your family was hurt?" Understanding dawned on Jackie—Mastana's reluctance to talk about her family or her home country. "How do you know it was the Americans? It could have been the Taliban."

"I saw them!" Mastana shouted. "They dropped their bombs from on high!" Her voice broke.

"So, to get even, you decided to take my husband?" Jackie's words were cold.

Mastana fingers sunk into the blanket at her side and replied through clenched teeth. "I did nothing."

"Then what's this all about?" Jackie pushed buttons on her phone to make the recording start. It was very quiet at first, so Jackie turned it up to full volume. It was still faint but recognizable.

When Mastana heard her husband's voice, she cried, "Where did you get this?"

Jackie ignored her question and held the recording closer to the bed. "He's talking about the base. What's he saying?"

"Why should I tell you?"

"I know you want to help me. You were the one who left the newspaper in my office."

"You have no proof."

"I understand you're having second thoughts. Did he threaten you?"

"You need to leave."

"Mastana, I can help you, but you have to help me. Tell me what he's done."

"Even if I had something that would help you, nothing good would come of it. Your husband would still be dead, and I would be sent away."

"My husband may still be dead, but what if others are killed? Do you want that?"

Jackie allowed the recording to play as she leaned into Mastana. "It wasn't only my husband who was murdered. A mother lost her innocent little girl because someone tampered with the aircraft." She pushed the stop button and slipped the phone back into her pocket.

She had struck a nerve and used it to her advantage. "That sweet girl whose only mistake was visiting her grandmother's grave at the wrong time. Now her mother will be visiting *her* grave."

Mastana's eyes filled with tears she was trying hard to hold back. Then her anger flared. "My son was also innocent when the American war planes killed him. Why is that acceptable to you?"

"It's not acceptable. No child should die."

Mrs. Austin's words caused the images of her village to flood Mastana's mind. When the Americans attacked, her settlement was not without its blame. Mastana remembered the many arguments she had had with her husband about the danger Hakimullah Mehsud's men brought to their village with their weapons. She and the other women were uncomfortable with the new arrivals and their harsh ways. At first, they claimed to only be passing through. Of course, the community welcomed them as followers of Islam. Soon it became obvious their view of Islam and Mastana's were very different.

The longer they remained, the more uncomfortable she and the other women became. Their talk poisoned the minds of the young men in the village, and the firearms they demonstrated so readily were dangerous around the children. The women often warned it would bring violence to their village someday. Mastana and the other women begged the elders to send them away. They should have listened.

She turned her face away from Jackie toward the window. "What will happen to me?"

"If you didn't have any part of this, I don't see why anything would happen to you."

"But without a husband to support me, what will I do? Where will I go?"

"There are programs in place. We'll find someone to help you." She held the phone out to Mastana again. "Now will you tell me what they're saying?"

# Chapter 48

A hundred things were running through Jackie's mind as she left the hospital. Did she have enough to take to OSI? They weren't thrilled with her investigating on her own. If this wasn't a slam dunk, would she be further jeopardizing her freedom? She needed to run this by someone to see if she had connected all the dots.

As she left the hospital, she pulled out her cell phone and searched her contacts for Captain Brody.

"Brad, it's Jackie." She couldn't keep the excitement out of her voice.

"Jackie, what's up? What did you find?"

"Can you grab Suitor and meet me at my house? I should be there in about twenty minutes. I have some stuff to show you guys."

"Will do. See you soon."

Thirty minutes later, Jackie opened the door to the eager faces of Brody and Suitor. She backed up and gave them room to enter.

"Ma'am, what happened to your hand?" Suitor asked with concern.

"Cut it on glass. Few stitches. No big deal. Come on in and grab a seat. Do you want anything to drink?"

Both gentlemen declined the offer and walked into the living room. Jackie continued to pace. She was too revved up to sit.

"Okay, spill the beans. What did you find?" Suitor asked.

"You aren't going to believe this." Jackie wasn't sure where to start. She tried to find a way to explain without wasting time on too much detail. "There's a lady who cleans the offices in the headquarters building. She came in the other day with cuts and bruises all over her face. I suspected it was from her husband and gave her my card. Yesterday the Wittlich Krankenhaus found my card in her things and called me. She was beaten pretty badly and was admitted into the hospital."

"I'm sorry she was hurt and all, but what does this have to do with the crash?" Brad asked.

"I'm getting there. So, I went to the hospital. Her husband was in the room with her, and they were fighting over something. I have no idea what they were saying because they were speaking Pashtun."

"That's from Afghanstan, isn't it?" Suitor asked.

"Yep! I picked up a couple of words that must not have a translation—F-16 and flight line."

"No shit!" Brad leaned forward in anticipation.

"Mastana's—that's the woman's name—husband seems to be a real piece of work. I heard him slap her, so I went in the room. He wasn't at all happy to see me."

"I can imagine not. Afghan men aren't overly fond of aggressive American women who get into their business," Brad said.

Jackie gave him a look meant to challenge his description of her.

He raised his hands in front of his chest, palms out in defense. "No, I think what you're doing is great. I'm fine with aggressive women."

Suitor burst out laughing as Brad tried to remove his foot from his mouth.

Jackie went on. "Mastana wasn't happy to see me either. Apparently, I wasn't supposed to see the family squabble. I didn't make a big deal of it and got out as soon as I could. While I was sitting in my car trying to decide what to do, her husband came out."

"Don't tell me!" Brad groaned.

"What?"

"You followed him, didn't you? Suitor asked.

"Of course. I don't know why. I was curious."

Brad threw his hands up in the air. "Why didn't you call one of us?"

"And tell you what? I hadn't even made the connection yet. At least not all the way. I had an inkling, but that was all."

"So, what did you find?" Suitor asked.

"I followed him to his house. He went in and came out. I decided to take a look around."

"I can't be hearing this," Brad moaned.

"Relax. I went through the front door—it was unlocked. Look what I found on the table!" Jackie grabbed the roll of paper from behind the door where she had left it. "Well, it wasn't this one exactly, but one very similar. What does it look like to you?"

They both studied the map. Brad was the first one to recognize it. "It's the base. What are they doing with base maps? They aren't for public use."

Jackie shrugged. "I have an idea. The one I saw had handwritten markings on it." She looked at Suitor. "Kind of like when you and I were tracking the placement of the aircraft before the accident."

Suitor's eyes got wide. "Are you kidding me?"

"Nope. I didn't get a chance to study it more closely because Mastana's husband returned with some friends."

Brad dropped his head into his hands.

Jackie saw him and quickly added, "I had a chance to hide though. There was a pantry off the kitchen, and I ducked in there. I couldn't see anything, but I heard three or four men talking. It wasn't in English."

"That doesn't really help then, does it?" Suitor asked.

She pulled out her cell phone and tapped buttons to get to the recording. She set it to full volume and pushed play. After a few minutes, she shut it off. Both men looked confused.

"So?" Brad asked. Neither of them understood Pashtun.

"So, I went back to see Mastana in the hospital—"

"Wait a minute," Suitor interrupted. "How did you get out of the house without them seeing you?"

"I waited for them to leave, and then I walked out the front door." She waved a hand dismissively. "That's not important."

Somehow, Brad wasn't convinced they were hearing the whole story, but he let it slide for now. "Okay, go on."

"Let me back up a minute. There were a bunch of these maps in the pantry, so I took one. I figured no one would miss one out of the group. I left the one in the kitchen because I figured that would be noticed if it turned up missing.

"So anyway, I went back to see Mastana this morning. She didn't want to help me at first. She's scared. I convinced her to listen to the recording, but when she started to translate it, she got really spooked and clammed up totally. I was right; her husband is the one hurting her. Brad, if she helps us, do you think we can get her assistance somehow? I'm not sure how that works."

Brad thought about it. "It depends on what she knows and what she does to help. That's out of my league, but we can ask your lawyer. What did she tell you?"

"She interpreted some of the recording for me. The men were arguing about the night of the crash."

"What was the plan?"

"She wouldn't give me details. She kept saying her husband would kill her if he knew she was talking to anyone."

Suitor asked, "Now what do we do?"

"We take all this to OSI," Brad stated emphatically. "Enough playing Nancy Drew."

Jackie nodded. "Why don't you two take the recording to Agent Marquette? I'll go by the hospital and see if Mastana is well enough to leave yet. If I can convince her to come, we'll need her to tell the OSI what she knows."

"I'll come with you," Brad said.

"No. She'll feel safer if it's just me. She's not likely to feel comfortable around men right now."

Brad and Suitor stood up together. Jackie handed Brad her phone. "I took off the password." She handed Suitor the map. "Take this too. It isn't a smoking gun, but it might make them listen to you."

# Chapter 49

Jackie pulled out of the driveway right behind the guys. They headed toward the base, and she peeled off toward Wittlich. So many questions. She had to remind herself over and over to wind the clock. She wouldn't get to the hospital any quicker by worrying.

She marched directly up to the nurses' station. *"Guten Tag,"* she said to the nurses with a smile. "I'm here to see Mastana again."

The nurse had a concerned expression on her face. "I wish I could help you," she said in heavily accented English. "Frau Mastana is no longer with us."

Jackie's heart sank. "What do you mean?"

"We went to serve her dinner, and she was gone. She didn't sign the release papers. The doctor is worried because she was very severely injured. She needs further care."

Jackie felt sick. "I'll see if I can find her." Mastana's statement that her husband would kill her rang in Jackie's ears.

"If you do, please convince her to come back."

"I will."

Jackie raced out of the hospital and jumped in her car. She reached into her pocket for her phone to call Brad then remembered he had her phone. "Dammit," she cursed under breath.

~

"Y ou have to be shitting me!" Marquette exploded at Emily Wright. He wanted nothing to do with another visit from Captain Brad Brody. It was clear to Marquette that Brody had gone over the wall into Jackie Austin's court. "You tell them to take whatever they have from Major Austin and get out!"

Wright bolted out of his office to deliver the message.

Marquette was as tense as he'd ever been on a case. He was exasperated that every piece of evidence they gathered against his prime suspect still left a small black hole at the center of the investigation. He could show how all the pieces implicated Major Austin—but only implicated.

She had made threats; there was a motive; there were tasty morsels of evidence. She was also conducting one of the most vigorous campaigns he'd ever seen a suspect perpetrate to point the finger anywhere else. She and her cop buddy had created a number of rabbit holes he was obligated to squat down and look into.

He was certain she was a scorned, angry widow and the killer of a U.S. fighter pilot, but he couldn't get anything to stick to her—the smoking gun, so to speak. It was keeping him up at night because it was all so crystal clear in his mind. She was the one, but he couldn't wrap it up tightly.

Marquette jolted at the noise of a scuffle and shouting in the bullpen. He knew his people could handle Captain Brody and was not about to get sucked into their squabble.

Finally, Agent Ramirez shouted over the din. "Okay! Okay! We'll listen to the damn phone!"

Marquette was pissed that Ramirez went against his orders to kick Brody out of the building. It burned him, and he stormed out to take charge. He kicked the security door open and found himself facing almost every member of the organization, either standing in the bullpen or craning from the hallway to see the dust-up. Ramirez was gone, leaving Wright standing between Marquette and the duo of Brody and a senior airman. The scene was incredibly unprofessional. Without a word, Marquette motioned for the two outsiders to follow him.

Captain Brody tried to talk, but Marquette shushed him until they were behind his softly closed door.

"What the hell do you think you're doing coming into my office like this!" Marquette exploded.

"If you would just listen to what I have to tell you! You've been going about this the wrong way," Brody shot back.

"You are so far up Austin's ass, I'm beginning to think maybe her husband wasn't the only one having an affair!"

Brody shook his head in disgust. "And you are so bloody arrogant, you only see what you want to see!"

Suitor jumped in. "We brought something—"

"Airman, you have no place here. Keep your mouth shut. I'll let you know when we need your interference." Marquette's sharp words froze Suitor in his tracks.

"Again, your arrogance is talking." Brody took the paper from Suitor's hand and began to roll out the map Jackie had seized. Marquette waved it away.

"What you don't get, Captain Brody, is that I have been an investigator for twenty years. I've seen it all. And I'm good at what I do. Major Austin's little act is not sucking me in like it has you!"

A sharp series of three raps of hard knuckles against his door stopped them both. Before he responded, the door swung open. George Ramirez was holding Jackie's phone, and he had a very nervous second lieutenant at his elbow. Agent Wright was on his heels.

"Boss, you need to hear what's on Austin's phone," Ramirez said with a tremor in his voice.

"Agent Ramirez, I can't believe you can't follow simple orders. I want all of this out of here!"

"No, boss, you need to listen." Ramirez placed the phone on the edge of Marquette's desk and motioned the nervous lieutenant over to him.

Marquette was incredulous. "Get the hell out of here!"

"Chris!" Ramirez shouted. "Get a grip! You were wrong! We were all wrong!"

Marquette was stunned into silence that his subordinate spoke so insolently. He threw up his hands to accede to whatever Ramirez intended to show him.

"This is Lieutenant Sameer Durrani. He's our computer network manager. Turns out, he also speaks Pashtun and is able to translate this recording. It's bad. These guys are talking about our F-16s." Ramirez paused and again tried to swallow. "They're all jaw-jacking about having sabotaged one of our F-16s. They intended to do a lot more."

Marquette cut him off with a guffaw of disbelief at Ramirez's sudden conversion. "Really? You really think Jackie Austin just happened to record that? A bunch of terrorists sitting around the campfire? Really? It doesn't seem odd to you that the killer somehow recorded that?"

The room was stone silent. Wright's mouth was hanging open. Ramirez showed shock at Marquette's unprofessional outburst in front of the others.

"Sir, we are in the middle of an investigation, and we have not determined that anyone is a killer." For the second time, Marquette was stung by Ramirez, but also cringed at his loss of poise in front of Brody and the senior airman.

Ramirez turned to Lieutenant Durrani and handed him the phone. "Sameer, you take control. Let it play as long or short as you like. Then stop it and translate for us. Also, try to give us a feel for how they are expressing themselves, emotion and emphasis, if you understand what I mean."

"Yes, sir."

As Sameer started and stopped the tape many times, Marquette slowly took his seat. He lowered his head into his hands as he listened.

After the lieutenant translated the segment about the flight line, Brody jumped in. "That's what I was trying to show you!" He snatched the map from where it had fallen to the floor and unrolled it in front of Marquette. He tapped his finger at the places mentioned by the voices Sameer translated.

As Sameer began the recording again, Suitor pointed out various areas as they were mentioned. Marquette somberly gazed at the chart and looked wherever Brody and Suitor pointed.

"'The wife of that pilot is searching around,'" Sameer translated. "'She was in my wife's hospital room.' The next man says, 'What are you going to do about her?' The first man answers, 'I will get rid of her. She is a mere woman. Accidents happen.' The men laugh." Sameer listened intently. "Now they are discussing drinking."

"Okay, okay, stop!" Marquette ordered in a strained whisper. Sameer paused the recording.

Marquette's thoughts were racing. What had he done? *She's playing with fire, and I pushed her into it,* he thought. As he tried to figure out how to salvage the investigation, he looked vacantly at the others in the room.

He stopped mid-thought and swung his head back at Brody and Suitor. "Where is Major Austin? How did she get this recording?"

Suitor and Brody looked at each other, not sure how much to tell.

"Dammit! Now is not the time to hold back on me!" Marquette yelled. "Where is she right now?"

"She went back to the hospital to talk to the wife of the guy on this recording," Brody said.

"What guy? Who's the wife? Who are they?" Marquette said, reaching for the phone on his desk. Suddenly, Marquette was in emergency mode.

Brody and Suitor exchanged glances again. "She didn't give us any names. She just told us to bring you the recording," Suitor said.

Marquette's career was flashing before his eyes. He had never even considered an outsider for this case. "Well, call her! Does she even know they are on to her?" He thrust the phone toward Brad.

"Ah, Agent Marquette," Suitor said. "Major Austin made the recording on her cell while hiding in a closet. That's her phone."

Marquette's urgency about Jackie's safety had energized Brad. "Have one of your agents call the hospital and explain we are looking for Major Austin who is visiting a local woman who works on the base."

Ramirez was writing notes as Brad spoke. "Which hospital?"

"Wittlich," said Suitor.

"Suitor, what the hell was her name?" Brody snapped his fingers in an effort to remember.

"It was Mastana, I think. I don't know her last name. She cleans Major Austin's office. She was able to interpret the recording, so she's probably Afghan."

Marquette couldn't believe what he was hearing. Major Austin had pulled all this together while he was only looking at her!

Ramirez bolted to the phone and dialed the operator. "This is Agent Ramirez with Air Force OSI, I need you to connect me with Wittlich Krankenhaus. Hospital security."

He turned to Brody. "Can you spell the lady's name?"

"M-A-S-T-A-N-A, I think," Brody said.

Ramirez rolled his eyes as he explained the urgency to a German officer who answered. He apologized for only having a first name but emphasized his need to find Jackie Austin. When he finished, he left his phone number and asked that the officer call him back as soon as possible.

With a bellow down the hallway, Ramirez retrieved another agent. "Call contracting and find out who cleans the IG offices where Major Austin works. We need everything we can get on a worker named Mastana; that's all we know. We need this pronto, got it? Stay on the line with them."

Marquette picked up the phone and dialed the command post. "This is OSI. Patch me through to the wing commander now." Marquette grimaced knowing there would be an accounting of why he ignored this possibility for two months.

To his surprise, the commander picked up the line in two rings.

"Sir, this is Agent Chris Marquette in OSI." Without waiting for formal niceties, he pressed on. "We have a recording that indicates individuals in the local area were associated with the loss of our F-16. I recommend—"

"What the hell? Where's this coming from?"

"Sir, we can brief you immediately. I recommend a level three recall of the Battlestaff, and we need the Threat Working Group assembled."

"Is there an immediate threat?" the wing commander asked.

"We don't know if there's an impending threat to aircraft at this time." Marquette paused for a second, wiping sweat that glistened across his forehead. "Although we are trying to locate Major Jackie Austin. I believe she's in danger. She recorded several individuals discussing the details of the sabotage and if she runs into them again it may become violent."

"You said Austin was behind this!"

Marquette squeezed his eyes shut and said in a tight voice, "Yes, sir. Austin *was* our prime suspect."

The wing commander's silence was deafening. Then in a cold calm voice, he said, "So you were wrong about Austin."

Marquette clenched his free hand into a fist as he spoke. "Yes, sir, I was evidently very wrong."

Brody grabbed his hat and tapped Ramirez on the shoulder. "I'm on my way to pick up the trail at the hospital. Tell them we'll be there in ten minutes. Suitor's coming with me."

"You have no jurisdiction in town. You can't do anything," Wright reminded him.

"I can find Jackie!"

Marquette hung up the phone and grabbed Brody by the sleeve. "I'm going to meet you wherever Austin is when you find her. Call me on my cell." He shoved a business card in Brody's hand.

"Got it."

Marquette pushed Brody and Suitor through the door. "Emily, get ready to be me. You're going to brief the Battlestaff in thirty minutes. The commander won't be happy I'm not there, but I've got to find Austin."

Wright nodded.

He continued to bark out orders. "Sameer, you need to make a quick list of the key points of the conversation and make a separate section about how you interpreted their tone. Then make a copy of the recording. Use my desk and don't lose Austin's phone." He swept away the papers on his desk and pulled the chair back for Sameer to get him on the task.

Marquette rushed to the door and called for two more agents. To one, he directed, "Initiate a BOLO for Major Jackie Austin. She may be in danger. Make sure everyone understands she is *not* a threat. Search everywhere within fifty miles of the base. Get the F-16 squadron to help if you need more manpower.

Call the unit commander. Tell them to take no unnecessary risks; locate her and contact the Battlestaff coordinator."

The "be on the lookout order" would get the maximum response from the military police. It would be sent out over the base police scanners and also passed along to the German police.

Marquette grabbed a file folder spilled on the floor and pushed it into the chest of the waiting agent. "The top pages have all her information. Now go!" The man fled the office, reading through the papers on the way.

Ramirez's phone rang, and he put it to his ear, covering the other with his hand.

Marquette then huddled with the other agent. "When Sameer is done with that phone, have him send you the recording. It goes to linguistics for a complete translation and analysis. Got it?" Marquette sent him away and shouted at Ramirez.

"George, what are they saying?"

"They're asking around the hospital now; nothing yet. I'm on the line with security. I told them our security forces are on the way."

"Okay, when Brody gets there, hand it off to him."

"Roger, boss."

Wright was already filling in a standard briefing form with a marker pen. Marquette sat next to her and engaged in a rapid-fire drafting of what Emily would brief the commander. They reviewed a page of quickly prepared notes written by Sameer. It was clear and concise. He may need to recruit Sameer from fixing email accounts to being one of his investigators.

With only minutes to spare before their meeting with the commander, Wright and Sameer gathered the last of their notes and bolted for the command center.

Marquette donned his shoulder holster and stood in front of the window. The entire area was abuzz with agents absorbed with the task of locating Major Austin and the cleaning woman only known as Mastana. His stomach was a hollow pit as the entire reality of his slanted investigation was in full view. He wished there was a sniper waiting to take him out to spare him from the questions he would have to answer later.

This was exactly what he hated most in one of his junior investigators—a closed mind caused by arrogance.

"You arrogant piece of shit," he hissed at himself. He spoke to his vague image in the glass. "Jackie Austin better not get hurt in this fiasco."

# Chapter 50

Jackie pulled up in front of Mastana's house. This time she didn't bother trying to be inconspicuous. She marched up to the front door and was about to knock when she heard a crash. She steeled herself and looked around. There was no one on the street at this time of night, and she didn't know who to trust anyway. If she left to get help, Mastana might suffer the consequences.

With a silent prayer, she grabbed the door handle. Like the previous evening, it was unlocked and turned easily in her grasp. She pushed open the door and walked in.

Marquette and Ramirez were speeding along the road to Wittlich when Marquette's cell phone rang. Ramirez answered.

Without preamble, Brody said, "The nurse said they had a Mastana, but she has gone missing. There was an American service woman here looking for her too. When they told her the woman was gone, the American raced out after her."

"Did you get the patient's address at least?" Ramirez asked.

Brody read it off. "It's in Minderlittgen. We'll meet you there."

"Wait!" Ramirez yelled at them. "You aren't going anywhere. We don't have jurisdiction. You don't know what you're getting into."

"You've backed Jackie into this corner, and she's strongheaded enough to confront him on her own if she thinks Mastana is in danger. We need to get her to wait for reinforcements," Brody said. "We'll go to the woman's house. We're closer."

"There's nothing that says Major Austin is there."

"Then there won't be any danger." Brody hung up.

"Damn it, Chris! Brody might be a cop, but that airman he's dragging along with him isn't!"

Marquette fumed. There was no way to make this situation any better. "We have to trust them for a change."

～

Enraged yelling echoed out of the kitchen. Jackie crept toward the sound, trying to make out how many people might be in the house. Aashna ranted nonstop in Pashtun. She thought she could make out Mastana's voice, much weaker and breathless. She was clearly in pain and pleading.

Jackie jumped as something heavy landed on the floor with a mighty crash. She threw caution to the wind and rushed through the doorway of the kitchen, her heart pounding wildly in her chest.

Mastana was lying on the ground, bleeding from her mouth. She clutched at her ribs, struggling to breathe. Aashna stood over her, raising his foot to stomp on her head.

Instinctively, Jackie lunged across the broken debris and struck Aashna low in a tackle. Catching him by complete surprise, he was forced backward. Their combined weight carried them over the kitchen table, and they landed in a heap on the floor, Aashna breaking Jackie's fall.

As she struggled rise, Jackie grasped the counter above to pull herself to her feet. One hand found a water-soaked rag, which she tossed angrily in Aashna's face. The other hand reflexively gripped the first thing it found—the handle of a wide drawer. Unfortunately, the drawer offered no resistance, breaking free from its stops. Jackie lost her balance and toppled over Aashna's legs, smashing into the stove. The drawer's entire contents of utensils and cutlery rained down on top of them with a deafening clatter.

Initially stunned by Jackie's explosive attack, Aashna recovered quickly. As Jackie rolled onto her hands and knees to scamper free from their entanglement, Aashna grabbed the back of her shirt. With one hand, he slammed her into the cupboards. The force of her head cracking against the wood filled her vision with sparks, then darkness. Her hearing cut to complete silence for a second before returning with a high-pitched hum.

When she could see again, she was on her back staring up into the red, puffing face of Mastana's husband. He was on his hands and knees beside her, eyes bulging and rage coursing through his entire body.

"Stupid bitch," he hissed through clenched teeth. Bloody spittle landed on her face. "I'll kill you!" He pressed down on her neck with one hand as he cocked the other fist back.

As she raised her arms to shield her head from the blow Aashna was about to unleash, Jackie caught a glimpse of movement to her left. Mastana scrambled to her feet. Unsteadily, she lifted a wooden chopping block above her head and brought it down on Aashna's back.

It was just enough to distract his swing at Jackie's head. Now Mastana was bracing herself against the counter, trying to catch her breath.

Aashna cried out something in Pashtun. Mastana flinched, and Jackie guessed the intent. He turned, still on his knees, and scooped one arm around Mastana's legs, jabbing a fist upwards to her abdomen. Jackie got to her feet as Mastana's eyelids flickered and her eyes rolled skyward. She slumped lifelessly to the floor.

"You bastard!" Jackie screamed.

Aashna swung around at Jackie's words. Diving forward onto his belly, he reached for her closest ankle. He sunk his fingers into the soft upper leather of her boot, cementing her foot to the floor. She braced herself against the countertop. Concentrating her strength into a kick, she drove her free foot into his right cheek.

His neck snapped back and blood burst from his nose. His hands flew to his face, releasing his hold on her. Jackie lost her balance and fell hard onto her back in the narrow space between the stove and the island cabinet. Aashna cursed with a long growling howl as a stream of blood poured through his fingers and onto his stained t-shirt.

Jackie struggled like a drunk to get to her feet and maneuvered to place the kitchen island between her and her attacker

Suddenly he grew quiet and lowered his hands. With his chest heaving and dark blood dripped freely from his chin, he said in a low voice, "No more games, *da spi zo*. I will finish you now as I did your husband."

"You miserable piece of shit!" She inched her way around the island toward the door.

Aashna circled the opposite way to stop her. "*Spei*! You know nothing!"

"I know you are an ignorant coward!"

"I am not stupid. *I* am the brains!"

"It doesn't take brains to beat a woman," Jackie spat.

He released a deranged laugh. "This isn't about some insignificant woman."

Jackie made a move toward the hallway.

Aashna once again blocked her path. "That airplane crash? Do you really think it was an accident? *I* am the one who decided what needed to be done. Your foolish pilots talk too much about their unbeatable machines! *I* beat them with very little effort!" With blood running from his nose and across his lips, he spattered crimson as he spoke.

Jackie's head spun. Aashna worked on base. *Where?*

"So cocky are they. Their arrogance makes them sloppy."

She searched the room wildly, looking for an opportunity. "You couldn't get close to a pilot if you wanted to. You're all talk."

Aashna struck out with a fist, but Jackie dodged just in time.

"I hear them babbling on their way to the jets. If not about flying, it is about women they bed. They are the ones with simple minds!"

*Did Aashna drive the truck the pilots took to their jets?* That meant he had a line badge!

He attempted another grab across the island. "Your aircrafts are not that special. It only takes a small puncture made by a fifty Euro awl to turn a fifty-million-dollar airplane into a pile of flaming rubble." His face was scarlet, and his nose continued to ooze dark liquid onto his shirt.

Jackie feinted one way, then made a bolt toward the door, but Aashna's leg shot out and tripped her.

She stumbled and Aashna caught her right arm, yanking her to her feet. She tried to push him away, but his strength was overpowering. Holding her upper arms, he drove her back against the kitchen wall, knocking the wind out of her. While she was still reeling, he hoisted her across his hip in a judo-like throw to the ground.

She landed in a grotesque, twisted heap and the tendons in her left knee let out a sickening muffled pop. As he approached again, she tried to kick at him with her other leg, but Aashna easily brushed her weak efforts aside. He pinned her down, straddling her body and wrapped his fingers around her throat. She pounded ineffectually at his arm and shoulder.

Jackie was in a mindless panic. She switched tactics and tried to dig her fingernails into his arms, but his sleeves were too thick. She clawed at his hands. The stink of his exhale infected her last breaths.

A dark tunnel filled her vision. She couldn't resist. It was impossible. There was no way out. This was her end. She stopped struggling and her hands hit the floor.

An image of Stan flashed through Jackie's mind. It was so vivid. He had cracked open the chilled Jeremiah Weed and was in a preaching mood. She heard his voice in her ears, and it was startlingly real.

The young lieutenants were standing in a close circle, and as he spoke, they hung on to his every word and movement. "Imagine being beaten in air combat. Your opponent has outmaneuvered you and is camped at your six o'clock. All he needs to do is get you to run out of airspeed and ideas so he can put his pipper on your canopy, squeeze the trigger, and turn you into a fireball. Imagine getting to the point that he's got the advantage, and he's waiting. You've ripped and strained every muscle in your body. You're soaked with sweat. You're gasping for air. You're exhausted from jinking your aircraft up and down, left and right. There's no way out."

The lieutenants waited for his revelation.

"We've been trained to respond to things we expect to happen. What about all the things we haven't been specifically trained to handle? In those cases, all you have is your ability to think." He tapped a finger to his right temple. "The best way to think is to slow yourself from the panic of certain doom; trust your training, trust your instincts, and trust yourself."

Stan was never so handsome as when he was like this.

"Warriors don't die as quitters or like squawkin' chickens. They might die, but they die with a cool head, thinking of how to survive until the last microsecond of life. As long as you keep thinking, you might find the edge, the way out, the advantage. But you have to breathe. You have to continue to move forward, even if you're scared as hell."

Jackie wanted to reach out and touch him.

"Warriors call that courage. It's not the absence of fear; it's the ability to act despite fear. We are American Airmen. Our DNA is about never quitting, never giving up."

Jackie felt the pain of Aashna's grip tighten as Stan spoke the words of the Airman's Creed. He hoisted his shot glass. "I'm an American Airman. I will not falter, and I will not fail."

The vision faded.

She was back on the kitchen floor, something cold burning against her lifeless hands. Her fingers searched, each hand finding a metal utensil. Summoning all her remaining strength, she swung first one arm, then the other, toward Aashna's face. A fork dug deeply into his left cheek until it would go no deeper. On the right, a knife pierced through his eye and embedded into the bone of the socket.

Aashna screamed and fell away, his hands furiously trying to wrench the utensils from his face to stop the pain.

Jackie scrambled to get free from him, gagging and sputtering as she strained to get oxygen to her brain. She tried to stand, but her damaged leg buckled beneath her, and pain racked her body. She reached high to the countertop and hoisted herself onto her good leg.

She was horrified at the sight of Aashna. He had pulled the fork from his cheek but had not been able to remove the object from his eye. His face was ghoulishly swelling as blood ran savagely from the socket.

But he was not done. Blindly, he searched the floor around him. His hand landed on the handle of a butcher's knife. Before he secured a grip, Jackie was on him, pushing the knife out of his reach as he collapsed onto his back. She placed one hand firmly in the center of his chest and pressed herself upward, her left leg useless behind her. With her right fist, she landed a punch square on Aashna's jaw that extracted another scream of anguish.

His hands tried to push her aside, but she screamed obscenities as she continued to land solid punches to the side of his head and neck until he ceased moving. Crippled and panting, she gazed into his deformed face. Then she lifted her fist to deliver another blow.

"Jackie!!"

She felt herself being lifted into the air as her name was shouted repeatedly by the voices of her allies. Suitor held her upright in his arms as Brody kicked every sharp object away from Aashna's unmoving body. He stooped to check for a pulse.

"Did she kill him?" Suitor asked anxiously while trying to assess the extent of damage to Jackie's blood-soaked body.

Brody did a quick assessment of the scene as his fingers waited for some sign of life. With a tone of disappointment, he pronounced, "Nope, he's alive."

"Mastana," Jackie said weakly.

Suitor eased Jackie down on the floor beside Mastana's still form. Mastana was barely conscious, but when Jackie took her hand, Mastana began muttering, "He did it, he did it, he did it."

Jackie shushed her. "It's okay now, Mastana. We're safe. You're safe. He can't hurt you anymore."

Mastana tried to say something else. Jackie wiped the blood from her brow. "You were so brave. You saved me. Thank you for being there for me."

The murmurs of the moment were cut short by the sudden arrival of Marquette. He was flanked by Ramirez and three German police officers who had unnecessarily kicked down the unlocked front door. They were frozen with their weapons drawn and pointing toward the ceiling, not knowing who the aggressor at the scene was.

∿

Marquette was stunned. The kitchen was a wasteland of breakage and debris. Blood was painted across every surface. He was shocked by the limp, gruesome figure at Brody's feet with a metal object protruding from his eye. Several feet away, Jackie Austin was covered with blood from her hair to her boots. She was stroking the forehead of another woman also spattered with blood.

Brody barked at the men Marquette had brought with him. "Stop, stop, stop, we're good! This one." He pointed at Aashna.

Marquette nodded, and the policemen holstered their weapons. One pulled out his handcuffs and forced Aashna's limp wrists into them. Another spoke rapidly into a radio, calling for an ambulance. The third dropped to his knees beside Mastana to assess her injuries.

Suitor and Brody lifted Jackie gingerly and guided her to a nearby kitchen chair that had been knocked askew in the tussle.

A faint moan came from Aashna. Jackie lunged in his direction. Brody and Suitor held her firmly in the chair. When the tension drained from her, the men tried to get her to her feet and out of the room.

She cringed. "Please, leave me here." She was pale and shaking. Suitor rummaged through cupboards until he found glasses. Efficiently, he filled one with water and handed it to Jackie.

"Water, that's it? After all this?" Jackie whispered in a hoarse voice. Gazing wearily into Suitor's eyes, she managed a ghost of a smile.

He smiled back and knelt beside her, placing his arm gently around her shoulder.

Ambulances arrived, sirens blaring.

Marquette knelt beside Mastana, taking notes furiously in small book he pulled from his jacket pocket as she muttered words in a weak voice.

Brad rested his hand on Jackie's shoulder and followed her gaze. "She's going to be okay," he reassured her.

The paramedics arrived, but Jackie refused to be seen until Mastana had been loaded onto a gurney and escorted safely away.

Next, Aashna was loaded onto a stretcher and strapped down tightly. A police officer stayed by his side the whole time.

Then it was Jackie's turn. A gurney was pulled in close, and the paramedics gently lifted her onto the cool white sheets. She laid her head back and sank into the pillow. Suitor held her hand while a medic gave her a shot of something to ease the pain.

Brad glanced around, taking in the devastation. He looked at Suitor. "I will never cross this woman."

Suitor grinned and shook his head in astonishment. "Me neither."

Marquette barked orders to Ramirez, trying to gain some control of the situation. Ramirez left obediently to call the command post and try to explain the unexplainable.

Only then did Marquette approach Jackie. He struggled for words as Suitor and Brad watched him. Placing a hand on Jackie's forearm, he said, "Seems you're pretty handy in the kitchen." He forced a laugh at his impromptu humor.

Jackie ignored him. She looked to her left where Brad and Suitor stood protectively. "Thanks for believing in me, guys," she said dreamily as the pain killer kicked in.

After the paramedics lifted her gurney, Marquette took another stab to break through Jackie's wall. "If you ever need a job, OSI can use a sleuth like you, Major." He patted her on the arm.

She slapped his hand away. "Kiss my ass."

Marquette tried to recover some of his dignity. "You still have a lot to answer for."

"Let's think about this." Brad tapped his head as if searching for something profound that was eluding him. "She cracked your case, caught your killer, nearly got killed doing *your* job, cleared her name, beat the shit out of a guy twice her size, and possibly uncovered a ring of terrorists." He paused for effect. "I think she's answered enough, don't you?"

# Epilogue

Jackie sat out on the deck of her house, looking over the cemetery. It was a beautiful German day, white puffy clouds drifting effortlessly overhead. She would miss this place when her assignment was over and it was her turn to head back to the States. Although she had to admit she was ready to start over. As she reached for her bottle, a sharp pain jolted in her knee, and she yelped. Suitor responded like a galley boy and worked to perfectly adjust the pillow under her braced knee lying across an ottoman.

"Better, now?" he asked.

"For now, thanks. Can't wait for the physical therapy phase."

Both Brad and Suitor had been sitting quietly with Jackie, sipping their beer. The events of the last few months would forever link them together, and she was totally at peace in their presence. She closed her eyes for a moment and enjoyed feeling a swirl of warm wind caress her face.

"What did OSI find at the house?" Suitor asked Brad.

Brad took another swallow before answering. "The stack of base maps Jackie told us about—including the one with the handwritten notes. There were markings indicating ramp locations and times. Even the perimeter fence in base housing that was cut was highlighted on the map."

Jackie nodded but didn't speak.

"There were a few other ramp spaces underscored. When compared to the layout of the F-16 parking you two came up with the weekend prior to the accident, they matched. The OSI thinks the intent was to damage more planes, but Aashna was interrupted. Seems like his cohorts got cold feet and bailed on him."

"It could have been a lot worse." Suitor instantly regretted his words and glanced at Jackie.

She nodded again and opened her eyes to gaze at the peaceful countryside. "We were lucky," she agreed. "I wouldn't want anyone else to have to go through what I'm going through now."

"Did they get the other guys?" Suitor asked.

"Aashna wouldn't give names, but Mastana did. The German Politzei rounded them up with no trouble. The Germans are working with the base on extradition."

"How did the guy get on the flight line?" Suitor asked. Jackie had already made the connection but let Brad answer.

"You won't believe this." Brad added a dramatic pause until Suitor turned from the view to look at him. "Aashna is the guy who drives pilots to their jets." Brad gestured with his beer as if the runway was lying at their feet.

Suitor's eyes widened, and he shook his head at the impossibility of it all. Jackie marveled at the fact that Stan's killer might have actually driven him out to the jet. It was too heavy an image to verbalize aloud in the restfulness of the moment.

They lapsed into a comfortable silence.

"Whatever happened to Captain Bennett?" Suitor asked, breaking the quiet again.

Brad looked over at Jackie to see if she would respond.

Eventually she sighed and took another long drink. "She'll get an article fifteen for conduct unbecoming an officer. Her career is over."

Article 15 actions were a kiss of death. It was broad enough to cover almost any incident and a catch-all when adultery, fraternization, or disobedience of military orders was involved.

"Did OSI find out about Colonel Carpenter?" Brad asked.

"Not from me. It seems that once word got out about Bennett and Stan, the gossip vine bled out with her many, many relational . . . ahhh." Jackie was searching for an appropriate euphemism.

Suitor jumped to her rescue. "Adventures?"

They all laughed quietly.

"Yes, relational adventures," Jackie concurred, and they all took a swig in unison.

"Carpenter's retiring," Jackie went on.

"They aren't going to bust him?" Suitor asked.

"Nope." Brad took another drink. "It's easier on the Air Force to let him retire, and then they don't have to deal with the court martial and paperwork."

"That's bullshit."

"Yep," Jackie agreed.

~

Jenn and Margaret took turns checking on Jackie and bringing her food. She was on convalescent leave until her knee healed to a point where she could more easily get around.

Margaret had checked on Mastana and reported back to Jackie that she was also healing. The American and German lawyers were working together, and there was no threat of Mastana being deported. She would probably lose her job because she had broken into the HAS and stolen from the U.S. government. The social workers on base were working to ensure she received proper counseling for the abuse she endured. She would have to testify against Aashna in court though. Jackie hoped she was strong enough.

As Jenn puttered around downstairs, Jackie ventured back into her room. She had been putting off the inevitable. With a heavy heart, she opened a cardboard box and put it on the bed. She hobbled on crutches to Stan's wardrobe and let her hand rest on the heavy German key a moment before turning it.

When she opened the doors, Stan's scent floated out. Jackie's heart skipped a beat, and she willed herself not to cry. Leaning on her crutches, she lifted out the top t-shirt and held it up. She smiled, recognizing the funny looking dragon on the front of the shirt, framed in a green shield. Stan had gotten this shirt from the 25th Fighter Squadron at Osan Air Base, Korea, where they first met. She hugged the cloth to her chest.

She was keeping it, she decided, and tossed it onto the bed. She went through the rest of his clothes, keeping some, folding others into the box to give away. As she picked up a pile of jeans and placed them into the box, a scrap of paper floated to the floor.

Jackie leaned over, carefully balancing herself, and picked it up.

> ~~I've been thinking a lot lately~~
> ~~Jackie, I've been an ass~~
> ~~I screwed up~~
> *I'm sorry and I want to make it right.*
> *I love you.*

A cold chill ran down her spine as she recognized Stan's handwriting. He was never one for love letters or even notes. He didn't like to talk about feelings, let alone put anything in writing.

Jackie knew this small gesture was significant, and she loved him for it. Yes, she admitted she still loved him. Even with everything that had happened. He wasn't perfect, but he was hers. 'Til death do us part was not an accurate sentiment of what existed between them now. He was actually there for her beyond his death.

He was there for her when she needed him the most. His presence in her life had saved her—twice. Among the infinite collection of memories she could have recalled about their time together, he chose the perfect memory to send her while she was trapped in a killer's grip. She would always carry a part of him with her. She placed the note back on the shelf and smiled. "Thank you, love."

####

## Excerpt from Truth Has No Agenda

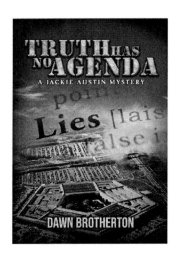

At Joint Base Andrews, thirty miles away, Lieutenant Colonel Dick Webster stood staring out the window at the airplanes on the runway. *It's happening again*, he thought. *What has the military become that sexual harassment is so common place?*

A knock at the door drew his attention.

"Sir, Senior Airman Amanda Nelson is here to see you," his executive office said from the doorway.

"Send her in," he replied.

Walking around to the front of his desk, he greeted her with an outstretched hand. "Good morning, Airman Nelson. Thanks for coming in."

The airman returned his firm handshake. "Thank you for seeing me, sir."

"Have a seat." He gestured toward a chair, then took one himself.

She nervously tugged at the hem of her air battle uniform jacket to pull it straight, then sat.

"I hear you had some trouble this weekend," he said. "Do you want to talk about it?"

Nelson cleared her throat. "Not really, sir."

Webster looked at her with sympathy in his eyes. "It does help to talk about it."

She stared at her hands fidgeting in her lap. "It was stupid. Nothing important."

"Your friend thought it was important enough to get the word to me."

"Who would that be, sir?"

"That's not important. Now at least I can help you."

"Whoever it was shouldn't have bothered you, sir. There isn't anything I need help with."

Webster knew that, at first, most girls didn't want to talk about sexual harassment. They felt it was a stigma put on them that would affect their work evaluations. Luckily for them, someone was looking out for them.

"Well, now at least we can deal with it," he said.

She looked at him shyly. "Sir, there really isn't anything to deal with. I was stupid and made a mistake."

"You have nothing to be ashamed of," Webster assured her. "We all make mistakes. In this case, the mistake may be more on the part of the young man, not you."

Airman Nelson shook her head. "That's what I'm saying, sir. He didn't do anything wrong. It was consensual."

"From what I hear, you were pretty hard on yourself after it happened."

She shook her head again and looked back at her hands. "I wanted it to happen. It wasn't until after that I was kicking myself. He didn't force me or anything. I just shouldn't have," she shrugged, "given in so easily."

"Maybe he shouldn't have pressured you," Webster suggested.

"He didn't. Really!" she tried to convince him.

"Since it's been brought to my attention, that makes it a formal report," he went on as if he hadn't heard her.

"Sir, I don't want to make any kind of report," Airman Nelson said.

"At this point, you don't have a choice. I already know about it. My exec will set up an appointment for you with the Special Victims Advocate." Webster stood, signaling an end to their conversation. Nelson stood automatically, following military tradition.

Webster walked behind his desk as Nelson departed.

# About the Author

Colonel (retired) DAWN BROTHERTON is an award-winning author and featured speaker. When it comes to exceptional writing, Dawn draws on her experience as a retired colonel from the U.S. Air Force as well as a softball coach, Girl Scout leader, and quilter. Her books include the Jackie Austin Mysteries, cozy mystery *Eastover Treasures*, YA Fantasy *The Dragons of Silent Mountain*, and romance *Untimely Love*.

She has also completed four books (*Trish's Team; Margie Makes a Difference; Nicole's New Friend,* and *Tammy Tries Baseball*) in the middle grade Lady Tigers series, encouraging female athletes to reach for the stars in the game they love.

With the help of former Disney illustrator Chad Thompson, Dawn has released her first children's picture book (ages 3-7) *If I Look Like You* and its accompanying activity book, *Scout and Her Friends*. These books help children explore STEM and non-STEM career fields as they learn they do not have to change who they are to fit in.

Under nonfiction, the *Baseball/Softball Scorebook* was created with instructions written for those not as familiar with the intricacies of the game.

*The Road to Publishing* is designed to walk writers through the maze of becoming a published author, whether self-publishing, traditional-publishing, or somewhere in between.

Dawn is a contributing author to the non-fiction *A-10s over Kosovo*, sharing stories from her deployment, and *Water from Wellspring*, a collection of short stories about how God has worked in people's lives.

For more information about Dawn's books and book signings, go to www.DawnBrothertonAuthor.com.

# A Special Thanks

I owe a special thanks to Lawrence "Stutz" Sutzriem for helping me with the parts inside the cockpit. As I am not a pilot myself, it was essential to have his expertise to make the cockpit scene come to life.